Deep Freeze

Deep Freeze

PATRICIA HALL

This edition published in Great Britain in 2002 by
Allison & Busby Limited
Bon Marche Centre
241-251 Ferndale Road
London SW9 8BJ
www.allisonandbusby.com

A catalogue record for this book is available from
the British Library.

ISBN 0 7490 0564 5

Printed and bound in Spain by
Liberduplex, s.l. Barcelona.

Chapter 1

The old woman lay under her thin blankets and watched the grey morning light filter through the window she had roughly blocked up with cardboard. Her limbs felt heavy and stiff and even though the heaped blankets were scant protection from the chill air, she felt disinclined to move. One day, she thought grimly, they would find her frozen to death here. Her smile was toothless. There were worse ways to go, she thought, to slip away alone in the dawn with only the sweetly singing birds for company.

As the light turned from leaden to silver, she eased herself off the narrow bunk, wrapped a blanket round her scrawny shoulders and edged open the rain-swollen door of the caravan and peered out.

The van, once white but now streaked with patches of green and black mould, was parked beneath a stand of trees where the bare winter branches were already dripping moisture onto the roof as the heavy frost began to thaw. The meadow beyond was empty, the cows safely indoors in a byre which she reckoned was probably warmer than her own dilapidated shelter. She liked the cows. When she came down here in the summer they often clustered around the old van in the shade of the trees, breathing their warm, grassy breath over her as she came and went.

She glanced at a string bag which hung permanently outside the door and her leathery face crinkled into a thin smile. Someone had left her a fat brown trout, its eyes as bright as when it had been plucked from the water just hours before. She took the fish the few steps to the bank of the river and pulled a clasp-knife from the pocket of her thick grey skirt, beheading and gutting the fish expertly and throwing the remains into the rushing water where the Maze ran noisily through a rocky defile. There'd been a time, she recalled, when she and her brothers would have landed finer fish than this on a moonlit night, higher up the river where the brown peaty water rippled through rocky shallows, the fish felt rather than seen between the fingers. She had thought she had heard voices in the night as she had dozed the restless sleep of old age. They were good lads in the village, she muttered to herself. Some on'em, any road. A cooked breakfast would do her the world of good, she thought, carrying the fish back to the van and lighting her small primus stove with hands that shook. Might even give her strength to go back to the other bloody place, she thought, where she had left her false teeth.

She ate the fish hungrily in spite of bare gums. She had neither clock nor watch in the van but she knew it was more than a day since she had last eaten. She would have to go back, she tried to convince herself, even if only to make sure she did not miss the meals-on-wheels woman who came to the bungalow twice a week with her plastic trays of unidentifiable lumps submerged in glutinous brown or yellow liquid, unappetising but better than nothing. As she sat on the bunk, enjoying the feeling of hot food inside her, she wondered how much longer she could keep up this double life with the caravan visibly decaying around her and the cold seeming crueller every time she woke here, where she loved to be, close to the river and the woods.

Slowly she pulled on an old duffle coat that she had picked up at a jumble sale, secured the door behind her with a padlock far too flimsy to hold it against a determined assault, and began the laborious climb up the track to the farm. Old Jenner knew that she still came down to the van, although it was more than a year since she had been given the spartan two room bungalow she hated. But Jenner was all right, she told herself. Jenner would say nowt. And however much the rest of them fussed and faffed about her welfare, she would do as she liked as long as she could get away with it. She hated the bungalow with a passion she carefully concealed. She would die in the van if she could. It was not the same as the open road, which was what her nomadic heart really craved, but it would have to do.

Passing the gate to the farmyard she saw Jenner leaving the milking parlour, his breath hanging in clouds on the frosty air, his coat collar pulled right up to the brim of his weathered tweed cap.

"All reet, Maggie?" he asked.

"All reet," she said, her voice almost as gruff as the farmer's. She had been coming to Jenner's farm since she was a long-legged, dark-haired girl and he a stocky blonde lad who had gazed at her hungrily from a distance, wary of the smouldering eyes of her brothers who had been hired to help with the hay-making and shearing.

But she wasn't all right, she thought as she stood like a scarecrow at the top of the lane, gasping for breath. The narrow road across the open moorland back to Shepley village stretched like a mountain ahead of her. The sense of foreboding she had carried with her up the long rutted lane grew suddenly intense and she doubled up, gasping in pain, as if the grinning skeleton with the scythe had caught her a preliminary blow. But it was not just pain which sent her reeling to lean against the dry stone wall, as much as dread. She closed her eyes trying to see through the mist which swirled in her brain but she could see nothing distinctly and the voices, which came to her more and more often, could not be heard clearly. Death, she knew, was very close, but it was not her own - this time at least. From the village just over the brow of the hill above her she heard the church clock strike nine.

* * *

They had tightened up security at the May Anderson hospital since the morning that one of the demonstrators had hurled a bucket of pig's blood and entrails all over Dr. Mahood as he arrived cheerfully on his bicycle for work. No one had ever been sure whether the insult had religious overtones or was

11

simply, and messily, ethical as the earnest young woman with a scarf wrapped around her face who had upended her plastic container so effectively over the defenceless doctor had slipped away into the milling demonstrators and vanished before anyone could apprehend her.

Dr. Mahood, an un-observant Muslim at the best of times and an ambitious man, had still indulged in more than one Arabic curse which he would have been very reluctant to translate as he had staggered into the hospital's pristine and hushed entrance hall wiping blood from his eyes and gobbets of nameless tissue from his clothes, looking more like the victim of a motorway pile-up than an obstetrician with his eye on a consultancy. He had chosen since then to travel to work by car.

A couple of bored police officers now kept a desultory eye on the permanent picket of protesters who had been confined behind portable metal railings on the opposite side of the street from the gates. The private clinic, housed in one of those heavy stone double-fronted Victorian mansions with which the north side of Bradfield had been endowed by its mill-masters in the nineteenth century, had invested in an electronic barrier and a uniformed security guard who scrutinised with ponderous care the passes which were now issued to all staff and visitors before he raised his barrier for them.

If anything the hospital's guardians were in a slightly heightened state of alert that morning, aware, as the previous day's Bradfield Gazette had made sure that the entire town was aware, that the regular local picket might be strengthened by a small contingent of Americans who were threatening to bring their country's more robust opposition to abortion to England in general and Bradfield in particular as part of a campaign tour.

But by five to nine that morning, while the grey winter light crept beneath the trees which shaded the hospital from the road, there was no sign of the promised reinforcements and PC Len Dickson, middle-aged and stolid, and his much

12

younger colleague, Craig Turner, surveyed the familiar small group of placard-wavers with benign contempt. The younger copper had offered his usual optimistic smile to one particularly pretty young woman who just as resolutely refused to meet his eye.

"You've no chance there, lad," Dickson said. "She's likely studying nuclear physics or summat. She'd gobble you up as a snack before breakfast."

"I got five GCSEs," his companion muttered defensively.

"Aye, but how many A Levels, lad? How many o'*them*? You're not exactly fast-track, are you? Be honest."

The younger man turned away, hiding his fury.

"It's not brains you need in this job," he muttered to himself, only too well aware he was deceiving himself.

The group they were minding was a mixed one, with a regular core of students from the university, cheerful, smartly dressed young people, in no way out of place on their hilly campus a mile from the hospital except perhaps for a certain earnestness around the eyes and an eager wakefulness which Len Dickson had never observed amongst students at this hour of the morning before. They were generally joined somewhat later by a handful of older campaigners, middle-aged women in sensible boots and heavy coats, and quite often a Catholic priest from the neighbouring church of St. Augustine reinvigorated by his early morning Mass.

There was nothing, PC Dickson swore to his superiors later, to single out this particular morning as any different from any other as Stephen Fenton-Green's BMW swept up to the barrier and the consultant waved his pass at the security guard with his usual buoyant greeting. Fenton-Green had parked the car in the space reserved for him close to the steps which led up to the main doors when it happened. Above him two women were just leaving the building as the consultant bounded up to the entrance. For a second, no more, the three of them manoeuvred round each other on the broad top step before Fenton-Green reached impatiently past the younger of the two women, little more than a girl in fact, with the merest nod of recognition, to push open the heavy glass door. It was then that the sharp crack of a single shot rang out.

It was another couple of seconds before anyone moved, before they realised what had happened and before the young woman's body, supported for a moment between the tall doctor and her dumpy middle-aged companion, began to slide awkwardly to the ground, blood pumping from the bullet's entry wound in her head. Then all hell broke loose. The driver of a taxi, which had been about to draw up outside the gates, suddenly thought better of it and accelerated away. Further up the road the roar of a motorbike shattered the stunned silence outside the hospital before it too fragmented into a confusion of screams and shouts of horror and alarm..

Instinctively it seemed, Stephen Fenton-Green flung himself through the entrance doors and onto the floor in the foyer shouting to the startled receptionist and a nurse who happened to be passing to get down. On the step, the heavy swinging door completed what the bullet had started, flinging the girl, who was probably already dead, like a rag-doll, face-down onto the floor and revealing in a mess of blood and dark hair what havoc the single bullet had wreaked on the back of her skull. Beside Fenton-Green, the girl's companion who had been knocked through the door by the diving doctor, hurled herself back outside and was the first to begin to scream, a terrible wailing sound, which was quickly taken up by the shocked young watchers on the other side of the road who began to scatter hysterically in all directions. They had read too many accounts of deranged assassins to believe that the first bullet was likely to be the last.

Glancing around him wildly for any sign of a concealed gunman, Len Dickson raced across the road, vaulted over the barrier, now apparently guarded by a uniformed zombie unable to move, and up the steps. He took one look at what was left of the young girl's head and choked down the bile which rose in his throat. Carried more by his own momentum than considered thought, he grabbed the shrieking woman who was now kneeling beside the body and pulled her roughly through the swing doors again into the foyer.

"Dial 999 and get an ambulance," he shouted at the ashen-faced receptionist who was helping Stephen Fenton-Green to his feet. "And you sir," he said to the consultant. "I take it you're a doctor. Could you see what you can do for these women before the paramedics get here." Fenton-Green, as white-faced as everyone else, gulped slightly and nodded while Dickson called his own control unit and began to explain as coherently as he could why he needed armed back-up urgently in the quiet suburban street.

"There's no hope for the girl," Fenton-Green muttered, nodding at the body which lay, crumpled and bloody, on the other side of the glass. "Do we know if the gunman's still there?"

"No, of course we bloody don't," Dickson said. "I've left my colleague to clear the street. That's the best we can do till I get some back-up. In the meantime can you tell everyone to keep away from the effing windows? We could have a mad-man out there."

"You look disgustingly cheerful for this time of the morning." The gravelly voice in her ear made Laura Ackroyd jump as she stood pushing entry buttons to unlock the main doors of the Bradfield Gazette only to find her boss, the editor Ted Grant, hard on her heels and breathing heavily. Laura sighed, followed him through the door and stood to one side to let him ease his heavy frame out of his thick coat and unwind his scarf.

"I just love these early shifts," she said, glancing at the clock above the deserted reception desk. It was just after eight o'clock.

"You're getting your beauty sleep then?" Grant asked, with a sideways leer.

"Not that it's any of your business," Laura snapped, her face slightly flushed. She had not tried to conceal the fact that

15

when she had moved to a new flat she had not moved in alone, but she still resented Grant's intrusion. Furious with him, and with herself for letting him get to her, she tossed her mane of coppery red hair back from her face and marched ahead of the editor into the newsroom where most of the desks were still empty and shrouded in early morning gloom.

Grant punched the light-switches as he followed his features editor in and the tubes flickered into life.

"Well, if you're all bright-eyed and bushy-tailed you'll get that series finished today, won't you," Grant flung over his shoulder as he made his way to his glass walled office in one corner of the open plan news-room. "We'll run it next week if you can just get your arse in gear."

Gritting her teeth, Laura dropped into her chair, punched her computer terminal on, and eased the top off the plastic cup of coffee she had collected from the new coffee shop opposite the office on her way in. Then, catching sight of her own reflection in the screen in front of her, she grinned. She did feel absurdly cheerful, she thought, though she had not realised it was so obvious that Ted Grant, that monument to male insensitivity, would notice.

Disinclined to hurl herself into work, she sat sipping her coffee slowly and taking stock of her situation. For the first time in several years, she thought, she seemed to have got her life together. Her decision to buy a new flat had been a much better one than she could possibly have anticipated: her enthusiasm for the ground floor and garden of the old Victorian house she now shared with a couple of contentedly middle-aged gays and a single mother on the floors above, had eventually persuaded Michael Thackeray to make a second attempt at shared domesticity. And this time, Laura thought, it really seemed as if it might work out. It might be a cold dark November morning, and work at the Gazette still more often than not a bore, but inside she knew she was glowing.

By nine o'clock the office had filled up and hummed with

activity as the first of the day's news deadlines approached. In the small enclave devoted to features, Laura remained insulated from the bustle at the top table where the sub-editors were planning the afternoon's front page. But even Laura's concentration was broken when Bob Baker, the paper's ambitious young crime reporter, suddenly flung down his telephone receiver, jumped up from his desk and dodged with the intensity and speed of a rugby forward towards the editor's office.

"What's the matter with him?" Laura's neighbour asked grumpily over the top of that morning's *Globe*.

"Oh, he's always looking for the scoop of the century," Laura said dismissively. "Most of them turn out to be very small earthquakes, not many dead."

But this time she had to admit her cynicism was not justified. Ted Grant, his face flushed and his belly bursting out of his shirt, emerged from his office within seconds, roaring like a bull elephant at his sub-editors.

"Hold everything," he said. "We've got a bloody hospital shooting - one dead - maybe more - armed police - patients besieged - the full Monty."

"Hold the front page," Laura muttered under her breath as Grant began deploying his reporters with all the panache of a Montgomery at Alamein. This was not a crisis where she expected to be drafted into the front line. Bob Baker and some of the other young men on the staff would be only too ready to volunteer for the fire brigade role. But she under-estimated Grant, who was determined to leave no angle uncovered.

"Laura," he bellowed. "Take charge of the human-interest stuff, will you? It's a young girl been killed. She'll have a family, school friends, whatever. Page three's all yours if you get it together in time."

"The Infirmary?" she asked, guessing that the fears of doctors and nurses facing daily mayhem in the casualty department had been all too bloodily fulfilled.

"That private place up towards Southfield," Grant said. "What's it called - May Anderson?"

"Right," Laura said, concealing the surprise she felt. The May Anderson hospital, specialising exclusively in women's medicine, seemed an unlikely scene for a shooting.

Laura slipped a fresh tape into her tape-recorder, shrugged herself back into her coat and sighed. As long as Ted Grant avoided the heart attack he courted with such assiduity, nothing at the Gazette would ever change, she thought. And that meant that if there were a victim to be interviewed and tears to be recorded on behalf of the great Bradfield public, then it would be a woman who carried the tissues.

* * *

It was almost two hours later that the Chief Inspector in charge of the armed officers who had closed the road, surrounded the hospital and sealed off the houses and gardens in the immediate neighbourhood, declared the area safe and allowed the police surgeon in to examine the body of the girl they now knew was thirteen-year- old Dana Smith. Detective Chief Inspector Michael Thackeray had spent much of that two hours sitting impatiently in a car parked a couple of streets away, waiting to gain access to the clinic where so far only PC Les Dickson had been able to talk to Dana's distraught mother. Mrs. Smith had been given a sedative by the medical staff as the only alternative to forcibly restraining her from pushing her way out of the doors to where her daughter's body still lay.

It had taken the police doctor only minutes to confirm Stephen Fenton-Green's conviction and pronounce the girl indisputably dead and to allow the forensic and scene-of-crime teams, in their space-age white cover-alls, to make what they could of the murder scene. And that was little enough when it was only too obvious that the girl had been just about as far away from her killer as it is possible for a murder victim to be.

Thackeray glanced through his curling cigarette smoke at

Sergeant Kevin Mower, who slumped rather than sat in the passenger seat beside him with his eyes half-closed and an empty plastic coffee cup almost crushed in his fist.

"Get hold of Dickson again," he said, as much to give Mower something to do as because he really needed to speak to the constable. He knew he would be informed as soon as he and the rest of the team standing by to launch a murder inquiry could approach the scene of the crime. Mower did as he was told. Mower had been doing as he was told, without dispute or any sign of enthusiasm, for months now, Thackeray thought irritably as he watched his sergeant pick up the handset. Mower was pale and tense beneath what was left of a summer tan, the dark hair longer and less fashionably cut than it used to be, his shirt putting in its third or fourth appearance that week, his silk tie slightly stained. It was ironic, Thackeray thought, that just as he was beginning to dare to hope that his own life was settling onto an even keel, Mower's seemed to be disintegrating. Although to an extent, he had to admit, their states of mind were not unconnected. The terrifying suddenness with which Mower's future happiness had been snatched away had grieved Thackeray and concentrated his own mind on Laura Ackroyd. It was time, he had concluded, to try to achieve what he had so miserably failed to achieve for more than ten years, and start afresh before Laura despaired of him.

"We can go in," Mower said. "They've finished searching the neighbouring buildings and found nothing. No sign of Lee Harvey Oswald, anyway. The SOCOs have done what they can, which is not a lot apparently. There'll be no DNA evidence with this one unless we can discover where the shot was fired from."

Thackeray smiled grimly. A shooting was uncommon enough in Bradfield to carry its own element of shock, although guns had made an occasional, and so far non-fatal, appearance in the sporadic gang warfare which flared around the drug trade on the estates. But at the back of his mind, as of every police officer's, lurked the fear that one day a deranged killer might spray random death around a school or playground. Thankfully, he thought, this episode did not seem to fit either of those patterns: thirteen-year-old girls out with their mothers seemed unlikely drug dealers, and the single shot implied malice rather than madness.

"Let's see what the hell we've got then, shall we?" Thackeray said starting up the car and gunning the engine unnecessarily. Blast Mower, he thought. His gloom was becoming infectious.

Thackeray steeled himself, as he always did, as he approached the steps where Dana Smith's body still lay, loosely covered by a blanket. He glanced at Mower, whose last sight of a young woman violently done to death had been so personal. But the sergeant's face was impassive, his eyes opaque, as he stared, apparently unmoved, at the body.

At the foot of the steps paramedics were helping a middle-aged woman in a coat streaked with blood into an ambulance.

"That's the mother," a uniformed inspector said as Thackeray approached. "In total shock. There's no emergency facilities here, of course, so they're taking her to the Infirmary. They say she needs looking at."

"I'm not surprised," Thackeray said. "Don't worry about it. We'll catch up with her later."

They were joined almost immediately by the bulky figure of Amos Atherton, Bradfield's pathologist who seemed uncharacteristically lost for words. He too had been waiting his turn to approach the scene of the crime.

"Bloody hell," was all he offered as he made his way up the steps, breathing heavily, and pulled the blanket from body and his Dictaphone from his pocket. Thackeray and Mower followed slowly, neither of them much wanting to see what was left of the girl.

"Not much doubt about the cause of death then?" Atherton said, his usually rubicund face pale as he surveyed blood and bone and what Thackeray could only assume was brain. "A President Kennedy job, that," Atherton said grimly. "Never knew what hit her."

"Can you get any idea which direction the shot came from?" Thackeray asked.

"Later maybe," Atherton said. "When I've done a proper examination. And if you know which way she was facing when she was hit."

"There were enough witnesses," Mower said. "Half the God Squad from the university were watching."

"Aye, I heard they were here," Atherton said, his face grim. "Can't leave well alone, can they, some folk? As if it's any of their business. How old was she, this lass? Thirteen? Fourteen? Nothing but a child herself, dammit."

Pale and taciturn, Thackeray stepped round the body and pushed open the hospital doors. Mower raised an eyebrow at Atherton and made to follow.

"As soon as?" he murmured.

"Top priority, lad," Atherton said. "I'll let you know when I'm starting the PM."

The spacious foyer was crowded with police officers, medical and nursing staff and even a scattering of patients in dressing gowns, all talking quietly amongst the potted palms and coffee tables.

"Les," Thackeray said sharply, as he recognised the constable who had first raised the alarm. "Let's get a bit of sense into this lot, shall we? Get hold of whoever's in charge for me, will you, and then clear everyone else out of here. I want an office, and I want to talk to the doctor who was coming in when the shot was fired, then anyone else who was in the foyer at the time, then anyone else who reckons to have seen anything significant." He turned to Mower. "You deal with the outside witnesses, Kevin, will you, assuming the uniformed lads have kept tabs on them."

"The buggers'll know about it if they haven't," Mower said angrily, turning on his heel. Thackeray watched him stride past Atherton and the girl's body without a glance in their direction and wondered what it would take to crack the shell which Mower had carefully sealed around himself over the last few months. And whether he would survive if anything did.

Sombrely he turned back to his own task in hand and found that the crowd in the foyer had thinned considerably and that Les Dickson was guiding a tall, good-looking man in an impeccable silver-grey suit, primrose shirt and subtly toning tie in his direction.

"Dr. Fenton-Green," Dickson said.

"*Mr*," Fenton-Green said holding out his hand, which Thackeray ignored. "A consultant, you know?" He smiled with a self-deprecation which Thackeray found irritating.

"Is there somewhere we can talk quietly, Mr. Fenton-Green?" he asked. "They've taken the girl's mother to A and E, so you're our best witness to what happened for the moment."

"I am supposed to be operating in half an hour..."

"We won't hold you up more than absolutely necessary," Thackeray said politely enough but his tone made very clear that he expected the doctor to comply.

"My office then?"

Fenton-Green settled himself easily behind his desk, looking relaxed, although the slight drumming of fingers on blotter indicated that he might not be as calm as he wished to appear. But then, Thackeray thought, being narrowly missed by a bullet was hardly the best start to a working day, particularly in a job where he guessed a steady hand was particularly important. He found it difficult to decide quite how old Fenton-Green was. His hair was greying at the temples but probably prematurely, he thought, and there were fine lines around the sharply blue eyes, but he was tanned and trim, clearly a doctor who followed the medical advice on diet and exercise. Much his own age, Thackeray concluded, pulling in his stomach defensively: in his forties, but considerably better preserved than he was himself since he had given up the rugby which had replaced religion in his life at an early stage.

"It must have struck you that the shot might have been aimed at the hospital in general or you in particular, rather

22

than the girl who died," Thackeray said. The drumming increased slightly in intensity.

"You mean it should have been me who died?" the doctor said. "You really think those people would do that? Shoot me? Of course, they've done exactly that in the States, haven't they, but here..?"

"Those people?"

"The anti-abortion lot. The ones who've been demonstrating for months," Fenton-Green said irritably. "They seem to miss the point that we do a lot more than terminations here. We've got gynae and maternity wards, for Christ's sake, new-born babies on the premises. I never regarded the demonstrators as much more than a bloody nuisance until today but now...," he shrugged helplessly. "I assume you've got files on them?."

"If we haven't we soon will have," Thackeray said. "Can you think of anyone else who might want to take a shot at you?"

Fenton-Green shook his head.

"There are professional jealousies, but they don't lead to this," he said. "If that bullet was intended for me I just don't know. I can't think of anyone who hates me that much."

"Family problems?" Thackeray persisted.

Fenton-Green shook his head even more vigorously.

"Of course, not," he said. "I'm divorced, haven't seen my ex-wife for five years or more."

"Children?" Thackeray asked.

"No," Fenton Green said. "I am happily settled at the moment with my girlfriend, but there are no children." He glanced at his watch.

"I can't think of anyone who might have wanted me dead, Chief Inspector," he said. "I'm happy to say. Unless one of those fanatics outside has gone completely off his or her head. And now I have an operating theatre waiting..."

"Just one last question for now, though we'll need to meet again quite soon," Thackeray insisted. "Dana Smith. I understand she had been a patient here. What exactly had you been treating her for."

"I don't suppose patient confidentiality applies now," Fenton Green said irritably. "Anyway I'm sure her mother will tell you all about it. I operated on her yesterday. A termination. She was very young so we decided to keep her here overnight and her mother arranged to collect her early this morning. She was obviously in the wrong place at the wrong time."

"Right," Thackeray said, hoping his distaste did not show.

* * *

"In the end it was a complete bloody disaster as a story," Laura said ruefully to Michael Thackeray that evening. "Not only had the girl just had an abortion, which made Ted terminally twitchy, but when I went up to Benwell Lane to talk to the neighbours they all had steam coming out of their ears about the Smiths. 'Bloody gippos' was the kindest description - marginally less unprintable than the rest. Most of them seemed to think that the loss of Dana was something they could quite easily live with. Is it me, or are human beings getting nastier by the day?"

Laura was sitting curled up in her favourite armchair close to the elaborate Victorian fireplace which dominated the sparsely furnished living room of the new flat. Thackeray had come home late, tired and drained, but still able to lift her spirits as she fussed over him and served the meal she had kept hot. Slumped on the sofa opposite her now, he listened with half-closed eyes as she described her day, which had touched tangentially on his own.

"I got the impression the family wasn't the most popular one up there," he said mildly.

"There was no one in at the Smiths' house. There are four sons, apparently, who come and go. Anyway, they'd gone, to the hospital I suppose. They're neighbours from hell, according to the woman next door," Laura said. "Not that many of

24

them would get brownie points for community values up there. It's where the council dumped the most difficult ten-grants when they pulled Bronte House down."

"The brothers seem to have been in and out of trouble almost since they could walk," Thackeray said drily. "Nothing major, but persistent. Dana we've got nothing on, nor the mother except for being bound over to keep the peace after some neighbourhood fracas a couple of years ago."

"Anyway there was no way I could dish up the innocent loveable victim Ted wanted. I ended up with a couple of para-graphs of heavily edited condolences at the bottom of page five and a tape-recorder full of abuse."

"Oh, I'd say that Dana's probably as innocent as a murder victim can be," Thackeray said sleepily. "The most likely scenario, I reckon, is that some nutcase took a pot-shot at the hospital in general rather than anyone in particular and the poor kid just happened to be in the line of fire."

"Can I quote you on that, Chief Inspector," Laura asked mischievously.

"You bloody well know you can't," Thackeray said. "You know we shouldn't even be talking about the case."

"Well, I dare say if you make it worth my while I could for-get about it," she said, getting up from her chair and taking Thackeray's hand in hers. He groaned, but it was only a half-hearted protest which he gave the lie to as he took her in his arms and kissed her even before she had turned out the lights and opened the bedroom door.

Chapter 2

Thackeray recognised the lips, although he had never met Dorothy Knight before. More usually pursed in piety on their way to the altar rail, today they were no less austere, drawn in a thin line like a red pencil slash through an unsatisfactory piece of schoolwork. Mrs. Knight's desk reminded him of a schoolroom too: papers and folders in neat piles, pens and pencils carefully ranged in a black leather holder, the screen-saver on the computer pulsating gently in pastel shades. Only the wall poster of an immature foetus, thumb in mouth, jarred. It was not, he thought, what most parents would want their young children to see and yet he knew that Dorothy Knight's organisation targeted schools as a matter of policy.

He glanced at Kevin Mower, who was sitting impassively on a hard chair close to the door, notebook in hand but apparently taking little interest in the proceedings, before he turned back to Mrs. Knight and the expression which so vividly recalled the absolute moral certainty with which he had once been condemned by women very like her.

"I shall want a list of your members," he said in a chilly voice which left no room for argument. "And the names of the party which is coming from America to join you."

"Not us particularly, Chief Inspector," the earthly representative of Saving Lives for the Lord said. "They have a busy programme of visits all over the country. Edgar Burridge is in great demand. I'm told he's an inspiring speaker."

"Do you know whether Burridge has arrived yet?" Thackeray asked.

"I believe he's been in London for a couple of days. He's due here for the meeting at the town hall on Saturday. I'm meeting him at the airport at two." Mrs. Knight visibly glowed in anticipation.

"Do you think in the circumstances it's wise for that meeting to go ahead?" Thackeray asked. Dorothy Knight gazed at him wide-eyed.

"Why ever should it not?" she asked. "This tragic business at the May Anderson is nothing to do with us. Absolutely nothing."

"You know no one, on the wilder fringes, who might have taken your message so seriously that they would use violence against the hospital? Perhaps intending to scare rather than to kill, but prepared to use a gun?"

"No one," Dorothy Knight said flatly. "We are a Christian organisation, Chief Inspector. We have all welcomed Jesus into our lives in a very practical way. We would neither encourage nor condone violence."

"You know as well as I do that doctors have been killed in similar circumstances in the United States, which is where your guests have just come from," Thackeray persisted. "You may find the idea shocking but it is not beyond the bounds of possibility that there are more hot-headed supporters of your campaign who would be less scrupulously non-violent."

"We don't tolerate hot-headed supporters," Mrs. Knight said, her look exuding a certainty untouched by even a scintilla of doubt and making Thackeray - not known as an unrobust copper - feel he was floundering in a jelly of liberal doubt. "As you know, we have been conducting entirely peaceful demonstrations outside the May Anderson Hospital for months now without any unpleasantness or disorder of any kind. We have had a great deal of support from Christian students at the university, and from some of the local churches. As you know it's a private hospital but Mr. Fenton-Green seems to be going out of his way to treat women the doctors at the Infirmary have turned down. I would be very surprised if the girl who was killed had paid for her abortion."

"You seem very sure that's what she was being treated for."

Dorothy Knight glanced away, momentarily embarrassed.

"It was easy enough to read between the lines in the *Gazette* yesterday," she said, but she was not distracted from the main

27

thrust of her argument for more than a second. "We do feel that Mr. Fenton-Green is operating what amounts to a policy of abortion on demand, which is not what the law permits. I am always astonished that the police take so little interest in what is going on in these places."

Thackeray flinched slightly, appalled at the idea of being asked to trample through the legal and medical minefield of abortion law.

"I'm sure if you had grounds for an official complaint it would be looked at," he said..

"Are you?" Mrs. Knight asked.

"Your membership lists?" Thackeray said, his irritation showing. Dorothy Knight turned to her computer, activated a programme and within minutes a list was being produced on the printer on a side table.

"We are not a big organisation in Bradfield," she said as the printer stopped after a page and a half. "I think our current subscribers number about 69, but of course some are more active than others."

"You were not at the hospital yourself yesterday morning?" Thackeray asked.

"No, Father Burke from St. Augustine's led the prayers yesterday, although I don't know how long he was able to stay after that. We like to keep the demonstration going until all the staff and patients have arrived for the day. Then we just maintain a token presence after that."

"And you were where, Mrs. Knight?"

"I man our advice centre here on a Tuesday morning," she said. "We always have an advertisement in the *Gazette* on a Monday evening which brings us some clients. They do a cheap rate on Mondays."

"But it didn't bring in Dana Smith, I presume," Thackeray said.

"Not to my knowledge, no," Mrs. Knight said. "More's the pity."

"You would have regarded her as a failure in any case, as

she had chosen a termination?" Thackeray suggested quietly. "Even at her age?"

"The law does not give her the right to choose, Chief Inspector, as you should know. The grounds for abortion are quite clear. And there is help available for these young girls who get themselves pregnant," Mrs. Knight said sharply. "That's the whole point of an organisation like this. We do not simply bear witness. We can help in practical ways if young women decide to do the right thing and keep their babies. We raise a great deal of money to help them."

"For twenty years?" Mower suddenly said explosively from behind them. Thackeray glanced round but the sergeant had already turned away, his face flushed, refusing to meet the DCI's eye.

"Really, I don't think that is acceptable," Dorothy Knight said. "I'm not here to defend myself or SLL, you know."

"You're right. I'm sorry," Thackeray said. "But you know better than most people that this is an issue which arouses strong passions on both sides of the argument. And it's an issue which may have killed that young girl, one way or another. Perhaps you'd just be kind enough to mark on this list for me the people you think were at the demonstration yesterday morning, and then we'll leave you in peace. The regular congregation, as it were. We were able to make contact with some of them while we were clearing the area, but there was a lot of confusion and some people quite understandably moved away quite quickly when they realised a shot had been fired."

"I'll try," Dorothy Knight said. "Father Burke will have a better idea..."

"Of course," Thackeray said. "I'll be seeing him shortly."

With ill-concealed displeasure, Dorothy Knight ran her eye down the list, ticking a name here and there.

"Those are the people I would have expected to turn out," she said at length, handing the list to Thackeray. With the paper in his pocket, they took their leave but it was not until they had reached the bottom of the stairs that Thackeray gave vent to his anger.

"I don't know what your views are on abortion, Kevin, and I don't really care," he said. "But I don't want those views getting in the way of this investigation. Is that clear? We've no idea what the motive was behind this shooting yet."

"Oh, come on, guv," Mower said, his face pale and tense. "This lot have been stirring the pot for months, working themselves up for the visit of this American fanatic, and you think there's no connection? This is a kid of thirteen we're talking about, with her head blown off on the steps of an abortion clinic. That's a coincidence? Please!"

"I'll tell you what I think," Thackeray said quietly. "I think there's going to be a storm of emotion around Dana Smith's death which, if we're not careful, will so muddy the waters that we'll never get to the truth. If I find you adding your three-penn'orth to the brew I'll have you off the case so fast your feet won't touch the ground."

"And that goes for all the women on the team too, does it?" Mower asked. "Because I can tell you, they're not happy bunnies."

"They'll behave as professionally as you do," Thackeray said. "And that will be very professionally indeed. Understood?"

"Right, guv," Mower said, turning on his heel so that he could leave the building ahead of Thackeray. The Chief Inspector could see from the set of his shoulders that his sergeant was still very angry and he wondered how much his warning was for his own benefit as anyone else's on the police murder team. Long buried emotions flared in unexpected places and at unexpected times, and he had been taken unawares when his horror at the death of Dana Smith had been compounded by an unexpected grief for her dead baby and all the others whose lives had ended before they had begun at the May Anderson Hospital. "Give me a child before he's seven," he said to himself with bitter mockery, but he knew it was not the priests who still touched him but the ghost of his baby son.

Mower pulled the car into the kerb, avoiding an over-turned dustbin, and a scattered pile of bricks which might at one time have propped up a disintegrating vehicle of some kind. He knew that their progress down Benwell Lane had been watched from the moment the car turned off the main road. It was a wide street of ageing semi-detached houses where the broad grass verges had long ago been pounded into mud and almost every other house had been at best boarded up and at worst gutted by fire. He glanced at Michael Thackeray.

"Welcome to Grosny," he said.

"The whole place was due to come down and be replaced by some sort of private development," Thackeray said. "But they ran out of money. They emptied the whole area out at one stage and then had to start renovating again. If you can call it renovating. You remember Bronte House up on the Heights? This is where they dumped some of the tenants when they pulled that down."

Mower glanced around him curiously. The fact that he had never visited this depressing urban shipwreck over the several years of his Bradfield career surprised him. But the reason he had missed it was obvious enough: the estate might show every sign of inner city dilapidation, but in fact it was small and isolated and on the very edge of the town. The Lane itself and one or two side-roads had been built adjacent to a cluster of old stone cottages around a chapel and a pub. Beyond that a strip of level ground took in a cricket pitch and a couple of scrubby fields where a group of slightly unkempt piebald ponies grazed before the main road to Millfield and Broadley plunged across a stretch of unfenced moorland and up a steep craggy hill to wilder country beyond. Unless some particularly notable villain had been decanted up here, it would be the uniformed branch which came face to face, day-to-day, with the cluster of adolescents who were sitting on a wall watching

31

their approach. And in Mower's experience, notable villains at the start of the new century inhabited considerably more attractive homes than these run-down council houses.

"It's a bit up-market for refugees from Bronte out here, isn't it? I've no doubt that a few executive residences would go down better with whoever tarted up all those bijou cottages over there. They can't think much of this lot as neighbours."

"Let's start at the pub," Thackeray suggested. "That always gives you a feel for a place."

They locked the car and walked past the unfenced green to what turned out to be, unsurprisingly, the Cricketers' Arms, another long low building in golden Yorkshire stone, with glass gleaming in the mullioned windows and well-cared for picnic tables ranged to the front, well out of sight of Benwell Lane. The main door was open but the bar was deserted, the tables showing signs of being recently washed down, the chairs still neatly arranged in a semblance of a Victorian sitting room, all carefully distressed oak, plush curtains and brass fittings glowing in the subdued light. Behind the bar a heavy man in shirtsleeves was refilling the cabinets of soft drinks.

"Can I help you, gentlemen," he asked, without much enthusiasm. Thackeray flashed him his warrant card, which did nothing to cheer the landlord's lugubrious expression. He glanced out of the still open door from which the end houses of the Lane could just be seen.

"Ben Robertson," he said. "How do? We don't see many coppers up here. Not often around when you're wanted, are you? I suppose you feel you've got to put in an appearance when it's murder, though."

"D'you get much trade from Benwell Lane, then?" Thackeray asked.

"We make damn sure we get *no* bloody trade from Benwell Lane, if we can help it," Robertson said. "We don't serve the buggers. There's nowt but trouble from over there."

"So where do they drink?" Kevin Mower asked, turning his gaze from the glittering optics behind the bar.

"How should I know?" the landlord said. "Next pub down t'hill towards town is the Fox. That's more your Benwell Lane sort o'place, isn't it? We're trying for a different class of customer altogether."

"Bar meals, that sort of thing?" Mower asked, running an eye down the menu chalked on a blackboard near the door.

"Aye, that sort o'thing," Robertson conceded.

"So you won't know the Smith family? The girl who's been shot and her mother and brothers?" Thackeray asked.

"Not the family as such, no. Just one of the lads - the youngest, I think he is, by name of Mick. He grazes his ponies on t'field at the back here. Pays me a bit o'rent. It's scrub-land really, not worth much, but every little helps, don't it? He's never caused me any trouble, hasn't young Mick, but I know nowt about his family. Didn't know he had a sister till she went and got herself killed. You're not safe anywhere these days, are you? The steps of a bloody hospital. I ask you."

"Mick Smith drinks here, then does he?" Thackeray asked.

The landlord looked at him pityingly.

"I told you. *None* of them drink here. I won't have any of those gippos and toe-rags on t'premises. Let one in and you'll be over-run by t' bloody lot. It's time they pulled them houses down and got the whole lot of them back to Bradfield where they belong. They've been talking about it long enough."

"Ponies?" Mower asked incredulously as he and Thackeray walked slowly back to Benwell Lane and the Smith's house. "What is this? The Wild West?"

"That's not the first time I've heard the Smiths called gippos, so perhaps that's what they are," Thackeray said. "Gypsies. It would go some way to explaining why they're so unpopular up here. When I spoke to Mrs Smith at the hospital yesterday she wasn't coherent enough to tell me her name never mind her ethnic origins. I just hope she's feeling a bit better this morning."

What had once been the front garden of the Smith's house now resembled a scrap yard. A couple of cars in a state of extreme disrepair were parked on the muddy forecourt which had long ago lost its fencing and gate. A pile of used tyres was stacked under the front window and several black bin-bags of rubbish bulged threateningly at the foot of the steps which led up to the almost entirely paint-free door in which panes of glass had been replaced by wooden boards. There was no sign of a bell or knocker, so Mower banged on the woodwork.

At first they thought that there might still be no one at home but eventually the door was inched open by a tall swarthy young man, his face pale and his eyes red-rimmed. He hardly glanced at Thackeray's warrant card before opening the door just wide enough to admit the two officers.

"Me mam's in t'kitchen. Straight through," he said. But the young man's assertion turned out to be optimistic. The woman who sat at the kitchen table in a too-tight maroon sweater with both hands clasped protectively around a mug of tea might have been corporeally there in her cluttered kitchen but not in any other way. She glanced at the newcomers with dazed eyes and nodded as Thackeray introduced himself but then her gaze returned to the milky tea and her mind to whereever it had been before they arrived. Grief took people many ways, Thackeray thought. Some people could not stop talking, wanting to analyse every minute detail of their loved one's last few moments on earth –the more sudden the death the more urgent the need to hear how it happened, what the causes were, what they had said before they were consumed by the dark cloud which had taken them from the earth. Others fell into a sort of panic, widows wanting to sell their houses for fear of destitution, children fretting over the details of funerals and hymns and headstones which would please the deceased, parents clutching at grandiose schemes to memorialise lost children who in the inevitable course of things would be soon forgotten. Others he had seen responded just as Megan Smith was responding, with a stunned disbelief which seemed to drain all consciousness from them. He did not think he would get much sense out of Mrs. Smith today.

He glanced at the young man who had opened the door.

"You are?" he asked.

"Gavin," he said. "Dana's brother. There's four of us lads. Dana were t'youngest, an after-thought, like, Mam always said." Gavin Smith looked at his mother helplessly but she did not seem to be aware of what he was saying.

"Are your brothers here?" Thackeray asked. Gavin shook his head.

"They're out," he said.

"Gone anywhere in particular?" Thackeray asked, suddenly suspicious.

"To find t'toe-rag who put our Dana in t'family way," Gavin said, suddenly on fire. "We'll kill that effing bastard."

"You didn't know?"

"She didn't tell us, did she?" Gavin asked glancing at his mother again. "She knew what we'd 'ave done about it an'all."

"Dana didn't have a regular boyfriend?"

"Dana didn't have a fucking boyfriend at all," her brother said. "She were only a little lass, for God's sake."

Thackeray was on the point of saying that thirteen was not unusually young these days for a girl to take a boyfriend or even a lover, but something about the young man's silent intensity held him back. Behind him they heard the front door open and close and suddenly the kitchen was crowded with three more young men, two of them as tall and dark as Gavin and as threatening, the third a slighter and paler version of the Smith template.

"Our Tom, our Terry and our Mick," Gavin offered. The brother ranged in age from mid-twenties to late teens and the four of them filled the space with an unstable cocktail of grief and aggression.

"Have you found the bugger yet, then?" Tom, who seemed to be the oldest of the quartet asked.

Thackeray shook his head noncommittally and glanced at Mower, who was leaning against a cluttered worktop and watching the proceedings with dark blank eyes. For the first time since he had known the sergeant, Thackeray felt constantly uneasy about his capacity to keep his head. The air in the room hummed with tension and he was painfully aware that they were outnumbered in a confined space by young men as heavy and as fit as they were themselves, and much more volatile.

"Finding a gunman is never easy," he said carefully. "We've a lot of scientific tests to do to give us some idea where the gun came from, where the killer was firing from, all that sort of thing. What we came up here for was to talk to your mother, to see if she has any idea who might have wanted Dana dead."

"Mam," Tom said, putting a protective hand on his mother's shoulder. "Can you talk to this copper?"

With what looked like a super-human effort, Megan Smith turned slightly in her chair to meet Thackeray's eyes, her own reduced to reddened slits in a face made blotchy and swollen with crying.

"What does he want?" she asked.

"I know this is very difficult," Thackeray said. "But I must find out whether it's possible someone was deliberately trying to shoot Dana - or you. You do understand that, don't you?" The woman shrugged wearily.

"Why would anyone want my little lass dead?" she asked.

"Did her boyfriend know she was pregnant, Mrs. Smith?" he asked, feeling the tension in the room rise another notch as he stepped onto what he guessed had become forbidden territory.

"I don't know owt about her boyfriend," Mrs. Smith said. "She only told me she were expecting when I asked her about getting fat."

"She never told you who the father was?"

"She did not."

"And she decided she didn't want the baby?"

Mrs. Smith glanced at her sons.

"I told her her brothers'd not have it," she said. "It'd not be wanted here. It were best to get rid of it."

"One thing puzzled me, Mrs. Smith," Thackeray said, trying to remain impassive as he felt Mower's eyes boring into the back of his neck. "The May Anderson Hospital is private and it's not cheap. How did Dana come to be having her operation there?"

"Aye, well, they told us at t'Infirmary that she were too far gone, didn't they? Kept her waiting weeks and then told her they wouldn't do it. But doctor from t'other place came up after and said he'd do it for her, free of charge. So that's what we did day before yesterday. I wanted to bring her home straight off but they said they should keep her in overnight because she were so young. I should have brought her back, shouldn't I, and she'd have been alive now. But it weren't to be. Fate's a right hard thing, mister, right hard."

Thackeray glanced around the young men who crowded the kitchen.

"I'm told you're not the most popular people on the estate," he said. Four pairs of unfriendly dark eyes were fixed on him as Tom Smith took it upon himself to speak for the family.

"That's nowt to do wi' Dana," he said. "There's folk up here who don't like me an't'lads because we don't go along wi'-some o't' stuff they get up to. Drugs an'that. But that's nowt to do wi' Mam or Dana. We give as good as we get, and don't get women and children involved."

"None of you?" Thackeray risked scepticism which was met with more glowers.

"We want this begger found, mister," Tom Smith said; his voice thick with anger and grief. "If it's owt to do with any begger round here we'll find out, won't we lads?" His brothers nodded.

"And tell *me*, please," Thackeray snapped. "I want no feuds over this. No taking the law into your own hands. Do you understand?"

"Mebbe," Tom said and with that Thackeray had to be content.

"If it's a choice between gang warfare up there or fanatical Christians down in town I'm not sure which frightens me most," Thackeray said sombrely as they eased back down the hill towards Bradfield.

"The road to hell or the road to heaven, according to taste," Mower said.

Chapter 3

Laura swam purposefully one final length of the pool to the shallow end where she took hold of two small dark-haired boys and towed them to the steps.

"You're a damn sight fitter than I am," said Vicky Mandelson, following behind with her small daughter bouncing up and down in the water with the help of electric blue arm-bands. Vicky glanced down at her one-piece black swimsuit and pulled in her stomach, looking enviously at her friend's slim figure.

"Does my tum look big in this? You can't believe these idiots who say you'll get your figure back," she said. "Not after three anyway."

"I wouldn't know," Laura threw over her shoulder as she helped Daniel and Nathan haul themselves out of the water and wrapped towels around their dripping bodies. Vicky drew a sharp breath as she followed behind. She knew that there was more than one reason Laura was so willing to come with her to the pool once a week to help with the children. She did not doubt for a moment the genuineness of the devotion her unmarried friend showed the three young Mendelsons, and particularly the daughter she and David had named after Laura, but she had also seen the covert longing in Laura's eyes when she thought she was not observed, the longing for children of her own.

"You could always stop taking the pill," she said softly, safe in the knowledge that the boys were too absorbed in their vigorous towelling to take any notice of the adults' conversation. Laura gazed at her friend for a moment, her eyes opaque.

"I don't think that's the answer," she said.

"Mum, Nathan's got my underpants," a naked Daniel Mendelson shrieked, chasing his brother half way round the changing room before his mother was able to catch his younger brother and restore order. Laura shrugged.

"It takes two," she said, her expression unusually wistful. Unwilling parenthood, she had decided long ago, was no way to welcome a child into the world. With much laughter they helped the two boys finish drying themselves and pull clothes onto still damp bodies, before Vicky bundled the baby into a thick towelling suit and chivvied all three into their seats in the back of her Volvo and strapped them in.

"You're sure Michael won't be able to get away?" she asked, back home, as she shooed the boys into the kitchen for their tea.

"He's up to his eyes in this shooting at the May Anderson hospital," Laura said shortly. She stood looking at Vicky, who had been her best friend at university, and not for the first time nor the last she was overwhelmed with envy for a marriage which looked as secure now as it had ever done, and for the brood of demanding children to whose needs Vicky had apparently entirely happily surrendered herself. "I suppose I'll have to get used to policemen's erratic hours. If it lasts."

Vicky caught the note of uncertainty in Laura's voice.

"This time, surely it'll last. I thought you looked two looked really happy last time you came to supper."

"Of course we are," Laura said brightly.

"And his divorce?"

"He's filed the papers."

"Good," Vicky said. "Now have a drink while I put Naomi Laura to bed and then you can tell me all about it."

"I'll read the boys a story," Laura volunteered. She kissed Naomi goodnight, letting her cheek rest for a moment against the little girl's silky skin, taking in the sweet smell of her, and she felt her eyes prickle.

"Come on boys," she said too cheerfully. "What's it to be?"

Later, after an excellent Italian supper and more than her share of the wine, Laura sat watching the local television news, which was almost completely given over to the shooting of the previous day. David Mendelson glanced over at his guest.

"I suppose this little lot is why Michael couldn't make it tonight? It could take a long time, this case. A single shot, no sign of the gunman - not a lot to go on is it?"

"He said he'd drop in to pick me up on his way home," Laura said. She let the word reverberate around her head, still unused to the idea that it now meant a place for two. With a faint smile, she turned her attention back to David, who as a crown prosecutor might ultimately find himself working on the case of the hospital gunman if a charge was ever brought.

"It doesn't seem possible that anyone could have deliberately shot a girl that age, does it," she said. "But the family's not very popular. I went up to do some interviews yesterday."

"It must be difficult for you two when your work touches on Michael's," David said. "Does that old bastard Grant put any pressure on you to bring him the extra tit-bit?"

"He'd better not," Laura said. "Michael would string him up if he thought he was trying it on. But I get the feeling that Superintendent Longley's not too happy with our living arrangements."

"Jack Longley's an old pussy cat when it comes to the point," David said unexpectedly. Laura grinned. She suspected that an old grizzly bear would have been an apter description of Michael Thackeray's boss.

Maggie Sullivan had lost track of how long she had waited for the bus by the side of the main road. She had wrapped herself up carefully against the bitter wind which was whipping through the village from the east, cutting through the layers of shabby clothing and the scarf she had wrapped around her thin grey hair. The bus shelter provided nothing of the sort. The glass had been shattered and lay in a frosted heap around her feet, and the seat, which some village benefactor had donated in anticipation of just such a day and just such a wait, had been made unusable through a combination of violent

41

assault and filth. She stamped her feet in boots which were barely waterproof and blew on her hands protected by woollen gloves worn threadbare with use. Her face seemed to shrink and shrivel under the assault of the wind but her watering eyes were determined. She had received no word from Bradfield but had woken that morning at her bungalow with an absolute conviction, confirmed to her own satisfaction by the dog-eared Tarot cards she dealt out on her table, and the voice which whispered with increasing persistence in her ear, that her daughter needed her and that she must make the journey as quickly as she could.

A small single-decker bus eventually veered erratically around the sharp bend at the far side of the village green and stopped with a wheeze of brakes and a gust of stale air as the door opened. Maggie handed her coins to the driver for the six mile journey to Eckersley and half fell into an empty seat as the vehicle lurched into motion again. It was a tedious ride, with calls at every village down the valley, picking up and dropping off a handful of people at each stop. At Eckersley she changed to another bus which would take her to the centre of Bradfield and from there yet another would, if she was lucky with the timing, deposit her at Benwell Lane a couple of hours after leaving home. The companion she couldn't see but only feel sat at her side murmuring incomprehensibly and occasionally making her wince with pain as he dug her in the ribs with a pointed elbow.

The wait in the gusty bus station at Eckersley was a long one and by the time she took a seat on the double-decker which would take her to Bradfield, Maggie felt exhausted and ill. She gazed out of the window with unseeing eyes as they bucketed and swayed down the main road which followed the winding river for most of the journey. Eventually the motion of the bus sent her into a fitful doze. She woke unrefreshed, haunted by nightmares which she could barely remember and with her conviction that something was desperately wrong with her daughter Megan's family only strengthened by her subconscious encounters with dread and desperation. The pain under her ribs had intensified now and as the bus lurched this way and that she increasingly gasped for breath. "Can't you leave us alone?" she asked her companion loudly and wondered why the woman sitting opposite her decided rather urgently to move away to another seat.

The bus-station at Bradfield was big and crowded and no one noticed a frail old woman when she sank to the ground in a doorway with her head on her chest, her breath coming in rattling gasps as she fought for air. But now Maggie's mind was quite clear as she saw Death approach again, stepping carefully over the severed heads and hands beneath his scythe, with one bony hand stretched out towards her, and then unexpectedly retreat, cursing and snarling as, in spite of the cold, she fell into a fitful sleep.

* * *

At police headquarters, Sergeant Kevin Mower had been trying not to breath in the vicinity of his boss all day. He had drunk the best part of a bottle of Scotch the previous evening, topped up again at lunchtime, in defiance of his doctor's orders, and was feeling the consequences, his hangover compounded by the familiar grinding pain in his stomach which had put him in hospital once already. DCI Thackeray sat at his desk and waited impatiently for an answer to his last question.

"Did you hear me, Kevin?" he asked.

"Yes, guv, the taxi," Mower said, shuffling through the files. "It had been ordered by Mrs. Smith to take her and Dana back home. Just as she said, in fact. He was just slowing down as he approached the hospital when he heard a shot and decided not to hang around."

"So no gunman there?"

"Nope. All above board. But we've not traced the bike. Several witnesses saw that at the end of the road, and then

43

heard it accelerate away just after the shot was fired but so far no one has given us any detail on the type of bike or who was riding it. Just that it was big and black and made a lot of noise."

"Not that a biker in leathers is easily identifiable anyway," Thackeray said gloomily. "We need a registration number to get far with that."

"They look like bloody astronauts these days, most of them," Mower said. His eyes met Thackeray's for a second and he looked away quickly.

"I'll get on then," he said. "There's still a lot of witness statements to look at. Someone must have seen something, probably without realising it was significant."

"So there's nothing much to report to the super?"

Mower shrugged.

"Not a lot," he said.

Thackeray let him go and made his way slowly up to Superintendent Jack Longley's office on the floor above and was surprised when he was met with something as close to a glower as Longley ever achieved in the normal course of their encounters. Longley and Thackeray, the bluff extrovert and the dour introvert, had learned to trust each other slowly but had recently constructed an unspoken alliance which they hoped would be the equal of anything their superiors might throw at them. They had tested each others strengths as well as weaknesses as silently as a pair of arm-wrestlers when the tragedy of Rita Desai's death had threatened both their careers. And together they had survived. Debts had been repaid and enough left unreported to bind them together irrevocably now until Longley's retirement, which hovered on the edge of both their minds like a faintly threatening cloud in a blue heaven.

"Owt happening, Michael?" Longley asked. "I've got county breathing down my neck, as usual."

"I'm still waiting for something definite from forensics," Thackeray said mildly. "Until we know what sort of gun it was we don't even know where to start looking."

"Is there a drug connection?" Longley asked. "Is some sort of turf war about to break out?"

"Nothing known as far as the girl's family is concerned," Thackeray said. "Things have a habit of going missing when the Smith lads are around but nothing major – car parts, electrical goods, even a horse once, though Michael Smith swore in court that it was his horse and someone had dyed its mane and tail to disguise its identity. He got three months regardless."

"You are joking?" Longley pleaded.

"No," Thackeray said with a faint smile. "These are tearaways, but not as we generally know them in Bradfield. They're Gypsies as far as I can make out, travellers anyway, who've settled down as much as they ever will. They still keep ponies, for God's sake, on some scrubby field next to the pub up at Benwell Green. They're about as far away from the clubs and pubs and the drugs scene as it's possible to get and still be in the same century as the rest of us. More *Heartbeat* than *The Bill*."

"So what's their little sister doing getting herself shot, for Christ's sake?"

"I still think it could have been an accident that she got hit. That someone took a pot-shot at the hospital – or at Mr. Fenton-Green, the surgeon – and hit Dana by mistake."

"Well, I suppose dotty Christians are marginally easier to deal with than a gang war," Longley said lugubriously.

"Harder to pin down, though," Thackeray said. He turned round as there was a tap on the door and Kevin Mower put his head round.

"I thought you'd want to know as soon as, sir," he said. "The message from forensics is just in. The bullet was from a semi-automatic pistol, something like a Walther PPK, they think." Mower hesitated for a moment with the understandable reticence of a bearer of bad tidings.

"There's more?" Thackeray said impatiently. The sergeant nodded.

"The bullet was damaged because it hit the wall after

45

passing through the girl, so they can't be sure, but they think they might have seen bullets from the same gun before," he said. "Two shootings in Manchester earlier in the year, Moss Side, drug-related, and then the one here in August, the lad with a bullet in the leg after that barney outside the Underground club. Those were definitely from the same semi-automatic. This one could be. You must recall Darren Cropper? See no evil, hear no evil, and keep stum if you know what's good for you – remember?" The two senior officers evidently remembered. No one had ever been charged over a shooting which left a nineteen-year-old crippled without a single wit-ness, or even the victim himself, noticing who pulled the trigger.

Longley's expression was grim as he dismissed Mower.

"Not drug-related, then?" he asked with heavy sarcasm.

"It's the first possible lead we've had," Thackeray said. "The rest is like trying to swim through born-again ambrosia."

"Aye, well, perhaps it's less messy if it's nothing to do with Mr. Fenton-Green and his controversial medical practices. At least we know which side we're on in a drugs war: nobbut our own."

"I'd best get back and read this forensic report," Thackeray said.

"All right, is he, young Mower?" Longley asked as the DCI moved towards the door. Thackeray shrugged.

"Not really," he said.

"Keep me in touch," the superintendent said. "I don't want any nasty surprises in that department."

"Sir," Thackeray said, knowing he had no choice but to comply but reluctant to even think about the inevitable moment when he would have to issue an ultimatum to Kevin Mower just as someone had once issued one to him.

Laura Ackroyd slid into the parking space the security guard had indicated and wondered whether she had pursued a point with Ted Grant several notches too far. With the shoot-ing of Dana Smith dominating the news pages of the Gazette,

46

Grant had arrived at the morning conference and dumped a heap of letters in front of Laura with a scowl.

"They're crawling out of the bloody woodwork," he said. "The green ink brigade mostly, but a few of them have summat interesting to say. It'd make a special page if you prune the nutters down to a nib or two."

With little enthusiasm, Laura had scanned a few of the readers' more printable comments on teenage pregnancy, abortion and the need to bring back corporal punishment, capital punishment and national service.

"I'd rather do it properly," she said, aware that Grant's scowl was deepening ominously, and his colour rising. She glanced at her colleagues round the table and found only expressions of gleeful anticipation at the sight of someone else tempting fate.

"Properly?" Grant had said, like the grumble of a volcano.

"Well, I could do a piece about the hospital. It's not just an abortion clinic you know. They do other things there, including fertility treatment. It would make a good feature. And I could interview the American anti-abortion man before his meeting at the Town Hall. Put all that together with the readers' letters and you'd have a good spread."

For a long moment Grant hesitated and the meeting held its collective breath, but then he grunted his assent.

"I don't want a load of bleeding heart bollocks about the need to help little slags too stupid to keep their knickers on," he said. Laura had drawn a sharp breath at that but said nothing, content to have got her own way, however grudgingly. But now she had negotiated herself past the public relations company in Leeds which protected the May Anderson Hospital from journalistic intrusion, she wondered if her instinct for a story had been as acute as Grant had evidently thought it was. The ranks of Range Rovers and BMWs in the hospital car park spoke of a clientele which hardly suggested that this was an institution devoted to the poor and needy, however apparently generous it had been to Dana Smith.

Laura stuffed her tape-recorder into her bag, locked up the car and went up the front steps which had been so carefully scrubbed down to the virgin stone that there was no sign at all of the tragedy which had been enacted there so recently. Through the swing doors she was met by a tall, dark-haired young woman in a very expensive suit with a very short skirt and very high heels who held out a hand in welcome. "Nadia Bellman," she said with a smile which did not quite reach her impeccably made up eyes. "We spoke on the phone. I'm so pleased we're going to have the opportunity of putting a more positive side of the hospital forward after the dreadful events earlier in the week. I don't think anyone here has really taken in what happened yet. That poor girl. Though as I said that's not really one of the things we can talk about."

"As I said, I want to write a profile of the hospital," Laura said, pushing unruly strands of hair out of her eyes and feeling scruffy. "My colleague Bob Baker is covering the murder."

"Yes, of course," Nadia Bellman said quickly. "I gather the police have no objection to the angle you're taking." Laura smiled grimly to herself. Nadia evidently did not know that she had her own hot-line to the police, should she need one, though she had arranged this interview so quickly that she had not had time to tell Thackeray anything about it yet. She followed Nadia into an office close to the front door and accepted the chair and the cup of coffee which was quickly offered.

"I've collected together a lot of information about the hospital for you," Nadia said as she settled herself at the desk and pushed a collection of glossy brochures in Laura's direction with long slim hands tipped with glossy red finger-nails. "I suppose you know something about its foundation. It was just a small maternity home but expanded after a bequest in the 1970s from Douglas Anderson whose two sons had been born here in the 1930s. Apparently there was some emergency after the second birth and the family was grateful for what the

48

doctor on duty did to save May Anderson's life. The bequest came with the condition that the hospital adopt her name."

"Right," Laura said, sipping her coffee thoughtfully. "And did Mr. Anderson approve of abortion as well as heroic child-birth?"

"I've really no idea," Nadia said. "That's a part of our remit we don't shout about from the roof-tops. Some people do get upset. But as far as I know they've done termina-tions here ever since the law was changed, which was before the Anderson bequest, so I can't imagine he found it a problem. It's not a problem to many people these days, is it, apart from these born-again Christians who keep waving placards around the gates. You're not one of those, are you?"

"Me? I'm neutral on these issues," Laura said, unsure why she chose to equivocate on an issue where she knew her own mind very well indeed. "When I'm working anyway."

"Right," Nadia said uncertainly.

"Do the Anderson sons take an interest in the hospital?" Laura asked.

"Not as far as I know. They're elderly themselves now. The place is run by a trust with a board of governors. It's all explained in that leaflet there." She riffled through the papers she had given Laura and selected one on the history of the hospital. "But you won't have space for ancient history, will you? What I really want to tell you about is the work Mr. Fenton-Green is doing in his fertility clinic. That's the cutting edge here. And no one can possibly object to that, can they? It must be so awful if you can't have a baby when you want one, mustn't it?"

Laura nodded non-committally, wondering why she resented the fact that Nadia Bellman was so anxious for her approval of everything the hospital did. After all, the young woman was only doing her job, even if it was a job which Laura, like most journalists, regarded with disdain if not downright contempt. But there seemed to be a personal commitment here which was undoubtedly more than the hospital trust was paying for.

"Mr. Fenton-Green is very busy in theatre today but he can probably spare you five minutes later this morning. In the meantime I've arranged for you to spend some time with the sisters in charge of the gynae ward and the fertility clinic. They'll be able to give you a good idea of just what goes on and how we're able to help women who simply wouldn't have been able to conceive up to just a few years ago."

"Great," Laura said, draining her coffee cup. Nadia led her down broad and spotless corridors with none of the noise and bustle which she associated with hospitals on television or in real life.

"Of course, every patient here has a private room," Nadia explained. "The facilities vary, of course. We have one or two suites at the top of the range, but most people pay simply for the privacy and the convenience of coming in when they want to rather than going on a waiting list."

"Presumably that doesn't apply to the maternity ward," Laura said tartly. "Or do babies arrive by appointment too in the private sector?" Laura could hear her grandmother's old-fashioned socialism in the question and was not surprised when Nadia threw her a faintly astonished look over her shoulder.

"Joke," Laura said defensively, but was not sure that she was believed.

"How come that someone like Dana Smith had her abortion here?" she asked.

"You'll have to talk to Mr. Fenton-Green about that," Nadia said, her expression still a little chillier than before. "He makes these arrangements himself. I think he sees it as some sort of personal charity, actually." It was not at all clear that Nadia Bellman shared the surgeon's enthusiasm for helping those unable to afford the hospital's usual fees. She eventually stopped outside a door at the end of the corridor.

"This is the staff sitting room," she said. "I arranged for

Stella Brady and Barbara King to meet you for a chat here. And Dr. Mahood said that he'd have a word. Then Dave Randall, Mr. Fenton-Green's technician, will show you where the cutting-edge fertility treatment is done. And you can meet Mr. Fenton-Green himself there when he comes out of theatre at about twelve. I think that should cover everything. If you do have any more questions you can get me by phone this afternoon." She handed Laura a card. "If I'm not in the office, try my mobile," she said. She opened the door and glanced in, waving Laura to enter.

"Stella, Barbara - this is Laura Ackroyd from the *Gazette*. She won't bite. Or if she does just let me know." With a smile which now definitely lacked warmth Nadia ushered Laura into the room and closed the door behind her.

Stella Brady was sitting in a low armchair with her feet on another, shoes off and the top two buttons of her uniform dress undone, smoking a cigarette. She was a slight, very thin woman whom Laura placed in her early forties. Her blonde hair was pulled back under the old-fashioned uniform cap and her face showed no trace of make-up. Her colleague, Barbara King, was older, plumper and altogether more relaxed as she stood by the sink and waved at a steaming kettle and coffee mugs beside her on the work-top. Laura shook her head and Sister King shrugged and brewed herself a large mug into which she liberally spooned sugar and powdered milk before crossing the room to join the other two women.

"I hope you're not going to write about the Anderson as if it's nothing but an abortion clinic," Stella said, her face full of suspicion. "Some of us won't get involved in terminations and think what we do in the rest of the hospital is a damn sight more constructive."

"It's mainly because we *didn't* want to give that impression that I'm here," Laura said carefully, only slightly surprised at the hostility she was meeting at every turn. She had no doubt that the entire hospital must have been traumatised by Dana Smith's brutal death and must be wondering whether new patients would be as keen to sign in after that as they had been previously.

Mr. Fenton-Green's too generous," Stella said, stubbing out her cigarette and lighting another with hands that trembled slightly. "He picks up these cases which have been turned down elsewhere without any idea of what he's letting himself in for and then look what happens. He could have been killed by that bullet just as easily as the girl."

"So I gather," Laura said. "Sister…Should I call you Sister? I thought that had gone as a title now."

"Here we even have a matron," Barbara King said with a broad smile.

"The patients like it and what the patients like the patients get," Stella Brady added.

"You sound as though you disapprove," Laura said, thinking again of her grandmother for whom the establishment of the National Health Service had been as near to a religious experience as Joyce Ackroyd was ever likely to admit to.

"I suppose you think that's odd as I work here," Stella said slipping her feet back into her shoes the better to lean towards Laura with something close to passion lighting up her face. "Well, I'll tell you what's odd. Working in an NHS hospital so understaffed that you don't even know the names of the patients you're supposed to be looking after is what's odd, until you're so tired at the end of a shift that you're no longer sure that you've given out the right drugs – or even if you've given out the drugs at all. *That's* odd. I did that for fifteen years, until my husband was on the point of leaving me and my kids thought I was a stranger who just popped into the house now and again to have a kip. When I didn't even notice that my own daughter was sick herself. That's what I call *odd*. And that's why I'm here."

"I'm sorry," Laura said. "I didn't mean to imply…"

"Oh forget it," Stella Brady said, buttoning up her uniform. "You just touched a raw nerve, that's all. Most of the staff are here because the pay's better and the working conditions are on another planet compared to the Infirmary."

"But why would the Infirmary turn down someone like Dana Smith for an abortion?" Laura asked. "I would have thought a kid of that age would be guaranteed a termination if that's what she wanted."

"The consultant down the road is a bit iffy about abortion," Barbara King cut in, and her disapproval was obvious.

"We don't know anything about the circumstances," Stella Brady said sharply. "She might have been pressured by her mother, there might have been medical problems – all sorts of reasons for her to be turned down."

"And Mr. Fenton-Green would have been easier to persuade?" Laura asked.

"You could put it that way," Stella said, glancing away.

"Or you could say he's just a more sympathetic doctor," Barbara King cut in.

"One of the great things about this place is that it can do some of the things that the NHS can't afford to do any more." She glanced at her colleague. "Isn't that right, Stella?" But her colleague just shrugged in response.

"Like what then?" Laura asked. "Not just easier abortions, surely?"

"No, no, like the fertility treatment." Barbara King's enthusiasm took over. "I'll take you down to see one of our new mums who's just had twins after trying for a baby unsuccessfully for about ten years. They'd told them it was hopeless at all the other hospitals they'd been to. The expression on her face is as much justification as this hospital needs."

"She was very, very lucky," Stella King said. "If you'd seen their records…" She shrugged. "There's no doubt Stephen Fenton-Green is very good at what he does. Those particular twins were well-nigh miraculous, if that's not blasphemous."

"You run the maternity ward?" Laura asked Sister King.

"I always loved midwifery," Barbara King said. "Stella here has much more to do with Mr. Fenton-King's fertility programme. She sees all the heartbreak when it doesn't work out. I only see the happy families when it does. It's much the easier option. Of course, not all our mothers go through treatment. Lots of them have babies perfectly naturally, thank goodness."

"Is it very expensive, having a test-tube baby?" Laura asked.

"Not all of them have test-tube babies of course, but fertility treatment is expensive," Stella Brady said. "But most of the patients have been able to raise the money from family or from loans. It's not prohibitive. I've never understood why the Infirmary is so reluctant to get involved."

"Mr. Fenton-Green will help out with that too, if he thinks it's a particularly sad case," Sister King said. "Stella's a Catholic of course, but this isn't one of the things she objects to, is it?" Sister Brady shook her head quickly.

"Bringing life into the world can't be a sin," she said. "Just so long as the procedures are ethical."

"But terminating a pregnancy…?"

"Of course," Sister Brady said. "We don't have that right."

"So you've some sympathy with the protesters outside then?"

"Some," Sister Brady said shortly. "But not if they were involved in this shooting. That was murder too."

The two nurses nodded sombrely.

"You've no idea what an effect it's had here," Barbara King said. "This is usually such a happy hospital. After all we're dealing mainly with positive treatments which aren't life-threatening even if they don't work. We're very lucky that way, we see very little of death – apart from the terminations, of course, and I don't really share Stella's views on that. I think there are circumstances…" Her voice trailed away as if this was old ground which there was little point in retreading, leaving a silence which Laura was reluctant to break.

"Tell me about Stephen Fenton-Green as a person," Laura said at length, trying to lighten the mood. "People speak highly of him."

"He's a very remarkable man, I think," Sister King said quickly. "He never gives up and he never lets his patients give up. Somehow he manages to keep hope alive even when the treatment seems to be interminable and the parents can see no end in sight. It's a great gift, that, to keep hope alive." If Stella Brady looked less enthusiastic she did not offer any reason why.

Behind them the door opened suddenly and before the nurses could tell Laura anything more about the consultant they were joined by a young Asian man in a doctor's white coat with the enthusiastic gleam of the convert in his eyes.

"Nadia told me I'd find you here," he said. "Imran Mahood, Mr. Fenton-Green's registrar. I've been delegated to show you the labs, though the research is not really my area…"

"I was just about to take Ms Ackroyd to Ash ward to talk to Mrs. Bailey and see the twins," Sister King said.

"Perhaps you could do that afterwards," Dr. Mahood said brusquely. "I have a window just now. I'm due at the Infirmary for an out-patients' clinic at eleven."

Laura got to her feet trying to hide her frustration as Imran Mahood took her arm and urged her out of the room leaving the two nurses, silently seething, behind.

"Mr. Fenton-Green and I both do some sessions at the Infirmary but the real advances in fertility treatment are being done here. We work with a team at Leeds, so we're right on the cutting edge. People think it all happens in London, you know, but that's not right. The first test-tube baby was born in the North of England and I know the boss is hoping to make a breakthrough here in the not-to-distant future."

"Do you have anything specific in mind?" Laura asked, her curiosity stirred now. She had developed little enthusiasm for science at school but she knew that many of the most dramatic – and controversial – developments were taking place on the frontier where medicine meets genetics. Mahood glanced at her, his eyes still gleaming, but an expression of caution there too.

"I think Mr. Fenton-Green would like to tell you about his experimental work himself," the doctor said. "I'm not up to speed on that. But I can show you how we do the *in vitro* work on fertility. That's the technique we used with Mrs. Bailey after all else failed. In spite of all the hype, it's a treatment of last resort and the failure rate is still very high. But with Mrs. Bailey it worked first time and she has healthy twins."

"That must be very satisfying," Laura said.

"Oh, it is, it is," Mahood said. He had led her to the hospital's third and top floor and was now unlocking a door labelled "No Admittance without Authorisation." Behind the doors was what even Laura recognised must be a state of the art laboratory, all gleaming glass and steel, where a solitary figure, dressed in white protective clothing and a face mask, was working at a bench at the far end of the room.

"That's Dave Randall, our technician," Mahood said but made no attempt to take Laura across the room for a proper introduction and spent the next ten minutes taking Laura on a whistle stop tour of the lab, lifting human eggs and sperm out of smoking containers of liquid nitrogen for her inspection, explaining exactly how fertilisation was achieved in a petrie dish and the egg re-implanted in the mother's womb, and flicking through a scrap-book of photographs of exhausted but ecstatic women clutching their miraculously achieved off-spring to their breasts.

"So what's next in reproductive technology?" Laura asked at last. "Will we soon be able to design our own babies? Choose the sex, the brains, the beauty, the child who'll play football for England?"

Mahood shrugged.

"It's almost possible already," he said. "But public opinion isn't ready for it. We'll be confined to eliminating some of the worst of the inherited diseases first – cystic fibrosis, muscular dystrophy, haemophilia, that sort of thing."

"Sounds pretty good to me," Laura said.

"But why confine ourselves to eliminating the bad?"

Mahood said, his face full of passion again. "Why not select the good characteristics? Why not improve the human race? What's so wrong with that?"

Long before Laura could marshal her thoughts to answer that most fundamental of questions the door from the hospital was unlocked again from the outside to admit a man Laura had not met before but recognised instantly from his photograph on the previous day's front page of the *Gazette*. Stephen Fenton-Green glanced around his domain possessively for a moment before holding out his hand to Laura and giving her the full benefit of his Robert Redford smile.

"They told me I might find you up here," he said. He glanced at his watch - a Rolex, Laura noted without malice. "Imran, you're going to be late for your antenatal clinic if you're not careful. Thanks for looking after Miss Ackroyd, but I'll take over now." Mahood shook Laura's hand without comment, closing the laboratory door carefully behind him while Fenton-Green took Laura's elbow and steered her towards the small office separated from the main part of the lab by frosted glass windows.

"We won't disturb Mr. Randall any further," he said. "He's very busy. But we can have a chat in here. He glanced again at his watch. "I've got about fifteen minutes free and then I'll take you back down to the wards." Stephen Fenton-Green, Laura thought, was undoubtedly a man who liked to be in control.

Chapter 4

Laura chopped root ginger and garlic and gazed out of the kitchen window at her recently acquired garden where the autumn leaves lay in umber drifts on the unkempt grass, gold in the light cast through the uncurtained windows. They would have to invest in a lawn-mower in the spring, she thought, and wondered how Thackeray would react to her desire for that most suburban of machines. She glanced at her watch. He was late. He was always late. She should have got used to it by now, she thought, and glanced again at the ingredients for her Thai supper which had the inestimable advantage of cooking in five minutes flat in her shiny new wok. She left the chopped chicken and vegetables under the cover of a tea-cloth and opened the French windows in the living room to take a deep breath of relatively fresh Bradfield air.

She felt as if she was living on the edge of a precipice and that at some point soon she and Thackeray would have to leap off and see whether or not they could fly. The day's work had unsettled her in a way which she could not have predicted. After she had been ushered back downstairs at the May Anderson Hospital by a Stephen Fenton-Green who had proved as charming, confident and personally inaccessible as she had expected, a beaming Sister Barbara King had taken her through to her maternity ward and introduced her to Karen Bailey, an angular woman with protruding shoulder-blades and a mass of bleached blonde hair who looked an improbable mother to the healthy pink twin girls who slept in cots at her bedside.

"Only two weeks premature," Sister King had said proprietorially. "A Caesar, of course, to be on the safe side. You can't take any chances with twins, can you, dear? But aren't they poppets?"

Karen Bailey had ignored the midwife and fixed an unfriendly gaze on Laura.

"I'm from the *Gazette*," Laura had said quickly. "I'm writing an article about the hospital. You seem to be the star patient at the moment. What are you going to call the girls?"

"What's it to you?" Karen had snapped back. "Their dad was thinking of Reggie and Ronnie, if they was boys, but they ain't so he'll have to put up with it, won't he?"

"We seem to have had so many baby girls just recently, you're very much in fashion, dear," Sister King gushed.

Laura had flinched slightly at that, but persevered.

"Would you have a picture taken for the paper?"

"No I bloody wouldn't," Karen Bailey said, her face surly now.

"Oh, Karen," Barbara King wailed but Laura turned away quickly, knowing that the rejection was final and that she did not want to get into prolonged negotiations with this fiercely hostile woman over the sleeping heads of her tiny babies who were doing unexpectedly unprofessional things to her tear-ducts.

"Oh, dear," Barbara King had complained as she ushered Laura back out of the ward to reception. "Such a shame. Mr. Fenton-Green has an international reputation in fertility, you know. We get so many celebrities coming in but I'm not allowed to tell you about those. Privacy, you know. Of course, once they're here they're treated exactly the same as any other patient. Even the lame ducks Mr. Fenton-Green picks up from the NHS get exactly the same facilities. I would have thought Karen could have cooperated with the *Gazette*, but new mothers can be very unpredictable. The hormones, you know."

"Karen Bailey's not one of Mr. Fenton-Green's 'lame ducks', is she?" Laura had asked. But Sister King had shaken her head.

"Oh, no, she's being paid for by her boyfriend. They've been together for a long time, I understand, and he's certainly not short of a bob or two."

"Oh shit," Laura said to herself as she snatched dead-heads off the late and languishing geraniums which were the first flowers she had planted in her patch of garden. "Oh hell and damnation, Michael. I wouldn't mind *triplets* with you."

Irritably she dashed the tears from her eyes and went back into the flat where she put Mozart's clarinet quintet on the CD player and flung herself into an armchair. She was, she thought, behaving like some fictional thirty-something in a panic over her biological clock. But the problem was not just one of timing. The subject of children was one which she had never found the courage to broach with a man whose son's death had destroyed his wife and almost destroyed him. It was a subject he avoided with bitter determination and she could not find it in herself to blame him even when, as today, she felt as if the imperative of motherhood might begin to tear her apart.

She heard the front door open and close as the last notes of the quintet faded.

"Right on cue," she said, jumping up and kissing Thackeray even before he had taken off his coat.

"To what do I owe this?" he asked wryly, pushing a whirl of copper hair away from her pale oval face and returning the kiss with interest.

"There's not really time for passion before supper," Laura said, trying to extricate herself for fear of having to postpone the meal for another hour or so.

"Which is?" Thackeray asked, without too much enthusiasm.

"Thai chicken with stir-fried vegetables," Laura said.

"God woman, you'll be giving me cod with garlic mash instead of honest Yorkshire fish'n'chips if this goes on much longer."

"We could try that new place which has opened at Eckersley some time," Laura said breaking free and heading back towards the kitchen. "It's supposed to be very good.

Some young chef who managed to escape the clutches of that grumpy bastard on TV – what's his name?"

"Simple coppers know nowt about such things," Thackeray said, coming up behind her and sniffing suspiciously. "There's enough garlic there to run the central heating. Are you sure about this?"

"Quite sure," Laura said. "Now sit down while I wield the wok. Timing is all with oriental cookery."

"If you say so," Thackeray said, evidently happy to go back into the living room and sink into the chair Laura had just vacated. "Who've you been tormenting with your impertinent questions today?"

"The May Anderson Hospital, as it happens," Laura called over her shoulder. "Ted wants a feature on it. You're not going to make an arrest, are you, and put the whole thing on hold while we wait for a trial?"

"Nothing's imminent, as far as I can see," Thackeray said. "What did you make of Fenton-Green then?"

"Most of them seem to think he's the second son of God," Laura said. "He does seem to be generous with his time for the poor and needy, considering it's a private hospital, but I can't say I warmed to the sainted Stephen. He's almost too good to be true."

"I've only seen him in a state of shock after he narrowly missed a bullet," Thackeray said. "Not the best moment to make a definitive character assessment. But I can't say I liked the man much."

"Do you think he was the target?"

"Increasingly unlikely, I'd say," Thackeray said slowly. "We're beginning to think that Dana might have been the victim of some family feud up at Benwell Lane. But you didn't hear me say that."

"Of course not, Chief Inspector," Laura said primly. "Now come and sit down. Eat and enjoy."

Detective Sergeant Kevin Mower sat in a secluded corner of

the back bar at the Fox and sipped his second scotch of the day. The clock over the bar told him that it was twelve thirty and although he knew that it was as inaccurate as most pub clocks it still meant that the informant he was waiting for was indubitably late. He ran a hand wearily over his dark stubble, knocked back his drink and returned to the bar for another.

The room was not full. A couple of men in work-clothes pored over a racing paper in one corner, and three women of uncertain age giggled over Bacardi-and-cokes in another, but the lunch-time rush, if the Fox boasted such a thing, had evidently not yet begun. Perhaps the location was a bit exposed for Tully, Mower thought. Although the pub was half a mile from Benwell Lane, which was the object of Mower's inquiries, it was possibly too close for comfort. He took his drink back to his seat, slung back another mouthful, and leaned back against the faded upholstery of the bench behind him and closed his eyes. Sleep, as elusive these days as innocence in a brothel, wound its fingers around his brain for a couple of minutes until he sat up convulsively, aware that someone was casting a shadow across his corner of the room. Jeff Tully was not an imposing man, small in stature, thin faced, scraggy necked and almost bald above the turned up collar of his worn donkey jacket, but he had come up quietly enough to startle Mower.

"You're bloody late," the sergeant said angrily, grabbing his glass and half rising in his seat.

"I were held up," Tully said, without apology. "I'll have the same as you."

Mower scowled but did not argue. He knew the conventions as well as his informant did and they included buying the drinks. He came back with two more glasses of Scotch.

"So what the hell's going on up this end of the town?" Mower said. "I expect to hear the word *before* things go down, not after we get a kid of thirteen in the morgue."

"Aye, well, it's a bit of a stunner all round, this one, isn't it?" Tully said. "Bolt from t'blue, it were, as far as I know."

62

"Come on, Tully," Mower said. "That won't bloody wash. You know as well as I do that guns mean drugs and that means endless trouble for every villain in Bradfield, including you. If we don't crack this quickly we'll have the drug squad, the serious crime squad, MI5 even, crawling all over the place. So what's the connection between little Dana Smith and the drug scene? Her brothers, is it?"

"I know nowt about owt like that, Mr. Mower," Tully said with enough vehemence to almost persuade Mower to believe him. "I keep out of that sort of mucky stuff, you know that."

"But the Smith brothers? Do they keep out of it? Or are they trying to muscle into it? There's enough of them to set up a firm with just the one family."

"Small time, they are," Tully said scornfully. "The odd bit of twoccing, nicking car radios, that sort of stuff. Nowt heavy as far as I know. No form to speak of. We're on t'edge o't'Country here and they're country lads, not city boys. I doubt they'd recognise a spliff if someone stuffed it up their nostril, never mind owt stronger. You must know that."

"We know what they've got caught for, and some of the stuff we can't prove," Mower said. "But maybe they got ambitious all of a sudden? Is that it?"

"If it were they might ha'got a good seeing to themselves," Tully said. "But their kid sister? I don't know anyone who'd do that. Honest, I don't. That's evil, that is."

"You live up here. Is there any word on who put her in the family way to start with?" Mower asked, but Tully shook his head over his empty glass. "Is that at the bottom of it?" Mower insisted.

"If I hear owt I'll let you know," Tully said.

"You do that," Mower said, a threat in his voice.

"Funny thing is, it's the mother in that family you hear most on," Tully said unexpectedly. "Right old battle axe, she is. Always rowing wi't'neighbours."

"Anyone in particular?"

"Anyone and everyone as I hear it," Tully said. "The

Smith's have been in Benwell Lane for years and I don't think they thought much o'some o't riff-raff that came up here after Bronte House were pulled down. Place went right down hill after that."

Mower smiled grimly at this unexpected sliver of social analysis.

"So you think there might be enough bad blood up there to provoke a shooting?"

"Aye, well, it's as likely as them gippo lads getting into drugs, isn't it?" Tully said, his voice querulous now. "Honest to God, I don't know, Mr. Mower. I've heard nowt about the lass. And if I do I'll be in touch."

"Do that," Mower said, weary now. Tully stood up, with a hopeful expression on his face but Mower shook his head.

"You've told me nothing I haven't heard already," he said.

"Ta very much," Tully said, turning on his heel and heading out of the bar with a silent fury which turned a few desultory heads in his direction.

When the door had clattered shut behind him, Mower finished his drink and followed him out of the bar. His car was in the car-park and it took only five minutes to drive up the hill to the cluster of run-down council houses on Benwell Lane and park outside the Smith's house immediately behind a VW Golf which he thought he recognised.

"What the hell's she doing here," he muttered, getting out of the car and looking around. For a moment he ignored the watching chorus of youths who seemed to spend all their time perched on a stone wall just across the road from the Smith's house. But then, when a swirl of raucous laughter greeted some sally which he could not hear, he walked towards them angrily, his warrant card in hand.

"Something funny, lads?" he asked, casting an experienced eye over the jeans and football tops in which most of the group braved the chilly November wind. "As funny as United's performance this season, is it?"

"What's that supposed to mean?" the tallest and meanest

looking of the boys asked belligerently, thrusting out his chest in its canary shirt.

"Let's just say the Yellows wouldn't last two minutes where I come from," Mower said. He knew that they could tell from his accent that he was not local but guessed that they would not be able to place him too precisely. "Last time I was at Highbury they leathered Man.U four-nil." The group made an extreme effort to appear unimpressed by that but the youngest boy, shivering in his thin top, could not sustain the pretence.

"Were you there, then? I saw that match on Sky."

"I get down there when I can," Mower said dismissively, his credibility established. "I had a season ticket when I lived in the Smoke. Now, let's get a bit of sense out of you lot, shall we? Which of you knew Dana Smith?"

All the boys looked away at that, although again it was the youngest who proved least able to maintain the defiance.

"At school, like," he muttered. "We saw her at school."

"And her boyfriend? One of you lot, was it?"

"Fuck off," the oldest boy said this time. "You wouldn't see us out wi' some gippo like Dana Smith."

"Well, someone didn't seem to mind," Mower said. "She was pretty fit, was Dana. She must have made a hit somewhere. Was it not anyone at school, then?"

More shrugs at that.

"Them brothers of hers would'a done their nuts if they'd seen anyone from round here wi'Dana," the oldest boy admitted at last. "They're mad, them Smith lads, you know? Bet they wanted to keep her for themselves. Right barmy beggars. I bet they killed her themselves an'all, if you really want to know. It's them you should be locking up."

"I'll bear that in mind," Mower said. "So as far as you know no one round here was going out with Dana?"

The head-shaking and expressions of bafflement at the question would have done justice to an acting class and Mower knew he would not get much further. He glanced across at the Smith house, where two of the ground floor windows were boarded up.

"Someone been chucking bricks, have they?" he asked.

"It weren't us," the youngest boy said quickly although the only response Mower got from the rest of the group was a sullen stare. He glanced at his watch.

"You come home for your lunch , do you? You'll just have time to get back to school for your first lesson this afternoon then, won't you? I won't keep you." The boys looked at him, puzzled for a moment, and then slid reluctantly down from the wall and began to walk away down the road, scuffing their feet. Mower did not think they would get as far as the secondary school a bus-ride away but at least the ploy had sent them on their way without overt threats.

Mower turned back towards the Smiths' house, where, as if in answer to his earlier question, the familiar figure of Laura Ackroyd, muffled in a bright green fleece against the chilly wind from the moors, appeared around the corner of the house, looking as surprised to see Mower as he was to see her.

"There's no one in," she said, with one of the blazing smiles which still had the power to send a shiver through the sergeant, who had nursed ambitions in Laura's direction until he had been comprehensively pre-empted by his boss. "I wanted an interview with Mrs. Smith, but the house is deserted. I thought she had half a dozen sons. They can't all be out, surely?"

"Four sons," Mower said. "That's enough journalistic exaggeration for one day, Ms Ackroyd."

"Point taken," Laura said, with a grin. "How are you, Kevin? I don't seem to have seen you for a while."

"Surviving," Mower said.

"Only just, by the look of you," Laura said, surveying Mower's unshaven face and unkempt hair. "Is there anything I can do?"

"Come and have a drink with me," Mower suggested,

glancing across the green to the Cricketers' Arms, where the car-park was filling up for lunch.

"Only if you eat something as well," Laura said cautiously. Mower shrugged.

"Whatever," he said.

They drove the short distance to the pub car-park and made their way to the bar where a comfortable buzz of patrons was sampling the lunch menu.

"I've passed this place dozens of time on the way up to Broadley," Laura said. "But I'd no idea it was so popular."

"New landlord, trying to impress, apparently," Mower said. "What'll you have?" Laura studied the menu for a moment.

"A V and T, and a ploughman's with Brie," she said. Mower came back quickly with the drinks, pushing the vodka in Laura's direction and keeping his hands on a glass of what could have been tomato juice. "They'll bring the food," he said.

"A Virgin?" Laura asked sceptically, looking at his drink.

"Not going to tell tales out of school, are you?" Mower said, his eyes opaque. "How's it going with you and the boss, anyway? Are you domesticating him at last?"

"Oh, I wouldn't go as far as that," Laura said with what she hoped was a confident smile, but suspected was not quite confident enough for the sergeant's sharp eyes. "And you? Surviving doesn't look as if it's doing you much good."

"Work's OK," Mower said. "Sitting in the pub's OK. Three in the morning's not."

"I can imagine," Laura said quietly. "Michael still won't talk about what happened to Rita."

"It wasn't his fault," Mower said, staring at his glass. "The inquest said so, the internal inquiry said so, no one thinks it was."

"Except Michael," Laura said. "So there you both are, busy blaming yourselves - and by the look of you, destroying yourself in the process."

"Leave it, Laura. You can't help." Mower turned away to

take two plates from the waitress who had brought their lunch, although as Laura tucked in to her bread and French cheese he merely toyed with his.

"Were you up here to see the Smiths as well?" she asked at last.

Mower nodded.

"There's still a lot we don't know about that family," he said. "And you?"

"I wanted to ask Mrs. Smith how Stephen Fenton-Green came to be treating her daughter in the May Anderson in the first place. I'm doing a feature on the hospital. He seems to be running a rather sophisticated version of pet-rescue down there, but how he picks his pets I just don't know."

"It's odd none of the Smiths are there," Mower said. "You'd think if people are putting bricks through the windows one of the sons would stick around to protect the house."

"Well, I don't think they've done a runner," Laura said. "There's a whole load of washing hanging out the back. I doubt the lads have gone far without their jeans."

"I'll get uniformed to keep an eye out till they turn up," Mower said. He drained his glass with more enthusiasm that its allegedly non-alcoholic contents warranted, glanced at the crowded bar and then shrugged wearily.

"I'd better get back or the guv'nor will have search parties out," he said.

"You'd better hope he's not got his breathalyser handy," Laura said as they got up to go.

"I'm OK, Laura," Mower said, controlling his anger with difficulty. "Don't interfere, right?"

"Right," she said cheerfully, although she did not believe him for a minute.

* * *

The smell of incense was so strong and so evocative that it caught at Michael Thackeray's throat as he stood at the rear of

68

St. Augustine's Roman Catholic Church and took stock. He had chosen very deliberately to interview Father Dermot Burke on his own. So when the sergeant had offered to grill one of his informants who happened to live in Benwell Lane, Thackeray had urged him on his way with an enthusiasm Mower had wondered at. But there were too many demons from the past lurking in the dark corners of churches for him to want Kevin Mower breathing down his neck when he tackled Father Burke about his involvement with Dorothy Knight's campaign.

The church was a huge, echoing Victorian edifice which must have been built when Bradfield's mill-workers were kept docile by piety as well as starvation wages and ill-health in the back-to-back cottages which had once surrounded this gaunt gothic construction of red and black brick. Inside it was almost dark. A couple of electric bulbs cast a faint glow over the sanctuary where the Sacrament light burned steadily, but most of the candles beneath the statue of the Virgin were guttering very low in their holders and the side chapels looked dusty and neglected.

The main doors had closed with an echoing thud behind Thackeray, but as he lingered behind the rear pews to take stock he dismissed the faint impulse to dip his fingers in the holy water as mere nostalgia and when he walked slowly down the central aisle, his feet ringing on the chipped tiles, he felt no urge to genuflect as he would have done automatically as a child. "It's gone," he thought to himself and his relief did not entirely suppress a faint sense of loss as part of his heritage and a prop which he knew that stronger men than himself still valued receded into the distant past.

Dermot Burke appeared suddenly from a wooden door which Thackeray supposed must lead to the vestry.

"Good morning, Chief Inspector," the priest said, holding out a hand in greeting. He was a rotund man in middle age, his dark hair greying above a florid face, but the blue eyes were intelligent and not unfriendly. "Shall we sit here?" He waved at the front pews. "It's not very warm in here, I'm afraid, but I don't run to a comfortable chair in the vestry and as I told you on the phone I need to be in church in half an hour to meet the builders. I think the roof may be in the final stages of decay."

Thackeray permitted himself a faint smile as he automatically glanced up at the flaking plaster of the ceiling above them.

"I should think the mosque does better business than you do round here these days, doesn't it?"

"This church was built after they brought a lot of Irish navvies over to help build the canal through the Pennines and many of them settled in Bradfield," Burke said. "Most of the families have moved on now and here we are with a virtual cathedral on our hands and no one to fill it. I expect the diocese will close it eventually and I'll move on too."

"But in the meantime you're a leading light in Saving Lives for the Lord."

"I wouldn't say a leading light, exactly," Burke said, glancing away for a second. "More a conscript, really. One feels a sense of obligation while the Vatican is so intransigent on these issues. But don't repeat that to my bishop, will you?"

Thackeray must have let his surprise show because the priest laughed suddenly.

"It's a long time since you've been in church, my son," he mocked. "Times have changed. Ideas are changing. You should come back. You might be pleasantly surprised."

"How did you know?" Thackeray asked, on the edge of anger now.

"Frank Rafferty in Arnedale's a good friend of mine," Burke said. "Your name cropped up. Don't worry. It's not a conspiracy. He regards you very highly."

"And I him, except when he's invading my privacy," Thackeray said through gritted teeth. He wondered just how much Father Rafferty had passed on about his former life.

"It wasn't like that," Burke said. "I just happened to mention

70

that I was going to be interviewed by a policeman and Frank guessed it might be you. He virtually instructed me to be as helpful as I could, which as it goes, is not very. I'm a member of the committee of SLL because a couple of the older women in the congregation here asked me if I would help. In principle I couldn't object without causing a scandal. I also flattered myself that I might be able to rein back the more radical elements a bit."

"Ah, so there are some radical elements, are there?" Thackeray pounced on the phrase with something like relief. "Dorothy Knight denies anything of the sort."

"Dorothy is so naïve she probably doesn't even pick up on the implications of what the hotheads are saying," Burke said.

"So just how hot are these heads?"

"Do you seriously think that SLL members might be involved in this shooting?" Burke said.

"It's one of the lines of inquiry we have to follow," Thackeray said. "Particularly with your American guest arriving in Bradfield so soon."

"When I say hotheads it's a relative term," Burke said. "I find it very hard to believe that anyone in SLL would get involved in murder."

"It's entirely possible that the shot could have been fired to intimidate," Thackeray said. "But a girl died, and whether the intention was to kill or simply to frighten, the end result is murder."

Burke nodded.

"There is a young man from the university who burns with an alarming self-righteousness. His name is Peter Bainbridge. He sometimes brings a young woman to meetings with him. I think her name is Jason, Felicity Jason. She hangs on his every word, but whether the attraction is ideological or sexual I really couldn't say. Perhaps a bit of both."

"Were they at the hospital on the morning of the shooting?" Thackeray asked.

"I don't think so, no. I arrived just at the crucial moment

and as you know after the shot everyone scattered. But I don't recall seeing Peter or Felicity. Is that good or bad?"

"No one saw the shot fired," Thackeray said. "So we can only assume that it was not fired by anyone who was on open view as part of the demonstration."

"Thank God for that, at least," Burke said.

"We'll have to interview these students, if only to eliminate them from our inquiries," Thackeray said.

"I understand that," Burke said. "Yours must be a difficult job, Chief Inspector, always delving into the darkest side of human nature. I do at least have the satisfaction of being able to absolve sinners when I've heard the details of their crimes and misdemeanours. And this is a particularly difficult case, isn't it, with so many issues in conflict. You must find it hard to remain uninvolved."

"Not really," Thackeray said. "My job is to uphold the law not necessarily to like it. If I carry baggage Frank Rafferty piled on my back years ago, it's really time I learned to distance myself from it even if I can't get rid of it."

"It's not always as easy as all that, though, is it?" Burke said. But Thackeray merely sighed as he got to his feet and buttoned up his coat.

"Thank you for your help, Father," he said. "I don't suppose I'll have to bother you again." But as he took the long walk from the central aisle, turning his back on the altar which now faced the people, he knew that some of his boyhood baggage still weighed heavily and could not so easily be cast aside.

Chapter 5

Twenty miles to the north, Megan Smith was travelling uneasily in the front seat of a dilapidated Ford which was being driven at a sluggish pace by her eldest son. Crammed into the back seat were her other three sons, looking increasingly disgruntled as the panorama of drab winter fields crawled past the car windows. "Won't this damn thing go any faster?" Terry Smith, who was crushed between his two brothers, asked as Tom swung the car onto the narrow lane which led to Shepley village, testing the suspension almost to destruction on the bend.

"You're lucky it's got us this far," Tom replied angrily. "If t'lad who owns it knew I were bringing it up here, he'd skelp us."

In the seat next to him his mother, bundled up in boots and a heavy winter coat, gazed unseeingly out of the rain-flecked windscreen at a desolate landscape of yellowing grassland sheltering in the lee of the looming moors above the valley. She kept her eyes focussed with difficulty on the winding road ahead because every time she closed them she could see her daughter's laughing face dancing in front of her, almost mocking her to follow wherever she led.

Dana had been a late baby, born eight years after Mick, the last of her sons, a beautiful, dark, curly-haired child who had entranced the rest of the family. They had adored her and spoiled her from the day she was born until the day she died. What Dana wanted, Dana had got, from the pretty feminine clothes her mother had scrimped and saved to buy her and the increasingly expensive toys which her father or one of her brothers used to smuggle into the house wrapped in black plastic bin-bags, their provenance never questioned, to the gold chains and rings her grandmother used to mysteriously press upon her from time to time.

When her husband Tom had died in a building site accident, and Megan had been left with the boys barely grown up and Dana not yet in her teens, the intensity of the girl's hold over her family had only seemed to increase. Megan scrubbed at her red, puffy eyes and moaned softly to herself as young Tom steered the car over the last few rutted miles to the village, her misery growing as the little close of old people's bungalows where her mother officially lived came into sight.

"Will you tell her, Tom lad," Megan said, her voice hoarse and throaty after hours of weeping. "I'll not get t'words out mesen."

"Nay, Mam, I can't," Tom said desperately.

"You're t'firstborn, Tommo," Terry chipped in again from the back seat. "You're always telling us that when you want first go at owt, or t'last spoon o'summat at table. Now you'd best do summat for being t'firstborn as our dad's not here. It's a man's job, telling our gran."

Tom's grip tightened on the steering wheel but he did not argue any further, and when he had parked the car outside his grandmother's bungalow he went round to the passenger side of the car and helped his trembling mother out, his face heavy with the responsibility the other four had thrust upon him.

He led the way up the short path to the front door and tapped lightly on the glass. For a moment the five of them stood uncertainly on the doorstep.

"She can't be out in this weather, can she?" Megan said .

"I'll go round t'back, Mam," Mick said. He was the youngest and slightest of the brothers and had a gentleness in his expression that the three older boys lacked. "She might be asleep in t'bedroom. All t'curtains are drawn."

"Don't bother," Megan said. "See if there's a key under that brick by t'dustbin, Terry. She sometimes leaves one there when she goes out."

They found the key and crowded into the Maggie's tiny living room, switching on the light and filling the sparsely

74

furnished room with an unshaded glare from the single bulb. Megan flung back the thin curtains to let in the fading day-light and drew a sharp breath when she saw what was scattered on the small dining table in the window.

"She knew," she said softly, almost to herself, as she ran her fingers across the Tarot cards on a purple silk square . She did not have her mother's skill in divination, but she knew enough to see that the reversed wheel of fortune would have alarmed Maggie and that Death, in the same unhappy orientation, might have panicked her. She shuffled the cards together quickly, wrapped them in the silk and put the bundle in her bag.

"We'll not have the bloody social seeing them," she said to herself.

"She's not in her bed," Tom said, having glanced quickly into Maggie's bedroom. "She's not here at all."

"Where is she, Mam?" Mick asked, his face full of anxiety.

"We'd best look down at that old van she likes down by t'river," Megan said, scrubbing at her eyes again with a sodden handkerchief.

As they filed out again an old man leaning on a stick on the other side of the road waved a fist at them angrily.

"I saw you," he shouted, his voice shrill with dislike. "I saw you, don't think I didn't. I've sent for t'bobbies. They'll be here shortly."

"Sod off, you old fool," Tom hurled back as he got back into the car and drummed his fingers impatiently on the steering wheel as the rest of the family packed themselves back into the passenger seats ready for him to take them down to the farm by the river where Maggie spent so much time.

"Where else could she be?" Megan asked helplessly. "She must'a gone down there to sleep last night after she found out."

"How did she find out, Mam?" Mick asked, but his mother did not reply. And when they had trailed single file past the farm and down the muddy track to the van, all they found was a rotting fish in a plastic bag hanging near the door and a new leak in the roof which had soaked the blankets on the bunk in the gloomy, musty interior.

"She knew," Megan insisted. "She saw it in t'cards. We'd best go home. She'll find us in her own good time."

"That must be him," Sergeant Kevin Mower said as a gleaming white BMW swept around the corner of Bradfield's open air market, where the Asian traders were busy packing up their stalls, and stopped on double yellow lines outside the offices of Saving Lives for the Lord. He and DCI Thackeray had been in an unmarked police car parked just as illegally for the last hour waiting for the Rev. Edgar P Burridge of Des Moines Iowa to arrive from Manchester Airport. They watched as a tall man in a long black overcoat topped by a mane of silver hair got out of the car and gazed around the street of tall dark stone buildings where the market litter, picked up by the sharp wind, drifted into deep doorways and scuttered along the gutter in the spitting rain.

"We'll give him two minutes to take his coat off," Thackeray said. "We don't want him getting the impression he's going to have a comfortable stay in Bradfield."

Mower glanced at the DCI out of the corner of his eye but said nothing. You could walk through fire with a man, he thought, and still not really know him.

"I hear there's going to be some sort of counter-demonstration at the town hall when he speaks on Friday," he said. "The feminists will be out, I guess. What's left of them, anyway." He wondered whether Laura, or her combative grandmother would be amongst them but did not dare ask. But he guessed that Thackeray would hate it if they were.

"That's uniform's problem," Thackeray said. "I simply want to let him know that just because there's been one American-style shooting at the May Anderson we're not going to let it become a habit."

"He's not been involved in anything like that, has he, guv?"

"Not as far as immigration are aware," Thackeray said. "They checked him out pretty thoroughly, apparently and he's got no convictions. But he's a pretty inflammatory speaker, by all accounts. It won't hurt to remind him that we have laws against incitement to violence here. And it's a chance to get a look at the man, just in case we're barking up completely the wrong tree over Dana's murder and it is some sort of conspiracy against the hospital. Right? Shall we get it over, then?"

They found Burridge in Dorothy Knight's small office, filling the space with his bulk and a deep, booming voice.

"I'm pleased to make your acquaintance," Burridge said when the two officers had introduced themselves. He had a smooth, tanned face beneath the thick silver hair and the fine lines around his eyes crinkled benignly when he smiled. It was obvious that Dorothy Knight, who was fussing over a coffee percolator in the corner of the room, was deeply impressed by her guest.

"Mrs. Knight tells me that she's hoping to fill the town hall for your meeting," Thackeray said. He had a rugby-player's breadth himself but still felt slightly over-awed by the sheer bulk of the American. He filled the room with what the DCI could only call charisma, which he reckoned was a dangerous quality in an enclosed space.

"Well, I hope we can rely on you and your sergeant being with us on the night, Chief Inspector," Burridge said. "We count on getting our message to the opinion formers and the high flyers where-ever we go, you know. Billy Graham used to say that you could never tell where the seeds you sowed one year would burgeon and grow the next."

"In this country we expect our police force to remain neutral in this sort of controversy," Thackeray said, his eyes chilly. "Our job is to protect the peace."

"Well, now, that's where we may differ," Burridge said. "There are those unfortunately on God's good earth who I don't reckon deserve much peace. And abortionists are top of my list as candidates for an unpeaceful life."

"Tell me, Mr. Burridge. Have you met anyone since you arrived in the UK who was eager to go further than a demonstration against abortion? Anyone who talked about violence – of any sort – as a serious course of action."

"Well, now," Burridge said cautiously. "As you know, in God's own country there have been one or two people who've gone a bit further than was strictly legal. But you have to understand that's not something I would ever encourage or condone, though I might understand *why* someone who feels so strongly about the millions of innocents who are being slaughtered could be tempted to take matters too far. But we are put here by the Lord to resist temptation, sir, and that's what I have always tried to do, even when the anger is a right-eous anger."

Dorothy Knight broke in irritably at that.

"We have been through this, Mr. Thackeray," she said.

"Not with Mr. Burridge, we haven't, Mrs. Knight," Thackeray snapped. "In the light of what happened to Dana Smith, which is still the subject of an intensive investigation, it did cross my superintendent's mind to ask the chief constable to ban Mr. Burridge's meeting on public order grounds. There's a lot of angry people out there after the shooting and we need to be sure that no one else is going to get hurt."

"Dorothy my dear, the Chief Inspector is quite right. But I can assure him that I don't intend to cast any blame on that unfortunate young girl who was killed. Believe me, Chief Inspector, my quarrel is not with teenage mothers but with the people who counsel them that sex outside marriage is cool, and the doctors who willingly kill the babies which inevitably result. This is a tragedy for the girls, Chief Inspector. I know that as well as you do. But it is adults who are to blame – parents, teachers, doctors, who should all know better."

"Are you travelling alone, Mr. Burridge?" Thackeray asked.

"Well, no, I have a driver with me. We rented a car in London but I brought my own driver from the States. He's just about got used to your freeways, I think. And I have two young assistants with me. They're back at the hotel presently, getting some rest. This is a whistle-stop tour and they're feeling the jet lag, I guess."

"Have you been threatened since you arrived in England?" Thackeray asked quickly.

"Why no, not at all," Burridge said. "We've been made very welcome. Very welcome indeed. Our meetings in London and – where was it Dorothy? – Chetingham?"

"Cheltenham," Dorothy Knight said.

"That's it. Cheltenham. They were well-attended and went off just fine. A lot of upstanding moral support, plenty of people willing to stand up and be counted on this issue. Very encouraging."

"Well I can't guarantee that you'll be made so welcome in Bradfield," Thackeray said. "So can I ask you to repeat to your assistants what I've just told you about the law in this country," Thackeray said.

"Of course you can," Burridge said expansively. "I want no trouble here, Mr. Thackeray. My message is too important for that. What Mrs. Knight and her brave people here want is a change in the law and I endorse that all the way. Violence has no part to play. And now, if you'll excuse us gentlemen. Dorothy has a busy programme planned for me. We should get on."

When they got back to their car Mower glanced sceptically at Thackeray.

"Did you believe a word of all that, guv?" he asked.

"Not a lot," Thackeray said. "I'll get uniformed to check out these "assistants". My guess is that they're bodyguards, and probably go around armed to the teeth in the States. It won't hurt to make sure they haven't got their hands on weapons while they were in London. It's not that difficult, after all."

* * *

"Do you really think so?" Laura Ackroyd asked Ted Grant,

79

wondering how much of the mutiny which was churning her stomach she could let leak out. Ted was sitting at his desk in shirt and braces, his stomach bulging against the restraint of buttons and elastic after a liquid lunch at the Lamb, and he showed no sign of understanding why Laura was objecting to his request that she should include an interview with Edgar Burridge in her coverage of the abortion debate.

"There's a whole lot of folk out there who agree with him," he said.

"Not a whole lot of women, there aren't," Laura objected. "This is for the women's page."

"Give over," Ted said. "There's all those nuns and devout Catholic ladies for a start. And the Muslims. They don't like it, either do they."

"Women believing what men tell them to believe," Laura said dismissively. "And anyway, I'm not just writing about abortion. The hospital does other things. Fenton-Green's a leading fertility treatment expert. There's a woman up there just had twins after years of trying. A really good story, but she didn't want her picture taken."

"Well, find out where she lives and we'll see about that," Ted said. "She'll be pleased as punch when she sees her little darlings on page 6."

"So we leave the protesters out of it?"

"No, we bloody *don't* leave the protesters out of it," Grant said, his annoyance getting the better of his post-prandial good mood now. "They're talking about filling the town hall for this Yank's meeting on Friday, girl. I want an interview with him, so get it bloody sorted."

At that moment there was a clatter at the door behind them and Bob Baker, the urgent young crime reporter, put his head round the door.

"There's more trouble up at the May Anderson Hospital apparently," he said. "That American bloke's joined the picket line, and the police have been called. I'll get up there, shall I?"

"Do that, Bob," Ted said. "And you can get up there too,

Laura. Have a look at what's going on and get an interview with Burridge organised. Strike while the iron's hot. By the sound of it he may be in a cell by the weekend and then it won't just be myself I'll be kicking if we've missed an interview. So get on with it girl, before I get really annoyed."

Laura swallowed her fury and did as she was told. She had often anticipated the day when she could throw her job at the *Gazette* back in Ted Grant's face and walk out in a flurry of righteous indignation over just such as issue as this. The temptation of a job in London had been dangled tantalisingly in front of her more than once but her reluctance to leave her grandmother without a living relative in Bradfield had always curbed her ambitions in the past and now there was Thackeray and their precariously established new life together. Grant, she told herself bitterly as she slammed her car door with a satisfactory thud, would simply have to be tolerated for a bit longer. But there were times when she wished him back on the London tabloid he had once dreamed of editing.

The scene at the May Anderson Hospital when she arrived ten minutes drive later, looked more like a battle zone than a quiet suburban street where women might safely come to give birth or undergo some more or less traumatic surgical procedure. On the furthest pavement from the hospital entrance police were erecting metal barriers to keep a hugely increased number of demonstrators off the carriageway, while further down the road another, evidently antagonistic, group of placard-wavers, most of them young women, was being held back by policemen with linked arms. Laura soon spotted a tall white-haired figure at the front of the SLL protesters whom she guessed must be the Rev. Edgar Burridge from Iowa. He appeared to be leading most of what she thought could best be described as his congregation in prayer.

Conscious of Ted's instructions, Laura worked her way through the crowd towards Burridge but before she could reach him she felt herself picked up and carried towards the barriers by a wave of emotion which seemed to be greeting some event outside the hospital which she could not quite see over the heads of the protesters in front of her. Wriggling her way to the front she caught a glimpse of a car arriving at the main entrance driven by a woman with a young girl in the passenger seat. A low moan ran through the protesters all around her and several missiles were thrown, one of which smashed against the back wind-screen of the car, causing the driver to accelerate convulsively right through the security barrier into the relative safety of the car-park beyond, sending splinters of wood like arrows in all directions. Catcalls and screams of outrage greeted this manoeuvre which were promptly answered by jeers and shouts from further down the street.

Shaken by the anger and hatred all around her, Laura extricated herself from what had so swiftly become a small but ugly mob and retreated down the road to the second group of demonstrators where she recognised one of the placard-wavers as the leader of the women's group at Bradfield University.

"You seem to be pretty heavily outnumbered," she said when the girl recognised her.

"You'd think we were back in the nineteenth century the way these people carry on," she said. "What the hell happened to a woman's right to choose?"

"It'll all blow over after the American's gone back where he belongs," Laura said. "They're stirring it up to get more publicity and the maximum turnout for his rally at the town hall I expect."

"Yes, well, they'll get a bit more than they bargained for there if I have anything to do with it," the girl said angrily. "We've got hold of dozens of tickets so he's not going to get an easy ride."

"Oh dear," Laura said, turning away to assess her chance of getting near Burridge again to raise the question of an interview. She had no intention of passing on the titbit of information she'd just been given to him, but she did wonder whether

82

she might feel impelled to tell Thackeray what she had learned. But as she watched Burridge raise his hands to heaven and lead his followers into a hymn, she rather thought that she would not.

"So fill me in, Kevin," Thackeray said at the end of another long day. The sergeant had slumped into the chair in the corner of Thackeray's office looking pale and drained.

"There's not a lot, guv," he said. "Amos Atherton's come up with his estimation of where the gunman might have been when the shot was fired, based on the angle of the injury which killed the girl."

"And?"

"According to most of the eye-witness evidence, she was standing fairly full-on at the top of the steps when she was hit. Amos reckons that puts the gunman to her right, at an angle of about 45 degrees, and judging by the path of the bullet, slightly lower than she was, which makes sense, given the flight of four steps."

"Can they work out the distance?" Thackeray asked.

"They're working on it, but it's a powerful weapon with a long range, so the gunman could have been some distance away."

"On the motorbike," Thackeray said. "That wouldn't put him too high, would it?"

"Probably not," Mower agreed.

"No trace of the bike, I suppose?"

"No, guv. We've been trawling through all the witness statements but no one seems to have seen it close enough to get anything except a brief impression, though a lot of people heard it roar off just after the shot was fired."

"Right," Thackeray said. "After the team briefing tomorrow morning I want you personally to go up to the university and talk to a student called Peter Bainbridge and his girl-friend Felicity Jason. They're regulars on the picket line at the hospital apparently. Talk to them separately and find out where they where on Tuesday morning. And whether either of them rides a motorbike. OK? And take Val Ridley with you."

"Guv," Mower said with just the slightest trace of reluctance which Thackeray ignored.

"Anything else from today's efforts?" he asked.

"We've just about completed the house-to-house inquiries around Benwell Lane but no one seems to have seen the girl with any of the local boys, or with a boy at all, come to that. Whoever she got involved with, they must have been damn careful about it."

"So what does that suggest?" Thackeray asked.

Mower shrugged.

"Someone she didn't want to be seen with? An older man? A teacher?" he suggested tentatively.

"Or just someone she knew her brothers would object to? Which, from what her mother says, could include pretty well anyone."

"I don't go for that, guv," Mower said sceptically. "You don't get lads on council estates behaving like that these days over their sister's boyfriends. It's bloody mediaeval."

"Or Muslim?" Thackeray said. "Or maybe some sort of Gypsy hangover? I just wouldn't know, would you? The mother implied they went for termination because of the brothers so what do we know? We need to talk to them all again."

"Right," Mower said. "Later tomorrow, maybe?"

"Do it yourself, after the university," Thackeray said. "And now, if you can stand an hour's overtime, there's one more thing I want to do today." Overtime, Thackeray thought, might be the best thing for Mower, if only to keep him from brooding over a bottle which was what he suspected he did most nights now.

"I'll just call Laura to let her know I'll be late," he said, knowing he would not be popular there.

* * *

84

Stephen Fenton-Green's house lay at the end of a track leading from a tortuous moorland road on the edge of Broadley, fifteen miles from the centre of Bradfield and some thousand feet higher. As Thackeray leaned out of the car window to speak into the entry-phone at the substantial gateway, the sharp wind buffetted him and a flurry of sleet left his dark hair sparkling.

"If this goes on we'll have snow," he said as they waited for the gates to open electronically and allow them to proceed up the drive to a spacious parking area in front of a triple garage. Mower's only response was a grunt of acknowledgement. Snow, Thackeray thought, was probably the least of the sergeant's problems.

Fenton-Green himself came to the heavy oak door of what had evidently once been a substantial stone farmhouse to usher them inside.

"We'll be glad of the four-wheel drive if this keeps up," the surgeon said by way of greeting. He showed them into a comfortable sitting room, with a log fire burning in the ancient stone fireplace, and where a slim blonde woman, who had evidently been watching television, half rose in her chair to greet them.

"This is my partner Fiona Madeley," Fenton-Green said briefly, but he put a proprietorial hand on the woman's shoulder as he spoke, as if he wanted to show off a woman considerably younger than himself and, when she turned her head, with a pale, glowing beauty which brought both the newcomers up short.

"Have you caught anyone yet, Chief Inspector," Fiona asked. "It's getting to the stage that I'm terrified every time Stephen's out of my sight."

"We're pursuing several leads," Thackeray said, far more optimistically than he felt. "As I said on the phone, we wondered whether you had remembered anything more about what happened that morning which could be significant?"

85

Fenton-Green went over to a side table where decanters sparkled in the firelight.

"Can I get you anything?" he asked. "Or is the TV cliché about not drinking on duty really true."

Thackeray saw Mower's mouth open and then close again abruptly.

"True-ish, anyway," he said quickly. "Nothing for us, thanks." Fenton-Green nodded and poured himself a whisky before coming back to the circle around the fire and sinking wearily into a chair.

"I've gone over and over it in my mind, and I can't recall anything significant at all. Wherever the shot came from, I was facing in the opposite direction, almost face-to-face with the girl and her mother." He glanced at Fiona. "We found blood on my suit and my shirt that evening. Quite horrible, Chief Inspector. Fiona was deeply upset…" Thackeray nodded sympathetically but he wondered at the squeamishness of a man who dealt with women's internal organs on a daily basis. Fiona toyed with her empty glass and steadfastly refused to meet anyone's eye.

"So you never looked in the direction from which the shot came?"

Fenton-Green took a long drink.

"I flung myself through the door," he said. "It wouldn't have saved me, of course, if it had been me they were aiming at and they'd fired more than the one shot, but it was an instinctive reaction. Neither very brave nor very dignified, I have to admit. I ended up face down in reception with the girl's mother underneath me. Quite an embrace."

"Did you think then that the shot was aimed at you?" Thackeray asked.

"I suppose I must have done," Fenton-Green said. "With the weeks of demonstrations we've had, and the stuff you read in the papers about what's happened to some doctors in America, of course it must have been in the back of my mind. Everyone's been very twitchy for weeks. Isn't there anything you can do to stop these demos? They're becoming quite intimidatory for staff and patients at the clinic. There was practically a riot there today when this American finally turned up."

"So I heard," Thackeray said. "And I'm sure the officers in charge of policing the pickets will be considering their options. It's not my responsibility personally, but I'll pass your comments on. But to get back to the murder, which *is* my responsibility. We are, of course, looking very closely at the anti-abortion campaigners. But I did also want to ask you again whether there was anyone else who could bear you a grudge? A disgruntled patient perhaps? Someone you've annoyed in the past in some way? Someone who has threatened or stalked you?"

Fiona Madeley sat up in her chair at that, her eyes full of fear.

"A stalker," she said. "Do you really think so?"

"Have you had any unexplained or threatening phone calls, for instance?" Thackeray asked. "Any reason to think you might have been followed or watched? Either of you?"

Fenton-Green shook his head irritably but his girlfriend continued to look at Thackeray with an expression of horror on her face.

"Ms Madeley?" Thackeray said. "Has anything of that sort been worrying you?"

"There was a phone call the other day," she said. "I was here by myself, and picked up the receiver but the line went dead almost straight away. I tried 1471 but they said the number was with-held."

"You never told me anything about this, darling," Fenton-Green said sharply. "When was it?"

"Oh, Thursday or Friday last week, I think. I didn't think any more about it at the time. Forgot all about it in fact. But now…" She stopped and shuddered.

"Nothing at all was said by this caller?" Thackeray asked, concerned by the real fear which seemed to have gripped the woman.

"Not even the traditional heavy breathing," she said faintly. "I gave the number and there was a slight pause, and then the dialling tone again. I just thought wrong number and someone too rude to apologise, you know?"

"This is an isolated house," Thackeray said carefully. "Have you noticed anyone up here you don't know recently? Prowlers, attempted break-ins, anything suspicious?" The surgeon and his girlfriend both shook their heads at that but Fenton-Green also now looked agitated.

"Fiona's up here by herself quite a lot," he said. "We have a woman who comes up during the day, but I'm often late home, sometimes away at night…"

"I'm sure there's nothing to worry about," Thackeray said. "I think you said you had no children, so they're not a worry…" It was obvious from the look which Fiona Madeley flung at Fenton-Green that this was sensitive ground and he left his concern for the surgeon's family at that. It must be a painful irony, he thought, for the fertility specialist if he had not been able to father children himself.

"The phone call was probably just what you thought, a wrong number," he said to Fiona Madeley. "But obviously in the circumstances it would be prudent if you took extra care with security until we know exactly why Dana Smith was shot. I've no good reason to believe you were the target, Mr. Fenton-Green, but it won't hurt to take precautions."

Fenton-Green nodded grimly.

"We'll move out," he said flatly. "We can stay in town until this blows over."

"I think that's probably an over-reaction," Thackeray said.

"It's my privilege to over-react," Fenton-Green said angrily. "If you don't mind."

"I'll talk to my uniformed colleagues to see what can be done in the way of additional protection, here and at the hospital," Thackeray said.

"After weeks of harassment by these dreadful people, I think that's the least you can do," Fenton-Green said. "If anyone lays a finger on Fiona, I won't be responsible for my actions, Chief Inspector. This whole thing is getting out of hand."

Chapter 6

Laura rescued a slice of smoking toast from the toaster and dropped it hastily onto her plate.

"Damnation," she said, sucking the fingers of one hand while trying to tune the radio into the local station with the other.

"Butter's supposed to be good for burns," Thackeray said, pushing the dish across the table in her direction, trying not to let her see his involuntary smile. To his surprise he had found that it was small domestic things like breakfast together, however hurried, which gave him an immense contentment with their new life as much as their fierce compatibility in bed.

"Another medical myth," Laura said, digging a knife into the butter instead and spreading her toast thickly. "Do you think in another life we might find a way of lazing around and reading the papers in the morning instead of listening to this crap and giving ourselves chronic indigestion so we can be at our desks by dawn?"

"You'd be bored witless in a week," Thackeray said, finishing his own toast and pouring milk into his coffee.

"Wanna bet?" Laura said. Thackeray looked at her consideringly.

"I am grateful for a second chance, you know?" he said quietly. "I know you wanted that job in London."

"I couldn't leave Joyce up here on her own," Laura said, not meeting his eyes. "And I did hope…" She stopped, aware that though this was neither the time nor the place, she had betrayed what she feared was rapidly becoming an obsession.

"What did you hope?" Thackeray asked.

"Oh, nothing," Laura said quickly. "It'll keep."

"Laura…" Thackeray began but stopped as the radio caught his attention with a familiar voice.

"You'd better listen to this," he said. "Didn't you say you

were interviewing the Rev. Burridge this morning? It looks as though Radio Bradfield's got there before you."

"Oh, damnation," Laura said, turning up the volume as the presenter asked Burridge to outline the reasons for his visit to West Yorkshire. As the American, with his rich, smooth drawl, launched into a well-rehearsed justification for what he called his crusade for the unborn, Laura's irritation grew. The interview was a short one and ended after a couple of unthreatening points from the presenter and a plug for a phone-in on which Burridge would answer questions later in the day.

"The arrogance of these people," Laura said angrily when the presenter had segued into his next piece of music. "It's always men making these unbendable rules, you notice. They don't have to give birth to unwanted children and see their lives wrecked by one silly mistake, do they?"

"There seem to be plenty of women in his organisation," Thackeray said, choosing his words with care. The conversation was heading into areas he would rather avoid. "What I find hard to understand is Fenton-Green working his socks off on a fertility programme with one hand and doling out terminations with the other. I find that very odd. "

"It's not odd at all," Laura said. "He obviously believes in a woman's right to choose. It works both ways. More wanted babies, fewer unwanted babies. You shouldn't have kids you don't want and can't cope with. I can live with Stephen Fenton-Green, even if he does think he's God. At least he's a God on the side of the angels." She glanced at her watch. Thackeray did not reply and she knew that he did not agree. She hesitated for a moment and watched Thackeray as he buttered his last slice of toast.

"I love you, you know," she said. "Never forget that, will you, even when we disagree?"

He looked up at her for a moment and as their eyes met Laura knew exactly why she had agreed to stay in Bradfield with this man, and why she desperately wanted the child which she did not think for a moment she could ask him for or that that he would willingly give her.

"I'm sure you'll give Burridge a hard time, and he'll probably deserve it," he said with a smile. He reached up and pulled her towards him for a kiss which promised much more.

"I'll try and get away at a sensible time tonight," he said. "Take care."

Sergeant Kevin Mower was even more evil-tempered than he usually was these days, DC Val Ridley thought as she drove him out of the town centre towards Branwell Lane. They had just spent a frustrating hour at the university tracking down the two students who had been unexpectedly absent from the protest line on the morning of Dana Smith's shooting, only to find that both of them had been out of town on a field course in Wales and had been for a week. The alibi would be carefully checked, but neither Mower nor Ridley believed that it was anything other than genuine. They had tracked down the pair of them in the students' coffee bar and neither had seemed especially pleased to see the police and it soon became apparent why.

Peter Bainbridge, small, bespectacled and self-contained was the more belligerent of the two when Val Ridley had explained why they had sought them out. But it was Felicity Jason, pale and fragile, who had seemed the most uneasy when Val raised the question of the demonstrations at the May Anderson, and it soon became apparent why.

"How often do you go up there then?" Mower had demanded aggressively. "Regular prayer meetings, is it?"

Felicity had shaken her head at that.

"I haven't been up there recently," she muttered at last "Since…" She trailed away and glanced at her companion who looked angrier than ever.

"Since what?" Mower demanded. "Since when? If there anything you need to tell us you can always do it down at the police station, you know? We'd be more than happy to oblige."

A tear had trickled down the girl's cheek at that and however hard Peter Bainbridge had gripped her arm, she had continued to stare at Mower like a rabbit mesmerised by a snake.

"Why did you stop going to the demos?" Mower had persisted.

"We were asked not to go again," the girl said.

"By?"

"By Mrs. Knight. She didn't want us there any more."

"Oh, leave her alone, for God's sake," Peter Bainbridge had broken in harshly. "If you must know, we were the ones who chucked the bucket of blood at that Asian doctor, what's-his-name? Mahood?"

They had left the two of them looking pale and shaken at Mower's promise that they would need to interview them again at police headquarters and that charges were highly likely.

"Self-righteous little wankers," he had snarled as he flung himself back into the car beside Val Ridley. "If that's what religion does for you, we're better off without it. I hope Mahood presses charges and the CPS throw the book at them."

Their next objective was to interview Mrs. Smith and as many of her sons as they could track down, but as the family had no telephone and Mower had found the house deserted on his last visit, they knew that they could be wasting even more time on the ten mile round trip.

Val glanced at her companion anxiously. He had slumped back in his seat and closed his eyes after his last outburst and she sometimes wondered whether his almost permanent hangover was concealing a more serious deterioration in his health. She had rushed him to hospital vomiting blood once since Rita Desai had died, and she did not want to repeat the experience.

This time however their luck was in. As they pulled up outside the Smiths' house, two of the brothers, in oil-stained overalls, scrambled from beneath a jacked up car which had been pulled into the derelict front garden of the house.

"Tom, Gavin," Mower greeted the brothers curtly as he swung himself out of the car.

"Have you found the bastard?" Tom Smith asked, wiping his hands on a grubby rag. "Have you got him?"

"Not yet," Mower said. "But we will."

"You'd better," Gavin said, kicking a large stone perilously close to the police car's door. "If you don't, we will, and there'll be no slaps on t'wrist then, I'm telling you. Hanging'd be too good."

"Of course, this whole thing might never have happened if your mother hadn't been so certain that you wouldn't have wanted Dana's baby in the house," Mower said. The brothers looked at him uncertainly.

"She were too young to be having a kid," Tom said.

"Do you know who the father was? Has anyone let on?" Mower persisted.

"No, they haven't," Gavin said. "They won't neither because they know he'll get a good hiding an'all if we get our hands on him."

"That's your reaction to everything, is it?" Val Ridley put in sharply. "It'd be more helpful if you reckoned on using your brains instead of your fists. Give a bit of thought to who got Dana pregnant and whether that might have anything to do with the shooting."

"Why should it if it were them demonstrators?" Tom asked, looking genuinely puzzled. "They're bloody nutters, them, aren't they?"

"But if it wasn't the demonstrators? If it was someone who had it in for Dana, or your mother or even you lads?" Val said. "What about that as a possibility?"

"Like whoever's putting bricks through your windows?" Mower said, nodding at the boarded up front of the house. "What did you do to provoke that?"

"That were all Mick's fault," Gavin said, his face sulky.

"Some kids were down in t'field bothering his ponies, and he chased 'em off. It were after that. They sent their big brothers round. Mick's a right softie, unless you go near his animals. Or Dana. Then he's got a temper on 'im."

"Is there anyone on the estate that you know of who's got a gun?" Mower asked.

The two brothers glanced at each other.

"What sort of a gun?" Tom asked, his eyes wary now.

"An automatic pistol," Mower said. "An illegal hand-gun. The sort of gun that Dana was shot with."

"Nay, nowt like that," Gavin said scornfully. "There's one or two might have shot-guns, for shooting rabbits, like, but nowt heavy. Not up here."

"And you? Do you like shooting rabbits?" Mower came back quickly.

"Not since we came to live here," Tom said. "When we lived in t'country, like, t'farmers used to want folk to keep vermin down. But not now. We do cars now." He nodded at the dilapidated vehicle they had been working on when the police arrived.

"Right, is your mother in?" Mower asked.

"Aye, she's indoors," Gavin said, waving at the half open door to the house. Mower followed Val Ridley as she knocked and pushed open the door.

"Mrs. Smith," she called. "Can we come in."

The only response was the sound of a chair being scraped on the floor in the living room and when Val and Mower looked inside they found Megan Smith hunched over a table with a scatter of Tarot cards on a silk square in front of her. She looked blankly at her visitors for a moment, her face still red and swollen with crying, her hair in damp straggles, before turning back to the cards.

"I can't do it," she said, her voice harsh. "She tried to teach me but I never listened and now when I need to find her I can't see what they're telling me. I can find the Lovers, that must be our Dana, but then I keep finding the Tower – look here, falling down. I can't make no sense of it. I need to find her."

"Her?" Val said. "Who do you need to find?"

"Me mam," Megan said. "She's gone off, hasn't she, because of Dana? And I need her here."

"Gone off?" Mower said, without much sympathy. "What do you mean, gone off? Where's she gone off to, for God's sake? Where should she be?"

"She should be in Shepley," Megan said. "We went out there to fetch her back and she weren't there. She hates houses but she'll not last long these cold nights if she's not under cover. She's not young any more."

Mower glanced at Val.

"How old is she? Seventy? Eighty?" he asked Megan.

"All of that," Maggie Sullivan's daughter muttered vaguely.

"We can ask the local police to look for her," Val said. "If you think she's in any sort of danger. If you tell us where she lives."

"O'course she's in danger," Megan said angrily. "She's out on her own somewhere. We looked in t'house, and we looked in t'van down by t'river, and she weren't there."

"We'll pass it on," Mower said impatiently. "But we came to talk about Dana. To see if you'd thought any more about the boyfriend. Or if anyone had let on locally who it might be? Someone must know."

Megan Smith turned slowly in her chair to face Mower.

"Forget him," she said, her voice full of contempt. "He took what wasn't his, whoever he was. I had great hopes for my Dana, for a grand wedding and a handsome groom, and all t'family coming from all over t'country to be there for Dana, like they came to my wedding. A Gypsy wedding. You've never seen owt like it, I'll bet. They pinned twenty pound notes to my dress, hundreds of pounds I wore that day. He took all that away, and he took my grandchild away, and lost me my daughter because of it. He didn't kill her, but he might as well have. He can rot in hell, he can."

They got no more out of Megan who told them where Maggie Sullivan lived and turned back to her cards to deal them again and moan faintly as she evidently tried and failed again to decipher a message from the horseshoe arrangement.

"Jesus wept, who are these people?," Mower asked, his voice hoarse when they eventually gave up and left her to her grief. "They'll be putting a curse on us next."

"They say some people go mad with grief," Val said. "She's as close to it as I've ever seen."

"And there's another old witch wandering about somewhere," Mower muttered. "You'd better get social services onto that one sharpish or they'll find her dead in a ditch."

"Right," Val said. She glanced at Mower curiously. Something about Megan Smith seemed to have reduced him to near incoherence, and his face was chalk white. Megan's two sons watched impassively as they made their way back to the car.

"Where are your brothers today?" Mower asked Tom Smith who had followed them out of the house.

"Terry's gone back up to Shepley to look for our gran," Tom said reluctantly. "I expect Mick's down with his horses. He usually is."

Val glanced at Mower.

"Got the strength for mucking out a stable?" she asked, in a desperate effort to snap him out of his depression. He did not smile.

"After that little lot it'll be a pleasure. My mother went in for that other-world garbage and much good it did her. It gives me the creeps."

They drove slowly out of Benwell Lane and across the common towards the Cricketers' Arms, where cars were beginning to arrive for lunch. Beyond the pub in one of the small stone-walled fields, they could see Mick Smith putting out hay for the half-a-dozen shaggy ponies who clustered round him eagerly.

"Get him out of the field," Mower said. "The only place I like those beggars is on the TV screen in the betting shop."

"Never had any ambitions to join the mounted branch then, sarge," Val mocked gently.

"Too right. I've seen what they can do in a scrap," Mower said.

They stood for a moment by the five-barred gate which led into the field, and after he had finished scattering his hay bale and given each of the ponies an individual titbit, Mick came slowly towards them, a much slighter figure than his brothers, fairer in colouring but with the same unmistakable signs of sleepless grief around his dark eyes.

"Hast'a caught him then?" he said.

"Not yet," Val replied. "We're working on it. We came up to ask whether you'd heard anything around the estate."

"What about?" Mick said, moving into the ramshackle shed crammed with hay bales and bits of tackle. "We don't hear nowt, us, because no bugger talks to us, do they?"

"Nothing about the lad Dana got involved with?" Val said, guessing that as the youngest Mick might have been the one of her brothers that Dana confided in. But Mick wiped his nose on his sleeve and gazed across the field at his ponies, his face closed.

"I know nowt," he said. "Though I'll tell you one thing. I wouldn't ha' minded a babby in t'house. I like babbies. Now bugger off and leave us alone."

"I don't believe him," Mower said as they walked down the rutted track back to the car. "He's not such a good liar as the others, that one."

"You don't think…" Val hesitated, appalled by her own speculation.

"One of the brothers, you mean?" Mower was less squeamish. "It's a thought. It's what some kid I spoke to the other day said too but I thought he was just an evil little bastard trying it on. But it would explain why Megan was so anxious to get rid of it. I wonder if forensics are doing DNA tests on the baby."

"If there's anything left to do DNA tests on," Val said. She glanced at her watch and then at Mower.

"You look wrecked," she said. "Do you want to come back to my place for lunch? Aren't you supposed to eat regularly?"

"For Christ's sake don't mother me, Val," Mower said. She shrugged and turned away, knowing that there were things she would much rather do to Mower than mother him and she would not like him thinking that there was anything incestuous in that.

Michael Thackeray looked almost as gaunt as Mower when he and Val Ridley came to him later that afternoon and outlined their thoughts on the paternity of Dana Smith's child.

"Incest?" he said incredulously. "And even if that were true, what bearing would it have on the shooting? You're not suggesting that one of the brothers might have killed her too, are you?"

"I suppose that would depend on whether Dana was going to make a complaint," Val Ridley said.

"She'd be in care before the words were out of her mouth," Thackeray said. "And where would Megan's family be then?"

He leaned back in his chair wearily and looked at the two younger officers.

"This was an unpleasant case from the beginning and it's getting nastier by the minute," he said. "I'm not prepared to wade into the family and turn them from grieving victims into suspects just on a hunch. We need hard evidence to even raise the issue. If we got it wrong the *Gazette* would crucify us." With Laura leading the chorus of complaint against victimisation and racism and worse, he thought wryly.

"So, let's take it a step at a time, shall we," he went on. "First the hospital. See if you can find out if the girl had any counselling before the termination and if so whether she gave even the slightest indication who the father might be. And ask Amos Atherton about the forensic possibilities. Can we find out that way who the father might or might not be? He can contact the May Anderson Hospital direct."

And if Mower and Ridley thought he was sliding out of that unpleasant necessity, Thackery thought, they were right.

"Then tomorrow we'll think about bringing the youngest brother in, if you think he's the most likely to crack. I'll talk to him myself if we get that far. "

"Right, guv," Mower said. "Oh, and I've asked the local man to keep an eye open for this grandmother of theirs who seems to have gone missing. That might be significant too, if she suspected what was going on."

"I think we're jumping way ahead of ourselves here," Thackeray said. "I mean, where the hell would any one of the Smiths get a semi-automatic pistol from, and learn how to use it – from a distance, mind – so accurately. Cover our backs as far as the family's concerned, Kevin. But I reckon that's all we'll be doing. So take care."

Maggie Sullivan woke from a dream in which the devil of the Tarot had taken her in a fiery embrace, and tossed her over his shoulder before leaping to the top of Shepley church tower and sitting there with Maggie on his lap, cackling wildly while the smoke from his flaming torch swirled around them. She was drenched in sweat and for a moment she wanted to grab hold of one of the shadowy figures she could see gathered at the foot of her bed to assure herself that they at least were real, but then the gist of what they were saying trickled through the dark mist of the nightmare which fuddled her mind, and she shut her eyes again.

"We need the bed," a firm male voice was saying. "You'll have to talk to social services again. She can't stay here cluttering up the ward."

"She's seriously under-nourished and dehydrated," another voice said. "I do think we should give her another day. They'll never find a nursing home to take her. It was obvious when they brought her in that she'd been living rough."

"That's what some people choose to do," the first voice came back. "You can't take every stray off the street. If they

100

need treatment we'll treat them. If not, there's plenty of people on the waiting list who do."

"I'll get social services to come in first thing in the morning to assess her," the second voice said and, with her eyes open no more than a glittering crack, Maggie watched the little group move away.

"No you bloody won't," Maggie muttered to herself, turning over and trying to see as far as the door of the long ward, which was only dimly lit. Alert now behind her half-closed eyes, she waited. Beneath the sheets she knew that she was wearing only a hospital cotton gown and she wondered what they had done with her clothes when they had brought her here. She could not remember arriving and did not know which hospital she was in, but she guessed from the size of the ward and the busy coming and going she had observed all day since she first regained consciousness that she must be in the Infirmary at Bradfield.

"Our Dana'll likely be here, an'all," she told herself and found the thought strangely comforting. She kept watching as gradually the ward settled down for the night and the lights were turned low. A nurse came round with drugs for some of the patients, but glanced only casually in Maggie's direction before taking her seat at a desk at the other end of the room. A sort of silence fell, broken by an occasional cough or moan and the heavy snoring of a man close to the nursing station. A clock above the head of the nurse, who was bent over paperwork at her desk, told Maggie that it was nine-thirty. Not too late, she thought, for what she had in mind.

Just before ten she saw a second nurse come onto the ward and begin a whispered conversation with the first. She could hear them giggling, and then they both glanced around the room and went out into the corridor, closing the door with its glass panels, carefully behind them.

"Gossiping, gossiping," Maggie said to herself. "Lasses are always gossiping."

"Come on now," said the voice in her ear. Very gently she

101

slid from under the bedclothes until her bare feet met the cold floor and made her way to the door at the furthest end of the ward which she knew led to the bathrooms. Infinitely slowly she eased open the door and slipped out into a corridor which, as she had hoped, led to a staircase going down. Tentatively trying door after door on her way downstairs she eventually found what she was looking for: a room full of lockers one of which had been left half open and from which she extracted a warm coat and a pair of outdoor shoes which more or less fitted her gnarled feet.

Maggie was not missed until the nurse going off duty found her bed empty at six o'clock the next morning.

Chapter 7

Val Ridley woke with a start the next day, unsure for a moment who was lying in bed beside her. Then the memory of what had happened the previous evening flooded back and she slid out of bed angry and naked, pulled on a robe and went to the bathroom, closing her bedroom door firmly behind her.

Over a cup of strong coffee, she reviewed her options, all of which filled her with self-disgust. She had invited Kevin Mower back for a meal the previous evening when they had finished work, and had been surprised when he accepted. He had followed her home in his own car, picking up a bottle of Scotch on the way which he had drunk steadily throughout their microwaved meal and afterwards. By eleven o'clock he had been drunk and incoherent and she had known that her hope of a romantic interlude was broken-backed. She had guided him to the bedroom, helped him pull off his clothes and rolled him under the duvet. But when she slipped in beside him he had turned away, snoring heavily, and her humiliation was complete.

"He probably won't even remember what we did or didn't do," she told herself bitterly as she made toast and smeared it lightly with low-fat spread. Since her marriage had broken up, wrecked, as so many police marriage were, on the rocks of long hours and mental exhaustion, Val had determinedly kept men, and particularly policemen, at arms length. But Kevin Mower was different. She had dreamed of enticing him into bed for years now in the teeth of his indifference, his philandering, his tumultuous and ultimately tragic affair with Rita Desai, and now his slow slide into a morass of alcohol-fuelled desperation. She ran a hand through her short fair hair and groaned, knowing that last night could only make her relationship with Mower even more difficult. She had made a desperate throw and lost, she thought, and it was about time she started looking for a transfer as far away from Kevin Mower as she could get.

She finished her breakfast and poured a fresh cup of coffee which she took into the bedroom for her guest. Mower was awake, his pale face rough with stubble, his hair black and dishevelled against the pillows, his eyes inscrutable. He sat up, propped on one elbow.

"Room service?" he said.

"More than you bloody well deserve," she countered, setting the coffee mug carefully on the bedside table.

"Sorry," he said. He sipped the coffee cautiously, wincing slightly although Val was not sure whether that was because the coffee was hot or whether it was irritating his inflamed stomach. For a moment she stood in silence looking at him, aching to take him in her arms, or at least touch his hand, but he avoided her gaze and she knew he would recoil, as he had done last night, even though he must by now be somewhat more sober than he had been then.

"This was a very bad idea," Mower said eventually. "Coming here, everything."

Val dropped onto the bed beside him with a groan.

"You need some help, Kevin," she said. "And if not me, who? Thackeray will have you out. You know where he's coming from. There's no one more unforgiving than someone who's been there."

"I'll be OK," Mower said thinly. "I just need a bit more time. Don't think I don't appreciate that you care."

He reached out and pulled Val towards him, kissing her roughly and sliding a hand under her breast but in spite of the flood of desire which threatened to overwhelm her she pulled away angrily and stood up, clutching her robe around her.

"I don't want your fucking charity," she yelled as she stormed out of the room, and was surprised when Mower fell back against the pillows in hysterical laughter, quite unaware of what she had said that was funny.

* * *

Thackeray closed the interview room door behind him without great force but Mick Smith, the youth sitting waiting for him behind the bare table, jumped like a startled animal, eyes wild with fear, as the big man approached and took his seat opposite him. Val Ridley was already in the room with a couple of audio-tapes in hand, ready to put them in the machine and commence the interview.

"Present, DCI Thackeray and DC Ridley," she said as she switched the recorder on. "Time 10.45 a.m."

"You're not under arrest, Mick, and this is an informal interview," Thackeray said. "You can leave whenever you want. But I would like your help in clarifying a few points about Dana and her boyfriend and your family. Do you understand that?"

The youth nodded nervously, his hands tying themselves in knots under the table, then pushing hair out of his eyes, fingers trembling. He was not as bright as his brothers, Thackeray thought, and that might be an advantage.

"Do you want to smoke?" Thackeray asked but Mick shook his head.

"Don't smoke," he said. "Don't like it.

"I want you to think back a bit, Mick," Thackeray said. "Back to when Dana must have got herself pregnant three months ago, that would be the end of the summer. Do you remember anything that happened around that time? Anything unusual?"

The youth shook his head, his eyes puzzled.

"Like what?" he asked.

"Well, I guess Dana had just gone back to school after the summer holidays. What did she get up to over the summer? Who was she spending her time with, for instance? Girl friends? Boy friends? Family?"

Mick sat and thought for a moment, as if casting his mind back three months involved an unaccustomed intensity of effort.

"I sold a pony at beginning o'July," he said. "Three hundred quid I got for her. That were in t'summer. For a little lass who were going to learn to ride."

"Did Dana like the ponies, Mick?" Val Ridley asked suddenly.

Again Mick took his time before he answered but then he shook his head.

"She did when she were little," he said. "She used to come down to old Jenner's field wi'me and ride bareback on old Charlie. He were right gentle were old Charlie. Didn't mind her hanging on his mane. That were when we lived in Shepley. But she weren't bothered once we come here and she went to big school. She liked reading then. Big books she brought home."

He shook his head, as if the thought of reading big books was difficult to conceive and Thackeray wondered if he could read himself at all.

"Did she have special friends at school? Anyone she brought home?"

"Lasses round about used to laugh at her because she didn't have mini-skirts and all that," Mick said. "Our mam wouldn't let her."

"So no best friend, then? No one who came round to the house, or went to town with her on a Saturday, anything like that?" Val persisted, thinking of her own teenage years and the interminable chatter of girls testing out their limits with each other, with boys and with the adult world.

"They called us gippos, didn't they," Mick said, suddenly venomous. "We kept out o'their way."

"So, going back to the summer, Mick," Thackeray said. "You sold your pony, Dana was off school. What else happened?"

"Dana went to stay with our gran out at Shepley," Mick said suddenly, as if conjuring a rabbit out of a hat. "To look after her, like. She used to like it there when she were a little lass an' all. We used to take her paddling in t'river and she laughed and laughed." He stopped suddenly as if the picture he had conjured up was too much to bear.

"She was a beautiful girl, your sister," Thackeray said quietly. "She must have had some lads chasing after her last summer, surely? As she was beginning to grow up. Can you not remember?"

"Can't remember," Mick said. "When she were little she used to say she were going to marry our Tom. But that was just joking, like. I used to say I were going to marry her, an'all. She were that pretty."

Thackeray drew a deep breath, aware that Val Ridley was doodling in her notebook and avoiding his eyes. He knew he would get no help there with the difficult questions.

"Who was her favourite brother, Mick," Thackeray said. "Was it you?"

"We all loved our Dana," Mick said, perhaps too quickly, Thackeray thought. "She were our babby. T'babby o't'family, our gran used to say."

"But who did Dana like best? Was it you, Mick?"

"She liked us all," Mick said, an obstinate look coming over his face. "There weren't no best brother, whatever Gavin said."

"But Gavin thought he was her best brother, maybe?"

"Anyone can think, can't they?" Mick countered.

Thackeray hesitated for a moment, casting about for a way to proceed.

"How many bedrooms are there in your house, Mick?" Val Ridley asked unexpectedly, filling the gap. The youth looked puzzled for a second.

"Three," he said eventually.

"That must be a bit crowded. Where do you all sleep?"

"Our Terry an'me sleep in t'back room," Mick said. "And our Tom and Gavin share. Dana used to sleep in wi'us in a little bed, but after our dad died Mam got two beds instead o'their big'un, and took Dana in wi'her. Said that room were t'ladies room and were private. Us lads were to keep out." He laughed. "Ladies," he said as if the word were unfamiliar. "We didn't think our Dana were old enough to be a lady."

"Or to have a boyfriend?"

"Nay, she were our babby, I told you. We all looked after our Dana. Till…." Mick stopped and they could see the tears in his eyes. "Till *that* happened," he said.

They let him go eventually, unable to persuade him into anything incriminating and increasingly aware that the boy simply did not understand what they were implying. Thackeray followed Val Ridley into the main CID office where Kevin Mower was sitting at a desk with a phone tucked under his chin and a sandwich in his other hand. He put the receiver down as Thackeray approached and squared his shoulders as if about to weather a storm.

"Nothing doing, guv," he said. "Amos has been on to the hospital but everything is disposed of immediately after any operation. Incinerated apparently. Very strict rules about it."

"I think we're flying up a blind alley here," Thackeray said. "We got nothing suspicious out of the lad, and he's naïve enough not to have worked out what he should have been covering up if there was anything to cover up. I think it's much more likely that there's a boyfriend somewhere out there, who was probably not very happy to learn he was going to be a father. Perhaps there's someone she met when she was staying with her grandmother in the summer. And where the hell is the old lady, by the way? Have the local bobbies or social services come up with any answers on that, by any chance."

"They haven't a clue, according to the duty sergeant at Arnedale," Mower said, as if no more could be expected of colleagues out in the sticks. "D'you want me to go up there?" he asked with little enthusiasm.

Thackeray looked at the sergeant speculatively for a moment and then shook his head.

"Not now," he said quietly enough for his voice to be muffled by the chatter of colleagues and the clatter of keyboards.

"In fact, you'd be a bloody sight more use to me, Kevin, if you got home and sorted your head out before tomorrow morning. You can't go on like this." He turned away and Mower watched him go before he glanced at Val Ridley, who had been watching the exchange from her desk.

"I suppose you think you're next in line for my job," he said venomously.

"Only if it's vacant," Val said. "And that's down to you, isn't it?"

Laura leaned back in her chair, sipped her drink and eyed the Rev. Edgar P Burridge with something close to admiration in spite of herself. The broad tanned face, the shock of almost white hair, the apparently guileless blue eyes, and that very American openness of expression, almost belied the implacability of his message. Almost but not quite.

"You say never, but what if a girl has been raped? Would you see her carry that child?"

"That is a terrible thing," Burridge said warmly. "But we are taught not to visit the sins of the father on the children. It is not that child's fault he was conceived in sin. I have known young girls made pregnant in the most terrible circumstances but with God's love and the help of Christian people, they have been able to come to terms with their situation and bring those children up in the Lord. It is, in the end, all about love, you see."

Laura was coming to the end of the hour which Dorothy Knight has allotted for her interview with Edgar Burridge and she felt distinctly weary, as if she had been headbutting his cast-iron defences for far longer than that. She knew she was wasting her time, and to some extent his, as her brief was to summarise his views, and those of his local supporters, unexpurgated, in the "debate" slot which Ted Grant was planning for his centre spread the following day.

"Doctors like Stephen Fenton-Green would argue that you're inflicting a second punishment on the mother who has already suffered enough," she said. "And on the baby who will never be wanted in the way a willingly carried child is wanted."

"*All* the Lord's children are wanted," Burridge said expansively. "We may suffer in this life but we move on to better things. The Lord gives life and the Lord taketh away."

"You'll be opposed to the death penalty then?" Laura asked, her face all innocence.

Just for a second Burridge's face darkened, as she guessed it would.

"That's a different issue," he said. "Let me tell you something, honey, if you really want a story. My friends in Bradfield tell me that your Stephen Fenton-Green is not above bending the law on terminations here, disgracefully liberal as that law already is."

"Bending it? How?" Laura asked, scenting a story, even if it was emerging from a source she instinctively distrusted.

"Just find out how far gone that young girl was who was shot the other day," Burridge said. "Even here you do have some limits on when a child can be ripped untimely from the womb."

Back at her desk half an hour later, Laura vented her anger by threatening to demolish her computer keyboard, so fast and angrily did her fingers thump at the keys.

"What rattled your cage?" Bob Baker, the crime reporter asked, coming up behind her and reading over her shoulder. "Tell me, is that lover-boy of yours getting anywhere with this shooting, or are we going to be left with another unsolved murder?"

"What's that supposed to mean?" Laura flung back at him. "Anyway, you're more likely to know the state of play than I am. Michael doesn't bring his work home with him. We've better things to do."

"I'm sure you do," Baker leered. "DCI Thackeray must have something going for him that's not immediately apparent to the naked eye."

"Shit," Laura muttered as her fingers hit several keys at once and the computer whined in complaint. Baker laughed unsympathetically.

"I hear you've got half the bloody paper for your so-called abortion debate tomorrow," he said. "According to what I hear your hero Fenton-Green has been bending the rules up at that private hospital of his."

Brought up short at that, Laura spun round in her chair to face Baker.

"You heard that too?"

"Well, it needs standing up. I only got it from the sainted Dorothy Knight. She's not what you'd call neutral, is she?"

"Have you mentioned it to Ted?" Laura asked.

"In passing," Baker said innocently. "I thought it might add a bit of spice to this big feature of yours."

"Thanks," Laura said, turning back to her screen irritably, but even before she had put the finishing touches to her interview with Burridge, Ted Grant's stentorian bellow reached her from the doorway to his office. Warily she crossed the room, aware that the eyes of her colleagues were surreptitiously following her progress. Laura's spats with her boss were legend in the office and she guessed that some of the men kept a book on how much longer she would survive at the *Gazette*.

"You called?" she said sweetly, as Grant lowered his enormous frame back into his black leather power chair. He glanced at his computer screen, to which he had evidently imported her barely finished article.

"You can't bloody say this," Grant said. "You'll have us in the High Court in less time than it takes Fenton-Green to bung another baby in the incinerator."

Laura drew a sharp breath at that, but said nothing. She knew if she got into a row with Grant on this particular issue she would regret it.

"You mean where he accuses him of bending the rules?"

"Of course that's what I mean. It's bloody defamatory, isn't it? You'd need chapter and verse and then some to get away with that."

"Bob Baker says he's heard the same story," Laura said reluctantly.

"Aye, he told me, and I told him the same as you. It's libellous unless you can prove it, and you'll never do that to satisfy our lawyers, I can tell you that for nowt. Jesus wept. The *Globe*'d think twice about publishing an allegation like that without a stack of sworn affidavits a mile high."

"Well, there's fat chance of that," Laura said. "I don't suppose there's a scrap of truth in it. They're just stirring up as much mud as they can to publicise this meeting Burridge is having. As far as I can see, everyone who's had anything to do with Fenton-Green thinks he's some sort of saint."

"Aye, well, you can leave that out too," Grant said. "I dare say he's as likely as the next man to bend the rules if the price is right. Proving it's another matter."

"So apart from that you're happy, are you?" Laura asked, watching him scroll his way through the feature, a scowl ribbing his heavy brow.

"It'll do," he said. "We'd better keep an extra page or two for readers' letters the day after. It'll bring every nutter in West Yorkshire out of the woodwork, this will. I'm still not sure it's what we should be doing in a family newspaper. But I suppose the murder's enough of an excuse. And the crusading Yank, of course. We can't ignore him."

"Right," Laura said.

"And you'd best tell your friends at the nick what he's alleging about our friendly neighbourhood abortionist," Grant added suddenly just as Laura was about to leave. "It's up to them to come up with the evidence for that sort of thing. I haven't got the staff for it, even if I wanted to get involved. So pass it on to DCI Thackeray, will you? I'm sure he'll love that."

"I'm sure he'll be enchanted," Laura thought as she made her way back to her desk feeling utterly depressed by her day's work.

112

Laura went home wrapping her bad mood around her like a dark cloak. She changed out of her suit into pants and sweatshirt and spent half an hour trying to jog herself back to sanity round the local streets. It was that quiet time after the schoolchildren had dawdled their way home and before the adults began to arrive, driving fast in the fading light or struggling from the buses with briefcases and shopping bags. There were few cars around and she found she had the pavements almost to herself as she worked up a sweat around the tree-lined streets of Victorian houses.

She knew very few people in this leafy neighbourhood to which she and Thackeray had moved together, and she regretted that it had taken her even further away from her grandmother, who still insisted on living in a tiny old people's bungalow on one of the now-decaying housing estates she had been instrumental in planning when she was undisputed queen of Bradfield town hall. She could do with a dose of Joyce's blunt common sense tonight, Laura thought, as she stopped for a moment and put her head between her legs, gasping for breath, and then stood gazing down from her vantage point on one of Bradfield's seven hills at the glittering evening lights of the town in the valley below.

She had missed this stubborn, grimy little town when she had been sent away to boarding school in the south at the age of eleven by her father and had obstinately returned to the local university when the time came. Now, she thought, she was beginning to resent its constraints, although she knew that if she could only persuade Thackeray to become a father again she might become a whole lot more contented with what she'd got.

She eased herself upright again and began the rather slower trot home, slightly surprised to see that Thackeray's car had joined her own much earlier than usual. She let herself into the flat and found him sprawled in an armchair in an old sweater and jeans, looking tired and crumpled, with a cup of tea in one hand and a cigarette in the other.

"You're early," she said, leaning over to kiss his cheek. "Do you want me to cook or shall we go out for a meal? We don't often get the chance."

"I needed to get away," Thackeray said. "You'd think after all these years I'd be immune to it, but this case is getting to me."

"I'd like you less if it didn't," Laura said, running a hand gently across his brow. "It's unpleasant enough without the allegedly reverend Edgar Burridge raising the temperature. He looks like one of those American TV evangelists – oozing sympathy and charm – but underneath there's a Salem witch-hunter trying to get out."

"It's Fenton-Green I don't trust," Thackeray said.

"Ah," Laura said cautiously. "Do I hear the echoes of your youthful brain-washing here? Or is there more?"

Thackeray shrugged.

"You don't need a priest to tell you some things are wrong," he said. "But might there be more? Did you inter-view Burridge today, as you planned?"

Laura hesitated for a second, thinking back to Ted Grant's instruction to pass on the American's more lurid allegations.

"I suppose I ought to tell you," she said. "Burridge is claiming that Fenton-Green is bending the law over termina-tions. Ted won't print it, of course, because it's wildly defama-tory, and there's no way we can prove it, but he suggests someone who can legitimately ask should find out just how late Dana Smith's operation was done."

Thackeray groaned.

"Dorothy Knight suggested he's ignoring the law the first time I spoke to her," he said. "It's an easy allegation to make and a difficult one to investigate. If it's true I'm quite sure he won't have recorded the fact on his patients' records. But if Burridge repeats it in public we're going to have to check it out, I suppose."

"Why don't you just leave the man alone," Laura said irri-tably, all her previous depression flooding back. "What does anyone gain from forcing young girls to have babies they don't want and probably can't care for properly? The whole idea's mediaeval."

"The law doesn't allow abortion on demand," Thackeray said, his voice tightening .

"And you approve of that, do you?" Laura said, the irritations of the day stoking a fierce anger which took her unawares and insulated her from the pain in Thackeray's eyes. "It's easy for a man to say. If you were faced with a pregnancy that was going to muck up your whole life you wouldn't be so certain."

"I hope I wouldn't sacrifice a child just for convenience," Thackeray said.

"Yes, well, it's a choice you'll never have to make, isn't it?" Laura said, infuriated now. "You should be so lucky."

"And you weren't?" The question dropped like a stone into a pool and Laura stared at Thackeray for a moment, knowing she had said far more than she intended but that it was too late to stop now.

"No, I bloody wasn't," she said.

"When did this happen?" Thackeray asked, gripped by what he knew was an irrational anger. "The father wasn't that bastard Vince Newsom, was it?"

"No, no, it was years ago, when I was a student," she said dully. "The usual thing, getting drunk, waking up in the wrong bed, the panic, the recriminations…"

"You had an abortion?"

"Of course I did," Laura said. "And no, it wasn't the wrong thing to do, it was the *right* thing, and I've not been filled with guilt ever since. It was a mistake then and I couldn't have coped with a child then…"

"But?" Thackeray said harshly. "Now you could?"

Laura turned away to hide her tears. This was not the way she had meant it to be and she did not answer Thackeray's question because she knew he did not need it answered. She went into the bedroom and picked up her coat, her bag and her car keys. When she went back into the living room Thackeray had not moved and his face was like stone.

"I'm sorry Michael," she said. "I'm going round to see Vicky. I need to talk to her." He did not reply.

When the front door had closed and the silence of the flat closed in around him, he flung back his head and cried out in pain for the son he had lost. He did not know how he could ever expose himself like that again.

Chapter 8

Thackeray had waited up till after midnight in the hope that Laura would come back. When she didn't he eventually fell into an exhausted sleep in front of a film on TV and seemed to have hardly rested when his mobile rang. He glanced at his watch before answering. It was six-fifteen, and not yet light, and his heart thudded as he heard Kevin Mower's voice at the other end of a line made indistinct with static.

"Can you hear me, guv?" Mower asked into the silence at Thackeray's end. "I said there's been a body found, a woman's body. Can you get down here?"

"Do we have an ID?" Thackeray asked, his mouth dry. He knew that his certainty that the body was Laura's was wildly irrational but that did not prevent the fear which almost paralysed him.

"It's one of the nurses from the May Anderson," Mower said. "We've not got a positive identification, but she's in uniform and they found her in the car park..."

"Shot?" Thackeray asked.

"Shot," Mower confirmed and gradually Thackeray began to relax slightly although there still seemed to be a lump of something solid and cold where his heart should be.

"I'll meet you at HQ in thirty minutes," he said. "Wait for me there and we'll go up to the hospital together. Have you got Amos Atherton out of bed?"

"With difficulty," Mower said. "We'll be there before him, I reckon."

Guided by the flashing lights of patrol cars parked at the back of the hospital, Thackeray and Mower arrived long before the winter dawn had broken. Lights had already been put up throwing a garish yellow glare under the trees which surrounded the staff car-park. A screen had been thrown around the huddled body which lay between two parked cars to shield it from the curious faces which could be seen at the windows of the wards and corridors on this side of the building.

"Where the hell's Amos?" Thackeray asked. "If I could get here why couldn't he?"

Mower punched a number into his mobile and spoke briefly.

"Just turning into the car-park, guv," he said, and almost before he had stowed the mobile away they could see the pathologist easing himself carefully out of his car, and moving towards them.

"A bit bloody early for this sort of thing, isn't it?" Atherton asked as he unrolled his protective clothing from his case and struggled into it. He glanced at his police colleagues and smiled grimly. "My God, you two look as rough as I feel," he said.

"No one's had much sleep," Thackeray admitted.

"Do we know how long she's been there?" Atherton glanced dispassionately at the person who would never wake again.

"Apart from the fact that she looks like a nurse we've no idea who she is or, assuming she works here, which seems reasonable, what time she might have been finishing or starting a shift. The alarm was raised by the security guard who took a turn round the car-park just before six after he'd heard some noise back here. He called us from his lodge and kept everyone else out of this part of the car-park," Mower said. "Showed a bit more common sense than a lot of people who find a body. Uniform were here just after six."

"Just so long as she was dead and didn't bleed to death before you lot got here," Atherton said. "It's not as if she was far from medical assistance."

"The guard reckoned she was dead when he found her, and the uniformed boys didn't have much doubt," Mower said. "We dragged the resident doctor out of bed to confirm it at 6.10. As far as I can see she's been shot in the head, just like the other one."

"Right," Atherton said. "She's likely still warm then."

"You can get inside now, Kevin, and find out who's in charge of the nursing staff. We'll want a formal ID as soon as we can," Thackeray said.

Mower nodded and made his way through the parked cars and back towards the main entrance of the hospital. Atherton pulled on his gloves and shook his head.

"Someone got it in for this place, have they?" he asked, as he stepped through the tape which had been hung around the murder scene and began to talk quietly into his tape-recorder as he examined the woman's head, which lay in a pool of blood. "Death would have been instantaneous," he said to Thackeray as he finished his first cursory examination. "No doubt about that. What the hell are these bastards trying to achieve?"

It was a question Superintendent Jack Longley repeated almost word for word when Thackeray reported back to him later that morning on the new outrage at the May Anderson hospital. Longley leaned back in his chair, his usually rubicund face pale and grim, and wondered whether it was merely a second murder which had created the dark circles under his DCI's eyes and the haunted look behind them.

"God knows," Thackeray said. "This is verging on terrorism."

"So who's the victim?"

"Stella Brady, 35 years old, sister in charge of the fertility treatment ward, married, two young children. She was due on duty at six thirty but quite often arrives early. She must have been shot as she got out of her car. She fell just by the driver's door which was still unlocked. As far as Amos Atherton can see before the PM it was a single bullet to the head, just like Dana Smith."

"Any obvious leads?" Longley asked, not bothering to hide his own sense of disbelief.

"Not yet. I'm just going to brief the troops and then go and

119

see the husband myself," Thackeray said. "He's been to the morgue to make a positive identification and has been taken back home to tell his kids, poor bastard. So far the only person who claims to have seen or heard anything is the security guard. He's downstairs with Kevin Mower making a statement but I've not seen it yet. We're interviewing everyone in the wards at the rear of the building too, of course, but the chances are that the patients were all asleep so our main hope is the night duty staff."

"There's no connection between Dana Smith and this nurse, apart from the hospital, that is?"

"It's early days, but no obvious connection, no. It looks as though the hospital was the target all along. We've been wasting our time on the Smith family. Dana was probably just a random victim." Thackeray did not hide his bitterness that so much effort had been expended for so little progress. "If we'd concentrated on the hospital we might have prevented this second death," he said.

"We'll step up security there, though uniformed won't thank us for tying up more officers," Longley said. He leaned back in his chair wearily. "This is a right beggar, Michael. Don't blame yourself. I've never heard of anything like it in this country."

"Yes, well, there is our American visitor. He'll be pretty high on my list of people to talk to, don't worry. Though to be fair, I thought it was the doctors they usually went for over there, not patients and nurses. Guilt by association seems a bit over the top, even by American standards."

"Talk to the Crown Prosecution Service," Longley said. "If there's a whisper he's involved in this I want him banged up on a conspiracy charge or else out of the country so fast his feet don't touch the ground."

"The thought had crossed my mind," Thackeray said. "Though it might not be easy. I'm told he's already making defamatory attacks on Fenton-Green. If the going gets rough, he could turn very nasty."

"If all else fails, get the beggar back to Idaho or wherever it is he hales from," Longley said.

"It's Iowa. I'll see what I can do," Thackeray said.

Half an hour later Thackeray and DC Val Ridley were sitting in the eerily silent front room of Stella Brady's neat semi-detached home on the outskirts of the town. Colin Brady, her husband, was sitting in the middle of a sofa with a pale and silent child on each side of him.

"We will get whoever did this, Mr. Brady," Michael Thackeray said quietly. "I promise you that."

"It's not going to bring her back, though, is it?" Brady said, his voice thick. His children watched him out of huge stunned eyes and he hugged them closer to him. "There's nowt you can do about that."

"Some time soon, when you feel more able to talk, I'd like to ask you more about Stella, who her friends were, what she thought about her job, whether she had any enemies…"

"Enemies?" Brady said incredulously. "Nurses don't have enemies, man. Her patients thought she was bloody wonderful. They always do, don't they? And up there, they were getting pregnant sometimes after years of waiting. They were over the moon with that place – with the doctors, the nurses, even the bloody cleaning women. Over the bloody moon. And she was conscientious. Not content with the actual nursing, always trying to keep up with the latest techniques, reading scientific stuff, all that."

Thackeray glanced at the two children, a girl of about five and a boy he guessed was a year or so older, both of them silent and tearless, no doubt unsure of exactly what had happened or perhaps even what death meant, and he stood up abruptly.

"Just one question now," he said. "Until you can arrange for the children to be looked after and we can have a longer talk. But I need to know. Did Stella have any contact with the termination patients?"

"She did not," Brady said flatly. "She were a Catholic, Mr. Thackeray, and she'd have nowt to do wi'that."

"Is there anyone we can contact for you, Mr. Brady?" Val Ridley asked. "To help you with the children? Stay with you? Anything?"

"My mother-in-law's on her way over," Brady said. "And the neighbours are very good. They'll be devastated when they hear." For a moment his face crumpled and tears filled his eyes, but then he hugged his children close again and swallowed his distress.

"We'll be right," he said.

"I doubt that," Thackeray said as they left the widowed father and made their way back to the car. "I doubt he'll ever be right again."

Laura Ackroyd launched herself into her twenty-seventh game of patience on her computer screen at the fag-end of a miserable day. The flickering cards served one purpose only, to occupy her mind until she could decently leave the office, at which point she knew that she would have to think about the things she had tried to avoid thinking about since she had arrived at work that morning.

She had spent the night at Vicky and David Mendelson's, after arriving at their house with a face so pale and eyes so tragic that Vicky had grabbed her friend, thrust her into a chair with a vodka and tonic and told David brusquely to leave them alone. Talking was supposed to help in these situations, she told herself bitterly, but on this occasion had not. As she repeated endlessly to Vicky, she had never intended to lie to Thackeray but the opportunity to drop a casual "Oh, by the way..." into the conversation had never come, and in any case the memory of her brief pregnancy had become almost unreal as time had passed. Now he had learned of it at the worst possible moment and it took no imagination at all to realise that news of her half-forgotten choice risked colliding with Thackeray's own memories made raw by his current investigations, with uncertain consequences

"I've blown it," Laura had told Vicky over and over again.

"I'm sure you haven't," Vicky said. "When you've both calmed down a bit, Michael will understand."

But Laura's certainty that he would never understand was only strengthened when she came in to work that morning, bleary-eyed and only semi-coherent, to find the newsroom in uproar after a second shooting at the May Anderson hospital and the second victim one of the nurses she had met. Fortunately for her career prospects, Ted Grant did not expect his female staff to play any great part in crime reporting. That, in his vast book of granite certainties, was a male preserve, so Laura was able to tap aimlessly at her keyboard, ostensibly working on a feature for Monday's paper, without attracting attention but in fact shaking inside with distress at the impact that she knew this new outrage would have on Michael.

But by lunchtime she had been dragged into the general mayhem when Ted Grant and Bob Baker approached her with their eyes gleaming with the excitement of the chase.

"The police have taken Edgar Burridge in for questioning," Ted said. "We'd best run your interview in the late edition, just in case he's charged and we can't run it at all."

"It's finished," Laura said dully. "It's in the file called Debate, along with the stuff about the hospital."

"Did you talk to Dorothy Knight, the local woman running this campaign Burridge is visiting?" Grant demanded. Laura shook her head. "Apparently they've got her down at police HQ as well. They must be pretty damn sure the protesters have summat to do with it. Bob here reckons they must have found a weapon this time."

"Your boyfriend's giving a press conference at two," Baker said.

"Did you meet this nurse when you went up to the hospital?" Grant said suddenly.

"Stella Brady? Yes, I did, briefly," Laura said.

"So why the hell didn't you say so earlier, girl?" Grant roared. "Give us as much as you can on the woman if you've met her – what she looked like, what she said, what the patients thought about her. Good God, girl, have you got no news-sense at all?"

"She ran the fertility treatment ward," Laura said defensively. "She said that she had nothing to do with terminations. She had conscientious objections to all that."

"All the better," Grant said. "Innocent victim, then. Piggy-in-the-middle, if all this really is down to the protesters. Bloody good story. Write it for God's sake. You've got fifteen minutes to catch the edition."

DCI Michael Thackeray stood on the steps of the Crown Prosecution Services' offices at an uncharacteristic loss as he gazed at the late evening traffic whirling around the town hall square. He had left the murder team to their largely routine tasks: interviewing Stella Brady's friends and neighbours, talking to patients and staff at the hospital who, it turned out had seen and heard very little at six that morning, and going over the security guard's statement. The morning frenzy with which he had insisted on interviewing Edgar Burridge and Dorothy Knight had dissipated itself as it became clear that there were no signs of a weapon at SLL headquarters or at Burridge's hotel, where Mower had apparently not been particularly light-handed in his search of the premises and the evangelist's two young acolytes. There was no indication at all that the two of them, and Burridge himself, had not been safely tucked up in their respective beds until long after dawn, just as they had said they were.

It had not needed the solicitor Burridge had summoned to his aid to make the point that there was no evidence to link either the organisation, its secretary or its American guest directly to either to the shootings. Although it was now clear that the shootings were undoubtedly linked to each other. Not only was the bullet recovered from Stella Brady's skull from the same gun which had killed Dana Smith, but the security guard clearly recalled hearing, though not seeing, a motorbike at the time of the murder, a bike which accelerated away noisily immediately after the sound of the shot. But Thackeray had still not entirely dismissed the idea that SLL might be indirectly connected to the murders, difficult as that might be to prove if the finger on the trigger had been someone else's entirely.

His temper had not been improved when just after he had allowed Burridge to leave, superintendent Longley had rung down to tell him to expect a visit from Special Branch the following day.

"Do they just fancy a breath of Yorkshire air or do they think there's some sort of national conspiracy behind the shootings?" Thackeray asked, loath to welcome the spooks onto his patch.

"Oh, I expect they're kicking their heels looking for summat to occupy themselves with now Northern Ireland's gone all cuddly," Longley said. "I know you'll give them a warm Bradfield welcome."

"Perhaps I'll have got rid of Edgar Burridge by then," Thackeray said. But he knew he was clutching at straws and David Mendelson at the CPS, when he called to see him at the end of the day, had been equally dismissive of Thackeray's suggestion that it would be a good idea to send Burridge back to America on some pretext before his meeting at the town hall could take place. David had put his hands behind his head and leaned back in his chair to gaze at his friend across the precarious piles of paperwork with which he was invariably surrounded.

"Nice try," he had said sympathetically enough. "But it's down to immigration. There's nothing you can charge him with, is there? We may not have a right to free speech in the constitution like they do, but there are limits. You'd cause an international incident. *The Guardian* would be screaming about a police state. You'd have cardinals and archbishops and every variety of born-again nut-case crying foul. It'd be more

125

trouble than it was worth. Just get your colleagues to police the meeting sensibly so we don't end up with a riot."

"Burridge is alleging that Fenton-Green has been doing late terminations," Thackeray said, his distaste showing. "What are we supposed to do about that?"

"You'd need evidence from a nurse or a GP to make that stick," Mendelson said. "I don't suppose you'll find the patients complaining. A can of worms, I'd say, unless you feel in a crusading mood and I should think you've got too much on your plate for that, haven't you?"

Thackeray had nodded slowly, wondering how much David knew about his row with Laura the previous evening. The silence between them lengthened and he realised that whatever he knew he did not intend to mention it.

"I reckon I'll call it a day," he said.

"You look exhausted," Mendelson said. "We're always complaining here about being overworked, but I reckon we're amateurs at it compared to you lot."

At the *Gazette*, Laura Ackroyd was still sitting at her desk, although most of her colleagues had long since gone home and most of the lights were off. She had played patience until her fingers could no longer click the mouse accurately enough to play any more. She had tidied the drawers of her desk. She had spend half an hour in the women's loo experimenting with her hairstyle. And now she could think of no more excuses to avoid the decision she knew she was going to have to make – to go home as if nothing had happened. Or not.

Guilt, she thought, was a slippery concept. She had heard Thackeray say often enough that many of his clients seemed to lack the ability to feel for their victims. The human empathy which prevents most people most of the time from carving up their family, their friends, and even strangers, was simply lacking in some criminals, he had concluded after sitting across bleak interview room tables from so many of them. While if Thackeray had a fault, and she knew he had many, it was his determination to take the sins of the world, as well as his own, on his broad shoulders. Guilt was his besetting failing.

And where, she wondered, did that leave her when the most powerful feeling she could summon up when she thought of the baby whose life she had quite deliberately ended was an almost imperceptible sense of regret for what might have been. Was she morally deficient in some way, she wondered, in that she did not grieve as Burridge and his friends and no doubt Michael Thackeray, thought she should grieve. Or was she, as most women she knew seemed to be, simply a realist in thinking that a bundle of cells created by a half-remembered coupling and wanted by no one was just that, and not in any real sense a child at all.

She groaned and reached out to switch off her computer until she noticed that she had email. The message was brief and to the point.

You think you have all the facts about the May Anderson Hospital, but there is a lot more to tell and you won't find out from Fenton-Green. He's not as lily-white as he makes out. It is time someone let you know what's really going on with his research. If you want to know more, let me know and we will arrange a meeting.

Laura stared at the screen for a moment before typing in her simple reply.

"Give me a time and a place."

She pressed Send and gazed at the address her response was going to which told her nothing except the fact that her correspondent chose to call him or herself Nemesis. It must be a joke, she thought. But she knew it might not be and felt a sense of relief that at least one decision had been taken out of her hands. She pressed Print and listened as the machine on the other side of the office reproduced the message and her reply. This was something she was going to have to show Michael Thackeray. And if, when they met, he told her that their relationship was over, then that was something she would have to learn to live with. What she could no longer do was put it off.

They agreed on neutral territory in the bar of the Clarendon Hotel where Laura found Thackeray sitting at one of the polished tables with a glass of mineral water in front of him alongside an ashtray that was already almost full. He got to his feet as she pushed through the swing doors, her hair flying, cheeks flushed, attracting the admiring glances which he still resented.

"Vodka and tonic?" he asked, his voice neutral, and went to the bar as she settled in the comfortable armchair in the corner which was waiting for her. He brought her drink and settled back into his seat without comment and for an awkward couple of seconds the silence hung between them.

"You said…"

"I had this email…" They spoke together and laughed awkwardly at themselves.

"Tell me," Thackeray said, but instead she just pushed the printout towards him across the table and waited while he read it.

"I thought it might be from Stella Brady," Laura said. "She might have sent it before…"

"Unlikely," Thackeray said. "Email is quicker than that. But it may be someone who's reacting to her death. We should be able to trace them through their email account, but it may take time. I'll get Kevin onto it. He's more computer literate than I am."

"It's easy for these people to make allegations and in the end some of the mud will stick," Laura said.

"It's not impossible that the allegations have some foundation," Thackeray said. "Fenton-Green's working in an area surrounded by regulations. He doesn't strike me as the most patient of men. The fact that you don't like the people who are accusing him doesn't mean they're not telling the truth."

Laura knew that what Thackeray was saying was fair but

she could not bring herself to agree and gazed steadfastly into her drink as she took another sip.

"Let me know if your emailer contacts you again," Thackeray said. Laura's head jerked up and there was fear in her eyes. "I'd like to identify him – or her."

"You're not coming home?"

"I'll stay at my place tonight," he said. He had not yet sold the bleak flat which had been his home since he came to Bradfield.

"Michael, we need to talk," Laura said, desperate now.

"I need to think," he said quietly, getting to his feet and running a hand lightly down the side of her face. "I'll call you tomorrow." And with that he was gone, leaving Laura to make her way to the bar and order another drink which she swallowed in a single gulp, to the evident astonishment of the sleek businessman who had begun to edge in her direction.

"Don't even let it cross your mind," she snarled at him, as she tossed her copper hair out of her eyes and marched towards the doors.

Chapter 9

By ten the next morning Laura Ackroyd discovered that the May Anderson Hospital had become an almost impregnable fortress. The security officer on the gate had been reinforced by two uniformed police officers and another stood at the main door like a guardsman at Buckingham Palace. Through the glass doors she could see more police at reception and she realised that even if she managed to sweet-talk her way past the gatekeepers, as she had spent a fruitless ten minutes trying to do, she would only have to start again – and very likely fail – further inside.

Irritated, she turned away. The opposite pavement was deserted this morning, she noticed, and she assumed that even the most vociferous protesters must have pulled back in deference to the dead nurse. She wondered why they had not had the decency to withdraw when Dana Smith had been killed. There had been no further message from her mysterious emailer when she got to work that morning, and she guessed that police efforts to trace the address might have scared him or her away. She had not yet told Ted Grant about the message and she was slightly relieved when he sent her up to the May Anderson hospital with instructions to talk to as many people who had known Stella Brady as possible.

But the assignment was proving problematic, and back in her car she attacked it from another angle, putting in a call to the hospital from her mobile and after a series of delays, finally getting through to Sister Barbara King, who sounded at the edge of her tether when she came to the phone.

"I can't get in, but I wondered if you got a coffee break and could come out for a chat," Laura said. The invitation was greeted with a long silence but eventually Sister King responded.

"I get an hour's break in about fifteen minutes," she said. "I was on early this morning, with a bloody police escort to work. My husband's going bananas. I'll meet you at the Kabin in the parade of shops at the bottom of Mornington Terrace. You can't miss it."

Barbara King arrived at the café with a winter coat fastened up to her neck to hide her nurse's uniform, refusing even to loosen a single button as they settled at a table in the corner of the small steamy room. The ebullient woman who had taken such pride in showing Laura her maternity ward only a few days before seemed to have shrunk as a result of the tragedy which had followed, her skin looked grey and her eyes were red rimmed behind slightly tinted glasses.

"I can't believe what's happening," she said after she had ordered poached eggs and coffee. "The whole place is shattered. Some of the patients are planning to leave as soon as they can, and it'll be difficult to persuade new ones to come in with the building under siege like this. There's all sorts of rumours flying around: it's a mad gunman with a grudge against hospitals, or nurses, an ex-patient who didn't get pregnant when they hoped to, or it was anti-abortion terrorists – is there such a thing? – or fundamentalist Muslims because of Dr. Mahood working there…It's a nightmare."

"I can imagine," Laura said.

"Everyone is wondering if they've done anything to annoy a potential lunatic, in case they're next."

"Could Stella Brady have annoyed anyone?" Laura asked.

"Of course some of the fertility patients go away distraught. It doesn't work for everyone. Mr. Fenton-Green couldn't even succeed with his own wife when she was treated there. But I can't think of anyone who could be *blaming* the hospital. They all have the possibilities explained to them before they come in."

"Fenton-Green's wife?" Laura was surprised.

"Well, he couldn't treat her personally. Dr. Mahood was in charge, technically. But it didn't work anyway and they got divorced soon after," Barbara King said. "It sometimes

131

happens that way, especially if one partner is very keen to have a family. A bit Henry the Eighth, I know, but I can understand the pressures. Then he went out with that public relations girl for a bit, what's her name, Nadia something?"

"Ah," Laura said, realising now why Nadia Bellman had been so defensive.

"Of course, the hospital gossips are waiting to see now whether his new girlfriend gets pregnant."

"Sounds a bit like living in a pressure cooker," Laura said.

"And even worse now. A pressure cooker with the lid screwed down tight," the nurse said. "My husband wants me to leave. But I like my job. Stella loved it too. She was always in a twitch, of course, in case anyone asked her to do anything she thought was unethical, but apart from that she really loved it when the treatment worked out, like it did for Karen Bailey. It gave her such a buzz. And she'd get heartbroken if it failed."

"So perhaps someone who didn't have a baby and then ended up divorced? They might bear a grudge and lash out?"

"Surely not enough to provoke them into shooting people at random?" Barbara King said. "It's too bizarre."

"And terrifying," Laura said. "Have your twins gone home? The ones you took me to see?"

"Oh, yes. Dad came round in the Merc yesterday. They're not married, of course. It's Miz Bailey and Mr. Something-else, Freeman was it? I can't remember now. You know she was joking about calling them Reggie and Ronnie, if they'd been boys? At least, I thought she was joking, but when I saw her bloke I did begin to wonder – a big, hulking brute in a cashmere overcoat, you could just imagine him with the Krays. Did you see that film? Someone said he runs the security firm that does the doors for all the clubs in West Yorkshire. They're all crooks, aren't they, the bouncers? Into drugs and stuff? He wasn't there when the twins were born, of course. Beneath his dignity, I expect. And it was funny – Karen didn't want to know the sex beforehand. P'raps just as well really. I

132

don't think little girls were exactly what daddy thought he'd ordered. Of course, Stella didn't like any suggestion that parents might be able to choose their baby's sex."

"Mr. Fenton-Green wasn't offering that, surely?"

"No, no, I'm sure he wasn't. In fact we've had a spate of girls, when what people generally want is boys. It was just Stella being twitchy as usual. She watched every move the doctors made in case she had to go to confession about it later."

Laura smiled faintly at this torrent of information after which Barbara King peered towards the door of the café anxiously and then waved at someone who appeared to be looking just as intently in their direction from the street outside.

"Who's that?" Laura asked, turning in her chair.

"Oh, just Dave Randall, the technician from the fertility lab. He sometimes comes in here for a late breakfast but he won't if he sees me with someone else. He's a bit shy, I suppose. A bit of a loner."

"I think I met him briefly when Dr. Mahood took me up there," Laura said.

"I suppose it must be an odd sort of job, fiddling about with other people's sperm all day," Barbara King said. "Not something you'd want broadcast around, is it?" She laughed but it was a strangely unconvincing sound and Laura wondered how long it would be before she succumbed to her husband's pressure to resign from her job at the May Anderson.

Kevin Mower stood at the bar in the Woolpack, CID's favourite watering hole, and ordered three double Scotches. When the barman pushed them towards him, the sergeant glanced quickly over his shoulder before picking up one of the glasses and knocking the drink down in one.

"I bloody needed that," he muttered to the startled barman as he took his money. "Been a bad day and it's not over yet."

The reason it was not over sat on the other side of the room at a table for two and took the glass Mower brought him without a word in the way of acknowledgement or thanks. He was a thin man who had hung his leather jacket on the chair behind him and sat, long legs awkwardly arranged under the fake oak table, in Chinos and black Ralph Lauren polo shirt, his fair hair flopping over his brow in a way which Mower found peculiarly irritating. Paul Cook, a DI in Special Branch, had arrived from London that lunchtime, spoken briefly with Michael Thackeray who had handed him over to Mower with the curt instruction to liaise. They had spent the afternoon going over the files on the two shootings at the May Anderson Hospital and by now Mower was at the end of his tether.

"Happy hour," he announced in a tone which left little room for dissent on the visitor's part as the office clock crept past six.

"Your boss always as chilly as that?" Cook had asked as they crossed the town hall square into the hilly shopping streets behind the brutalist headquarters of the building society which was one of the town's major employers.

"Chillier most of the time," Mower said unhelpfully. "He's that rare breed. In nobody's pocket."

Cook cast him a sceptical look as he dodged a dilapidated taxi undertaking a deadly U-turn round one of the square's traffic islands.

"You're not local yourself, are you?" he asked.

"South London. Started in the Met," Mower had admitted, knowing that if Cook really wanted to know he could easily find out. "I like it up here."

"No accounting for taste."

Now settled across the table from Mower, Cook sipped his drink while Mower made a superhuman effort not to knock his second slug back as quickly as he had the first.

"I think we met once," the DI said eventually. "Weren't you at Paddington Green?"

Mower laughed mirthlessly.

"Briefly," he said and Cook nodded as if cogs were slipping into place.

"It was after that bomb on the railway at Paddington," he said. "You remember?"

"I wasn't involved in that investigation," he said.

"No, I seem to recall you had other things on your mind. So that's why you're up here in the sticks, is it?"

Mower looked at his interrogator with dislike in his dark eyes.

"I said I *like* it up here," he said again, although it was a protestation which drifted further from the truth with each day that passed. Cook shrugged and grinned and turned his attention to his drink.

"So do you really suspect the anti-abortion campaign is getting violent?" Mower asked. "You've got hard evidence?"

Cook tossed his hair back and stared at Mower for a moment from hooded eyes.

"I wouldn't say that. But little old ladies who love pussy cats have been known to get violent recently," he said. "Middle-aged mumsies have thrown themselves in front of lorry loads of calves leaving the country. Who knows what these pro-life buggers might get up to. Put sweet ickle babies and fundamentalist religion together and light the blue touch paper? Of course it could be getting violent."

"So that's what you lot get up to now is it?" Mower asked. "Now the IRA's a spent force and the only problem at Paddington is Railtrack."

"Well, I wouldn't bank on that, but in any case terrorists don't always come with a balaclava and a Kalshnikov," Cook said. "An incendiary device in a department store's been just as effective. Or in this case, maybe, a single handgun and a fast bike. We're not just talking the odd half brick thrown in anger. We're talking organised here. Plans made on the internet. Guns and bombs and hate mail."

"But the nurse who died is opposed to abortion," Mower said. "Don't you think they'd have checked that out before shooting her in cold blood."

"What makes you think they're that efficient?" Cook asked.

"My guess is they were aiming at the surgeon in the first attack and killed the girl by mistake. As far as they're concerned, all the nurses and doctors are equally guilty so it doesn't make much difference which particular one gets wasted."

Mower drained his glass, disturbed that he was disturbed at the Special Branch man's matter-of-fact tone. He had been working too long with Michael Thackeray, he thought. He was losing his edge.

"Another," he asked and when Cook made a token attempt to go to the bar himself he waved him back into his seat. "Be my guest," he said. This time DI Cook watched from under half-closed lids as Mower repeated his order and again drank one of the glasses at the bar before picking up the other two. Being a methodical man, he filed the information away for future reference. Kevin Mower, he thought, might turn out to be more of a liability than a help as a minder during his time in Bradfield and he wondered just why DCI Thackeray had lumbered him with a sergeant who had evidently exchanged a problem with women for a problem with booze.

"Have you had any luck checking out bikes?" Cook asked when Mower had sat down again. The sergeant shook his head.

"There's not a single name that's come up – in the hospital, in the campaign, amongst the witnesses, who's the registered owner of a bike," he said.

"Patients, ex-patients, their families?"

"All being checked. We had to work hard to persuade the hospital to give us access to their lists but after the second shooting they caved in."

"If it was an NHS hospital we could have got hold of them, no trouble," Cook said.

"Yeah?" Mower's scepticism evidently nettled Cook.

"No problem," he said. "Anything you want to know that's on an official computer these days, we can get."

"Big Brother's arrived, then."

"You don't look that fucking naïve," Cook said suddenly,

136

the languid drawl which had got on Mower's nerves all afternoon replaced with a harsher sound altogether. "D'you think we shouldn't be using the same gear as the bloody criminals then? All tooled up with mobiles and encrypted email and a black market in Russian weapons that makes the UK arms industry look amateur. You must have gone soft since you left the Met, sergeant. Getting too matey with the sheep-shaggers, are we? Woolly-minded as well as woolly-headed up in Yorkshire? Get real. If these anti-abortion protesters are taking people out at the rate of two a week in Bradfield, that may be just the start. How do we know they're not planning a national campaign? If this is just a little local feud of some sort, then you can treat your suspects with kid gloves if that's how it's done here. But if I get even a hint that it's part of something bigger, then I tell you, it's no holds barred. It's terrorism and we don't mess about with terrorists."

Mower finished his drink and did not offer his visitor another.

"Right," he said. "Can you find your way back to your hotel OK?"

"Oh, I think I might manage that, Kevin," Cook said. "I thought I might check out one of Bradfield's famous curry houses? You're not up for that then? Soak up some of the sauce?"

"Not tonight," Mower said. "I've other plans." He shrugged himself into his coat and left Cook finished his drink and watching his departure speculatively. Outside in the slanting rain which was ripping down from the Pennine hills above the town, Mower shivered as he made his way further up the hill and into the narrow network of streets off Aysgarth Lane where prostitutes huddled for shelter in doorways and Asian men watched them and him with unfriendly dark eyes. Eventually Mower slipped into another pub where he knew he could sit in a corner undisturbed until closing time and ordered another drink and then another. The need for sleep was becoming urgent and this was the quickest way he knew to attain the oblivion he desperately needed, though he knew that tomorrow he would probably feel worse than he had done today.

A young woman in a thigh hugging leather mini-skirt, shivering with cold, slid into the seat opposite him, questioning, propositioning, with blank blue eyes. He looked her up and down, from her streaky blonde hair and pale thin face to the scuffed toes of her red boots and shook his head.

"If I had the energy I'd take you down the nick just to get warm," he said. The girl stood up quickly, her face contorted with anger, hands clenched into impotent blue-white fists.

"You can keep your sympathy, an'all," she said. "I've seen you staggering down t'road with a skinful often enough, pukin' up in t'gutter. You want to get *yourself* fixed up, you do, before you start on me." She spun on her heel and went out again into the bitter night and Mower crouched over his glass, shaken by the force of her assault. He was in deeper than he thought, he told himself, if a complete stranger could pin him so clinically to the floor.

"Why the hell did we take Rita on that bloody raid?" he muttered into his drink for what must have been the hundred thousandth time, and as usual the answer which Rita herself would probably have given came drifting back through the whisky fumes. It had been blind chance, bad luck, a malign fate which had put her in the wrong place at the wrong time and killed her. And now, he thought, the same thing was killing him.

In a row of lock-up garages at the back of Benwell Lane, Gavin Smith slid his hand under the sleeveless top of the girl he was with and struggled to unhook her bra. He had pulled his companion onto a pile of sacks in one corner and her face was hardly visible in the light which filtered through the open door but she did not seem to object to his attentions and he felt himself becoming more excited even though he had told himself that sex was not what he wanted from Melanie Todd. He knew she fancied him. He had known it for months in spite of the reluctance she and her gaggle of girl-friends showed whenever he or any of his brothers glanced across the lane in their direction as they worked on their cars. And until now he had ignored her and her giggling mates. But now, he thought, Mel might provide the crack he was determined to find in Benwell Lane's defences.

Mel's bra gave up the struggle and she let him fondle her breasts, with every indication that she was enjoying the experience. He kissed her and he knew that she was his for the taking so he took her with an angry passion which she returned in kind. And when they were finished he despised her even more than he had done when he had met her in the street and chatted her up.

"Enjoyed that, did you?" he asked. "Right little raver, aren't you?"

"Tecks one to know one," Melanie said. "Are all your brothers as tasty as you?"

"Oh aye, all except our Mick," Gavin said. "He's more interested in his ponies than in lasses."

"I've seen him down in that field all hours," she said. "Right farmer's boy, en't he? Not as good looking as the rest of you neither. Sad, really, but my mam says you always get one runt in a litter."

"But you're not the runt in yours," Gavin said, running a hand experimentally down the inside of the girl's thigh and wondering whether she would be up for it again. But she pushed him away.

"I've got to get back," she said.

"Did you know our Dana then?" Gavin asked, forcing his mind back to the object of the evening's adventure with some difficulty.

"Might 'ave," Melanie said, trying to insert feet still clad in boots through the legs of her knickers without great success.

"Must 'ave," Gavin said. "And I reckon you girls must 'ave known who she were seeing an'all. In't that right?"

139

"Might 'ave," Melanie said again. "But so what? She's dead now, in't she? What good does it do knowing?"

"Well, we thought we should invite him to't funeral, like?" Gavin said. Melanie succeeded in wriggling back into her pants and giggled.

"You're kidding," she said.

"Nowt like that," Gavin said, suddenly sounding deadly serious. "Wi'us Gypsies if you sleep with a lass you're reckoned to be married to her. So Dana's boyfriend should be at t'funeral. Stands to reason, don't it?"

"Now you are kidding," Melanie said. "If that were true you'd be married to me an'all. Fat chance."

"Aye, well, it's just a tradition, like. Not everyone sticks wi'it these days, do they? But if that lad were fond o'our Dana it's not such a joke, is it? We could invite him to't funeral. It'd only be t'decent thing to do."

"Aye, well you'll not get Nick Bailey anywhere near owt you lot are doing," Melanie said. "If he had it off wi' Dana – and I did say *if*, mind – I reckon it'll have been a quickie in here, just like you an'me. Nowt more than that. Reckons he's a hard man, does Nick. And randy with it. Had more lasses than hot dinners."

Gavin put his head between his knees, fists clenched as he tried to stifle the red-hot wave of anger which threatened to burst from him. Melanie was struggling into her denim jacket and did not appear to notice. She leaned over and kissed him on the back of the neck.

"Don't matter to me if you are a gippo," she whispered. "I think you're gorgeous. D'you want to meet me here again tomorrow after school?"

Gavin swallowed hard.

"Mebbe," he said. "But me and Tom have to go to Wakefield tomorrow about a car."

"You'd best send Terry then," Melanie said. "It's all t'same to me."

When she had gone, Gavin walked slowly round the end of

the garages towards home feeling sick. He knew Nick Bailey, a stocky sandy-haired lad of about eighteen who rode around the estate on a beaten up motorbike terrorising any of the older residents who had the temerity to complain about the absence of a silencer. He could not imagine how Dana could possibly have got involved with someone who took such pleasure in his own thuggishness and he wondered, not for the first time, whether the child she had been carrying was the result of a rape she had not dared to admit. He groaned in frustrated fury, knowing that there were questions to which he would probably never find the answers.

"I'll kill the bastard," he promised himself as he approached his mother's house where the curtains at the unboarded upstairs windows were all tightly drawn against prying eyes. "I'll bloody kill him."

It was not until he was edging his way past the heap of old tyres which were stacked close to the back door of the house that he became conscious of a low moaning sound.

"Hey up, who's that?" he said and when there was no response he opened the door so that the light from inside the house spilled out into the front garden where a car still rested on bricks and the rest of the muddy patch was littered with wheels and heaps of other junk. Even then it was only just possible to see that a dark patch which might have been just another rubbish bag lying close to what was left of the garden gate was in fact human. Cautiously he approached the bundle which began to move.

"Who's that?" Maggie Sullivan croaked. "Is that my Micky?"

"Jesus," Gavin said. "What are you doing there, Gran? We thought we'd lost you. How did you get here all the way from Shepley."

Maggie Sullivan groaned as she tried to straighten out her stiffening limbs. She did not know how long it was since she had collapsed within sight of her daughter's front door, when the voice which had urged her on since she had left the town

141

centre suddenly fell silent, but she knew it had only been dusk then and now it was a cold dark night and she was frozen to the marrow.

"Help us up, lad," she commanded, though her voice was faint. "Get us into t'warm before I catch my death." With one swift movement Gavin reached down and picked his grandmother up, conscious that she was little more than a bundle of bones beneath the over-large coat she seemed to have wrapped herself in. He carried her into the house and through to the front room where his mother and his brother Mick were sitting close to a blazing open fire.

"Oh my God," Megan said jumping up and helping Gavin put her mother on the sofa. Mick, sitting on the other side of the room seemed transfixed by the new arrival. "Where've you been, Mam? We thought you were lost. What have you been doing all this time?" Maggie had begun to shiver convulsively.

"Put kettle on, Mick," Megan said urgently. "She's frozen to death here. Meck a big mug o'tea quick, lad. Plenty o'sugar."

Gradually as her daughter massaged her mother's icy hands and feet in front of the roaring fire, Maggie felt some life begin to return.

"We went looking for you, Mam," Megan said. "We thought you might be down at t'van, but you weren't. Where've you been? Wherever have you been?"

"I saw it in t'cards," Maggie managed to say at last. "I knew summat had happened. It were all in't cards. It were our Dana, wa'n't it? Has she gone?" She showed no surprise when Megan nodded, her eyes filling with the tears that had never been far away for days.

"I needed to come. I needed to tell you to come away from here," Maggie said as Mick came back into the room with her tea and helped her sip it slowly.

"It's too late now," Megan said.

"Nay, nay, you must still come away. There's nowt good'll

142

come o'this place now. You must get the lads away from here, all o'them. Folk like us don't belong here, in houses."

"That's what the beggars who live round here would like," Gavin said angrily. "They've been trying to get us out o'here ever since we arrived. Well, I'm not going, for one. And Mick won't leave his horses." Mick looked from his grandmother to his brother nervously.

"There's nowhere to go, Mam," Megan said. "Where would we go, me and four great lads. It were hard enough getting this place out o't'council. We'll never get owt else."

"I can't leave my horses, Gran," Mick said, his hands clenched tight with anxiety.

"And there's Dana's funeral," Megan said. "I don't know when they're going to let us have Dana's funeral…"

Maggie finished her tea and handed the empty mug back to Mick. She was still wearing nothing but the thin hospital gown under the coat she had stolen and she shivered intermittently in spite of the heat from the fire. Utterly weary she turned away from her family and buried her face in the back of the sofa, closing her eyes and letting sleep claim her.

"You'll do as you like," she said, although whether her own voice was confined now to the inside of her head or whether it reached Megan and the others she was not sure. "You always did as you liked. Teck no notice o'me. I should have stayed on t'road till it were time to burn t'van. I came to tell you. I can't do no more than that. I've walked as far as I can and I'm finished now."

"Told you so," said the other, increasingly distinct voice in her head triumphantly.

Chapter 10

DC Val Ridley watched her boss circumspectly from behind a
tight, closed face which gave nothing of herself away. That
Thackeray was in a filthy mood was not in doubt, although
she had no idea what had caused it or even whether it was
anything to do with her or anyone else in CID. Not that there
was no good reason for anger and distress. They had sat outside Stella Brady's neat semi-detached house in silence for a
moment as Thackeray apparently steeled himself to keep the
appointment with the dead woman's husband that they had
made by telephone.

"The kids are with his mother-in-law," Val ventured.

"Right," Thackeray said. The silence lengthened until at last
Thackeray shook himself into action and got out of the car. Val
followed him up the short drive to the Brady's front door
which was opened wide almost as soon as Thackeray pressed
the bell.

"I saw you sitting there," Colin Brady said, his voice full of
hurt accusation. "I'll not bite, you know." Thackeray nodded
bleakly knowing that his own unprofessional reluctance to
enter a house in mourning would probably have been echoed
by enough of Brady's friends and neighbours now for him to
realise that the bereaved were a sort of modern leper from
whom fear of contamination kept many people away.

Brady led them into his sitting-room, untidier than the last
time Thackeray had seen it, the loss of a woman's organising
energy already apparent in the over-full ashtrays and the collection of dirty coffee mugs on the table. He was more surprised to see Father Dermot Burke, a pale blue sweater
straining over his clerical vest and collar, waiting to meet them.

"Father." Thackeray's greeting was curt enough to verge on
rudeness. "This is DC Val Ridley who's going to act as our liai-
son with Stella's family."

144

"That at least is something civilised in this appalling business," Burke said. "Colin's not one of my flock but I felt I had to call for Stella's sake. I was just saying that I hoped her deeply held convictions could not have played any part in this tragedy."

"We don't know yet what played a part in this tragedy and what didn't, which is why we're here to talk to Mr. Brady again," Thackeray said. "Obviously we have to look at Stella's beliefs, in the light of the protests which have been going on at the hospital. But we have no way of knowing whether they have any bearing on her death."

Burke smiled grimly.

"It would be the ultimate irony if she were to have been shot by anyone sympathetic to SLL, in view of the fact she was a member," he said.

Thackeray glanced at Brady, who had slumped onto the sofa in a corner where the squashed cushions told of hours spent in that exact position and he wondered how long it was since he had been to bed.

"Is that right, Mr. Brady?" he asked. "She was a member of an anti-abortion group?" Colin Brady nodded.

"She felt very strongly about it," he mumbled.

"Did she discuss her rather ambivalent position at the May Anderson with you, Father?" Thackeray asked.

"She wasn't ambivalent about her role," Burke said. "She felt entirely comfortable with the work she was doing. But she was unhappy about the terminations which also went on there, obviously. And latterly I did get the impression that this was troubling her more rather than less."

"Did you get the feeling Stella was unhappy about anything particular at work, Mr. Brady?" Thackeray asked, but Brady just shook his head.

"Father Burke?"

"She was never specific. Just a certain mistrust, I felt. A feeling that what rules there are were being bent," the priest said, looking uncomfortable.

"Operations being carried out too late, you mean?" Thackeray asked. "I keep picking up that rumour but no one comes up with any hard evidence."

"That was possibly part of it," Burke said. "But I felt that there might have been more to it than that. Don't get me wrong, Mr. Thackeray. Stella never made any specific allegations to me about the hospital, either in the confessional or outside it, so you need have no worries on that score. But she seemed unhappy. Or uneasy perhaps might be a better word."

"SLL wasn't using her as some sort of spy? Their line to the inside?"

"Not to my knowledge," Burke said sharply. "That might have put her job at risk, I'd have thought, and she certainly wouldn't have wanted that."

"But don't you think that she perhaps felt in some danger? Particularly after Dana Smith was shot?"

"Oh, no, I never got that impression," Burke said quickly. "If I had, I would have told her to go straight to the police, naturally."

"Mr. Brady," Thackeray said turning to the murdered woman's husband. "Did Stella seem at all unhappy to you before she died? Did she have any worries at all that she told you about?"

Colin Brady shook his head dully again.

"She been on the early shift for two weeks," he said. "When she's on that shift she goes out before I wake up and then needs to get to bed soon after we've had our supper. There's not much time for talking when I come in of an evening. It's getting the kids to bed, cooking summat to eat and then a quick look at telly before she turns in. You know what it's like with a young family."

Thackeray nodded sympathetically enough although Val Ridley knew that the reassurance was standard police issue with no connection at all with Thackeray's actual experience.

"Surely after Dana was killed you talked about what was going on at the hospital," Val put in carefully.

"It was a difficult subject," Colin Brady said. "She approved of them demonstrators but I knew that if it were one of them that shot the girl she'd be right upset about that. I could see the whole thing was tearing her in two. I didn't raise the subject. She looked tired out by it all. Completely shattered. I thought it were best to leave well alone till she wanted to talk about it herself. You know what I mean?"

"Did she come to you, Father? After the shooting?" Thackeray asked Burke but the priest shook his head.

"I haven't spoken to Stella since I saw her at Mass ten days ago with the children. She didn't come last Sunday, as far as I'm aware."

"She was working," Colin Brady said, his voice hoarse.

"I know it must seem an unacceptable question, Mr. Brady, but I have to ask it all the same," Thackeray went on. "You and your wife obviously had different views on religion, but apart from that was your marriage a good one? Were you happy together?"

Brady looked at the Chief Inspector for a horrified moment before jumping to his feet with his fists clenched so angrily that Thackeray thought for a moment he was going to hit him. He wouldn't really have blamed him. Father Burke evidently feared the same and took Brady's arm, urging him back into his seat.

"You mean did I shoot Stella, don't you?" Brady said, his voice thick with suppressed emotion. "Well, sod you, inspector. Sod you to hell. My kids and me, we're just devastated by all this. I'm not a crying sort of man, but that doesn't mean I don't care. I'm bloody wrecked, if you want to know the truth, and I don't know how I'm going to cope with those little ones. So the answer to your question is yes, we were happy together. *Very* happy. Maybe you don't see too many happy families in your job but I loved my wife, and she loved me."

Thackeray left Val Ridley with Brady to go through his recollections of the last few weeks of Stella Brady's life, in case they offered any sort of clue to her violent death, and drove back to police headquarters alone. He had felt deeply depressed all day and had chosen to accompany his DC as much to get himself out of the oppressive atmosphere of his office as because he thought his visit would serve any particularly useful purpose.

He resented this case with an intensity which frightened him. No murder case was easy to handle, but the deaths of the two women at the May Anderson Hospital had a quality of random viciousness which he found hard to equate with the self-proclaimed morality of so many of those involved in the debate about the hospital's activities. If this really was the work of the anti-abortion protesters then it was terrorism in the purest sense, dealing out death without reason to terrify those who remained. The irony that they had killed one of their own might not be lost on whoever had fired the fatal shots, he thought, but he suspected that Stella Brady's death would probably be regarded by fanatics as a price worth paying.

And then there was Laura, about whom he hardly dared think at all.

Back at HQ he glanced into the busy CID office where he found Kevin Mower at his desk with Paul Cook slumped in a chair beside him, neither of them obviously engaged in anything which could loosely be described as work. Cook straightened up at the DCI's approach but Mower remained as he was, gazing at his blank computer screen apparently oblivious to his surroundings.

"My office, please," Thackeray said. Mower looked up at that and scrambled to his feet as he ran a hand across his eyes.

"Sorry, guv," he said. "We were waiting for you to come back." He shuffled together a bundle of files which has been lying untidily on his desk and followed Cook and the DCI to his office.

Back at his desk Thackeray gazed at Mower with evident disfavour as he shuffled his files some more.

"Bring me up to speed, Kevin," he said.

"Right, guv," Mower muttered. "A fresh report from forensics is the main development. It was the same gun killed Stella Brady as killed Dana Smith. No doubt about that, they say."

"So we have to assume the same killer, and the same motive?" Thackeray said.

"I guess so," Mower agreed. "Unless, as we said in the beginning, Dana was hit accidentally and Fenton-Green was the target."

"Any sign of the weapon?"

"They've finished searching the car-park, the road, the gardens – the same as last time. No sign of a gun or even cartridge cases. Presumably if he hung on to it once he's done the same again this time."

"Ready to take another pop," Cook offered. "Sounds like a contract killing to me. Have you thought of that?"

"Of course we've bloody thought of that," Thackeray said. "But who'd take out a contract on a thirteen-year-old girl and a nurse with two small children, for God's sake?"

"Well, I reckon the gun's your best lead," Cook said. "Ride-by shootings, an automatic pistol, even in a one-horse town like Bradfield you must have a few suspects who'd fit the frame."

"It's being looked at," Thackeray said tightly. He glanced at Mower, who looked even more haggard than usual in the direct light from the office window.

"Do we know how the killer got his bike round to the car-park at the back, Kevin?" he asked. "Did he go past the barrier or is there another way in that a bike could use? Did the security guard see him go in? Did he hear him? Was he asleep, for Christ's sake?"

"He says not," Mower said. "I'll look at his statement again, guv."

"Both times people have been talking about a bike making a lot of noise, in other words something big and powerful," Thackeray said. "The first time we know the shot came from further down the road so there's no problem there. But this

149

time the killer was much closer, Amos Atherton says, possibly just a couple of yards away. So see if you can find out exactly how he got there, will you. And if it doesn't fit with what the security guard is saying, bring him in for another chat. He was there to prevent this sort of thing happening, so I'd like to know why he didn't."

"Is the security company kosher?" Cook asked. "Anyone looked at that?"

"If not, they will," Thackeray said. "Right, get on with it - and Kevin, keep me up to speed this afternoon. I'm seeing the superintendent at four and I know he's taking a lot of flak from the hospital and from county."

"We had a session with Fenton-Green," Cook said thought-fully. "Very full of himself, isn't he? Thinks he's God's gift to suffering women."

"Which he may well be in some cases," Mower said sharply.

Thackeray looked at the sergeant again and thought that he could almost see the raw nerves quivering beneath the skin. Cook stood up and shrugged, throwing Thackeray a look which evidently tried to combine sympathy and mock despair, unaware of how utterly it repelled the DCI he was trying to impress.

"Come on, Kevin," Cook said. "Bugger the motive behind all this. Let's see if we can find the gunman, shall we? There must be something on record that'd help."

Laura Ackroyd sat at a table in the bright glass and chrome coffee shop that Bradfield's main bookseller had just opened and considered her future. On the plus side, she thought, she was single, attractive - or so she was told - and youngish although she could only just recall the boozy party she'd had for her thirtieth birthday. The down-side was that she was sin-gle, not attractive enough, it seemed, to hold on to the man she really wanted and getting too old for the sort of career development she had lived in hope of for more than ten years.

On top of that she had a grandmother who depended on her and a boss who would dearly like to find an excuse to get rid of her. The balance sheet, she thought, looked a bit skewed from where she sat huddled in her bright green fleece over her skinny latte pretending to be one of the in-crowd and very afraid that she was on the way out.

She did not see Vicky Mendelson come into the coffee shop and jumped when her friend put a hand lightly on her shoulder.

"Can I get you something to eat?" Vicky asked, her face flushed as though she had been running. "Sorry I'm late," she said. "I had it all sorted for Naomi to stay with a little friend from the mother and toddler group when she rang to say Rory had a cold so I had to start ringing round all over again."

"Right," Laura said. "I wouldn't mind a sandwich. Something salady, on brown."

She watched Vicky join the queue at the counter and shook herself mentally. Vicky was the only person she had ever confided in about her sometimes stormy relationship with Michael Thackeray, and if that relationship was finally over, as she feared it might be, Vicky and David, who had introduced them, should be the first to know.

"You look tired," Vicky said when she returned with a tray.

"I'm not used to sleeping on my own," Laura said wryly.

"Ah," Vicky said. "You two haven't made it up then?"

"He says he needs time to think," Laura said, fiddling with her paper napkin. "He's staying at his own place."

"Men are such fools," Vicky said. "It's not as if there's nothing in his past he didn't try to hide."

"It's this murder case," Laura said. "It's got everyone on edge. And anyway I didn't try to hide anything. It just didn't seem significant any more, it was so long ago. I never even thought about it."

"Yeah, well, you know what they say. Once a Catholic, always a Catholic. Just the same with Jews, so David says. I wouldn't know. I was brought up in agnostic Anglican bliss.

But this case is bound to get to Michael, isn't it? You showed your usual brilliant sense of timing with that particular confession."

Laura nibbled at her sandwich without enthusiasm.

"If this really does go pear-shaped, I'll have to get out of Bradfield," she said. "If necessary I'll take Joyce with me, but I can't stay here much longer."

"It won't come to that," Vicky said, hoping that there was enough conviction in her voice to convince Laura. "He'll be back. You'll see."

"Maybe," Laura said, pushing her plate away. "I thought I knew him by now, you know? And now this." She grinned ruefully. "In the meantime I'm going to throw myself into work. Ted is keen to do something more on the May Anderson set-up, looking at fertility treatment and where it's going. I think he envisages some sort of baby Frankenstein monsters emerging from all this manipulation of nature. Personally I'm more interested in what it does for the women. There was this quite ordinary woman in there when they showed me round, must have been well the wrong side of thirty, and she'd had these gorgeous twin girls and she was absolutely over the moon. She'd make a bloody good case study if I can track her down. And there must be lots more. There's a good series of features in it."

"Is it a good idea to go careering around maternity wards if you're feeling so broody yourself?" Vicky asked, her face serious, but Laura leaned back in her chair and brushed her hair out of her eyes with a flamboyant flourish.

"Sod it," she said, laughing. "If I get too desperate I'm told I can always use a turkey baster."

* * *

Tom Smith sat on the steps which led up from Benwell Lane to a narrow back entrance which ran the length of the terrace of houses opposite his own home. It was half past eleven and the night was dark and beginning to feel frosty. The street light at the bottom of the steps was not working. He and his brothers had made sure of that. Even so he was in full view of anyone who walked up the Lane towards him and that was the way he wanted it. His brothers, on the other hand, were concealed behind the remnants of a field hedge on the other side of the road. They had been there for a good three-quarters of an hour and were beginning to shiver when they heard the footsteps they were waiting for.

As Nick Bailey rounded the corner on his way home from the Fox, full of lager and an extra large portion of chicken vindaloo, he felt at peace with the world. Even the sight of Tom Smith sitting in the shadows on the steps, his arms wrapped around his knees, did not prick the bubble of his self-satisfaction. On this estate, with his wide circle of friends and admirers of both sexes, he felt invulnerable. No one could touch him here, and no one was likely to try. Even as Tom stood up, a good six inches taller than Nick and broader, he felt not the slightest intimation of danger.

"Got a light, mate?" Tom asked. "I came out for a quiet fag to get away from nagging women, and found I'd only got one match." He approached Nick, cigarette at the ready in his mouth and watched with dark, hate-filled eyes as the younger man reached into his pocket and pulled out a disposable lighter.

"Keep it, mate," Bailey said magnanimously and flicked the flame a fraction too close to Tom's face. It was only then that he must have sensed that something was very wrong because he began to spin round just as the other three brothers approached him silently from behind taking his legs from beneath him as Tom grabbed the outstretched arm and twisted it viciously behind his back.

"That's for Dana," Tom said as he forced the arm up behind Bailey's neck until he grunted with pain.

Taken completely by surprise, Bailey could offer little resistance to the blows which rained down on his head and the kicks which soon found his belly and ribs as he fell to the floor. Outnumbered and outmanoeuvred, he curled into a ball with his arms over his head until a boot caught his jaw and snapped his head backwards and he lost consciousness.

The four of them left him lying on the pavement no more than a hundred yards from his home and melted silently away again into the darkness, circling round to the back of their own house and in through the kitchen door where they held bruised knuckles under running water and Gavin wiped a smear of blood off his left boot. Tom glanced at his brothers without any sign of excitement or even satisfaction in his eyes and nodded.

"He'll remember our Dana now," he said flatly.

Behind them, the door from the living room opened and Maggie Sullivan's fragile frame eased itself into the room. She glanced, sharp eyed, at four pairs of freshly washed and more or less bruised hands and her face was split by what might have been a smile.

"It'll do thee no good, but," she said. "There's four of you but he'll find an army if he wants one. And he will. Best if we're on our way tonight. He'll not find us then."

"Give over, Gran," Tom said, taking his role as the oldest man in the family seriously now. "We're going nowhere."

Outside the sound of a siren told them that Nick Bailey had been found already. Tom took the stairs two at a time, closely followed by his brothers and they watched from the front bedroom window as an ambulance pulled up at the spot where they had left Bailey, and paramedics jumped out. A few minutes later a police patrol car arrived and the whole street was eerily illuminated by the blue flashing lights.

"Dost'a reckon we killed him?" Mick asked, his voice high with tension.

"We never," Tom said. "Just remember, we've bin in t'house all evening watching t'telly. Never went out at all. Not that he'll shop us. Tha knawst them sort. He'd rather settle his own scores than have t'coppers involved."

They stood in silence as Bailey was lifted onto a stretcher and the ambulance shot away down the hill, blue light still flashing.

"I told you he weren't dead," Tom said, sober reality beginning to seize him now as the adrenalin drained away. "They don't bother wi'lights unless someone's alive, do they? No point, is there?" Gently he let the threadbare curtain down to cover the window again and urged his brothers in front of him down the stairs.

"They're bound to come knocking," he warned the entire family as they settled in the living room. "Just remember noone's been outside t'door tonight and we'll be fine." He was very aware of the dark eyes of his mother and grandmother watching him intently as he spoke with a new authority.

"I were telling our Tom it's time to be moving," Maggie said faintly to Megan. "You won't listen to owt I say, but I know it's time. There'll be no peace here now, no peace and no rest either. Not for any of us. When I were a lass, people would listen to the old folk. No one listens now." She slumped back into the corner of the settee which took up most of one wall in the cramped living room. "It's time to be moving," she said, repeating what the voice in her head was saying with increasing persistence, as someone thumped loudly on the front door.

Chapter 11

Laura Ackroyd parked her car on the broad main street of Arnedale and sat for a moment to take stock. She knew the small market town at the head of the Maze valley well, having spent an eventful few months on the local newspaper, the *Arnedale Observer*, two years before. Unlike some of the other small Dales towns, Arnedale had not let itself be smothered by tourists: the weekly livestock market still flourished, although no longer in the town centre which it had once filled with bellowing cattle from the green dales and lowing sheep brought down from the high hills. The crowds of shoppers who flooded in to pick up bargains at the market stalls which crammed both pavements on three days a week still included a good number of well-swaddled country folk from the outlying moorland villages in town for their weekly supplies. But in amongst the traditional ironmongers and suppliers of country clothes, spanking new boutiques and fancy goods merchants and purveyors of country delicacies quite foreign to any farm kitchen were increasing in number and it was one of these Laura was seeking.

Laura left the car and strolled up the sunny west side of the street, past the Bull, where an enticing aroma of roast beef and woodsmoke wafted from the doors, past the shop selling an array of traditional toffees and fudges, and the sadlers which claimed to have served Arnedale's country folk since 1876, and probably had, until she found the narrow entrance and single curved display window of The Potter's Art. It was, she thought, a surprising place for the divorced wife of Stephen Fenton-Green to have ended up.

She opened the door, which activated an old-fashioned shop bell above her head, and went inside. The showroom was completely empty and Laura was not surprised. With winter approaching, Arnedale was no doubt returning to the relative calm of life before the population of industrial Yorkshire discovered the charms of the countryside on its doorstep and the internal combustion engine allowed them to explore it. And Laura doubted very much whether the local women who shopped in Arnedale whenever they could reach it from communities often isolated by snow would be impressed by the delicate examples of ceramic art which Jennifer Fenton-Green displayed on her black and chrome, carefully back-lit shelves. Beautiful the richly coloured and hand-painted vases and dishes and plates undoubtedly were; practical they were not.

It was a few minutes before Laura realised that she was no longer alone. A tall woman in a pale gold silk suit, with fine, snow white hair held away from her face by a velvet band, had emerged from the back regions of the shop and was standing looking at her with a diffident smile on her carefully made up face and an inquiry in her wary, pale blue eyes.

"You must be Laura Ackroyd? You rang?" Laura suddenly felt scruffy in her black trousers and green fleece.

"It was good of you to see me," Laura said, wondering what had motivated this slim and elegant but fragile looking woman, who could not be as old as the white hair suggested, to agree to the invasion of her privacy that the *Gazette* was proposing. She had persuaded her that her testimony was essential to the profile of Stephen Fenton-Green that she was writing, and had been surprised when the consultant's ex-wife had agreed to see her, and she wondered now just what Jennifer Fenton-Green's agenda was.

"Well, I was naturally interested in what's been going on in Bradfield," Mrs. Fenton-Green said. "After all I was married to Stephen for ten years. It's not often that some random assassin comes so close to achieving what you've felt like doing your-self so many times, is it? I am assuming that it was really Stephen that this gunman was aiming for."

Laura smiled faintly, completely taken aback by the quiet but unmistakable venom in Jennifer Fenton-Green's voice.

157

"I take it I can quote you on that," she asked carefully.

"Oh, I think you know better than that, Ms Ackroyd," Jennifer Fenton-Green replied and Laura realised that in spite of her slightly ethereal appearance, she was dealing with a sharp intelligence. "It might encourage Inspector Plod to come hammering on my door, mightn't it, although I have to say that I am slightly surprised he hasn't arrived already."

"I take it you didn't part from Stephen on what they call civilised terms?" Laura said.

"I've made tea," Stephen's ex-wife said. "Come through and I'll tell you all about it."

The room behind the shop was furnished as a small living room, with comfortable chairs, pale carpet and a tea-tray already arranged on a low table in front of a Victorian fire-place. For a moment the two women sized each other up as Laura was provided with a cup of pale Darjeeling tea with milk and a slice of coffee cake. Then Jennifer Fenton-Green arranged herself carefully in a chair opposite Laura, crossed her slim legs and raised an interrogative eyebrow.

"Just exactly what is it you want to know?"

Jennifer Fenton-Green turned out to be candid to the point of total exposure. She had met Stephen when he was a recently qualified registrar in a London hospital and she had just left art college and was planning her first exhibition of ceramics. They were successful, ambitious, attractive, apparently a match made in heaven according to their friends, Jennifer said wryly, in spite of the fact, which Jennifer had not discovered until after they had married, that Stephen's previous marriage to a nurse had lasted only a very short time.

Pursuing his career through hospitals in the Midlands and finally to Bradfield, Jennifer had been content to follow her own interests as and when she could. But the prefect match had quickly turned out to be less than perfect. They had both wanted children but no children came, she said. Working in the field himself, Fenton-Green made sure that Jennifer got all the treatment available but nothing worked, they drifted apart and had divorced five years earlier.

"The problem was on your side?" Laura said.

"So Stephen insisted. He had all the necessary tests as well…just in case. At least he told me he did. It was galling of course, knowing that he was having success with so many of his patients, but nothing they could do seemed to produce a baby for us."

"You were treated at the May Anderson?"

"Latterly, yes, when we moved up here, though I'd been to hospitals in London and Birmingham earlier."

"Is it usual for a husband to treat a wife?" Laura asked.

"Technically I was being treated by other doctors," Jennifer said. "But of course Stephen was taking a close interest. How could he not? He was even more desperate for a child than I was. Since we parted, I've come to terms with the whole business. There is more to life than having children, you know."

"I'm sure there is," Laura said, though without as much conviction as she would have liked. She glanced at the delicate ceramic bowl on the table between them.

"You're still working?" she asked. "Is all that stuff out there your own work?"

"Sadly, no," Jennifer said. "I buy most of it, mainly from people I've met over the years whose work I admire. I did almost nothing myself when I was married to Stephen. He was a very demanding man."

"I can imagine," Laura said.

"I found it hard to rekindle the inspiration I had when I was young. This place is a sort of compensation. It just about makes me a living, with what Stephen is gracious enough to allow me in the way of maintenance. He kept the house and I took some capital but it was before property prices went through the roof so I lost out on that. "

"In some ways working on fertility treatment must be a sort of compensation for him," Laura suggested. "Not having been

159

able to have children himself. Perhaps he'll have better luck with his new girlfriend."

"Yes, I heard there was someone new. She isn't the first, of course. He seems to need someone with him all the time. I'm just the opposite. After the divorce I preferred my independence."

"You're not lonely," Laura asked.

"No. Conventional wisdom has it that you have to have a partner. But I have my work. I have a reasonable social life. The occasional romance. But no live-in lovers. Never again. "

The words struck so many chords for Laura that she gazed down at her coffee cup, wondering if she would ever have a live-in lover again. She doubted that she could ever accept a life of such ascetic isolation as Jennifer Fenton-Green's with such equanimity. She wanted her live-in lover, desperately, and increasingly a gaggle of children to go with him. She sighed and glanced at her host.

"All these girlfriends but still no children? Doesn't it strike you that maybe it's your husband who had the fertility problem, not you?"

"I really don't care any more," Jennifer said. "I'm too old now to be bothered with all that myself. If he still wants to be a father of young children at almost fifty then good luck to him is all I can say. Not that I can imagine him as much of a new man, changing nappies and taking a day off work when they're ill. Fat chance. He just wants kids as trophies, as proof of his masculinity. That's why it all became so impossible for us in the end because I did reconcile myself to the facts and he couldn't. I was fed up with tests and attempts at *in vitro* fertilisation and the rest of it. I just wanted to get on with my life. Do you think that's so unnatural? He did, as he never tired of telling me."

"No, of course not," Laura said. "We're supposed to have the right to choose, aren't we? If after all that your choice was to give up trying, what's wrong with that?"

"Ask Stephen. I could never understand it."

"He couldn't be seen to fail?"

"Oh, no, Stephen doesn't like to fail at anything and I suppose I was his biggest failure. I often wondered what his first wife did wrong to be dumped so quickly. He would never talk about her. Just said it was a terrible mistake. There were no photographs, souvenirs, nothing. It was as if he'd just erased the relationship from his mind. It was not until much later, when we were in the middle of the divorce, that I discovered that her mistake, with dreadful irony, was to have a child. A child who turned out to be disabled in some way. I never discovered what was wrong with him."

Laura looked at Jennifer in astonishment.

"So he *could* have children himself? He never told you that? That's weird."

"I thought so. I only discovered by accident when a letter came which appeared to be addressed to me but was in fact intended for him. It was a begging letter from a hospital in London which claimed to have treated his son years ago. When I gave him the letter and asked him for an explanation he went mad, said it was his wife's child and he didn't believe he was the father, she had been a slut, all that sort of abuse. And anyway the child had died. I didn't know what to believe. But by that time our own relationship was so bad that it didn't make much difference what had happened before I even met him. I didn't make a big thing of it."

"You never made any attempt to find his first wife?"

"No. You don't understand about Stephen. When things go wrong he cuts you out of his life. You become a non-person as far as he's concerned. I assume that's what happened to this unfortunate woman who married him. I suppose I'm a non-person too now, as far as he's concerned. He does it to colleagues as well. One day they're in favour, the next they're out."

"Do the police know that?" Laura asked curiously. "There must be a lot of people out their who don't like your ex-husband much."

"I don't know what the police know. As I said, no one has been to see me so I assumed they weren't interested in all this old history. There's no particular reason why they should investigate the potential victim of a crime, is there, and I assumed that was what he was."

"They will have an interest in a possible motive," Laura said. "But it's not as if you were difficult to track down. It's an unusual name. I'm sure Inspector Plod can find you if he wants to. Why did you stay here? You don't sound like a native."

"I like this part of the world," Jennifer said. "I saw no reason to move away after we split up, though I know Stephen would have liked me to. He likes to block people out when he's finished with them. He hates it that he still has some financial obligations to me because he kept the house. That was the deal. Fair enough, I'd have thought, but he still resents it. We only communicate through his solicitor. But presumably he had to make the same sort of deal when he walked out on his first wife and child."

"When you go to the hospital he seems such a hero," Laura said.

"Oh, yes, he cultivates that in public all right," Jennifer said. "But the public and the private face can be very different. He's a control freak and if you decide you don't want to be controlled – at work or at home – then he can be mean, vengeful, even violent on occasion. When he hit me for the second time, after I told him I didn't want any more treatment, I packed my bags and left."

DC Val Ridley looked at Kevin Mower and saw in his dark eyes the same blankness she had just faced from Nick Bailey, who was lying in a hospital bed at the Infirmary recovering from cracked ribs, a broken arm, and lacerations and bruises too numerous to itemise.

"He'll say nothing," she said. "His mother's sitting by his bedside like the proverbial Gorgon saying there'll be no complaint. It was just the drink. No problem. It's quite obvious they don't want us involved." The Accident and Emergency Department at the Infirmary had called the police the previous night when Bailey had been delivered to them, bloody and unconscious, but now he was squinting at the world through blackened eyes, the sight of uniforms brought something as close to a sneer as his swollen lips could manage. Whatever had happened at Benwell Lane the night before, Val Ridley had concluded, the Baileys were not going to tell them what it was.

"Yes, well, it could be the Smith lads if they reckon he was Dana's boyfriend, but if Bailey won't complain there's nothing we can do about it," Mower said, his lack of enthusiasm plain. "I guess if my sister had been shot after playing around with a toe-rag like Bailey, I'd quite like to knock the grin off his face too. But unless he owns a powerful bike and an automatic, I don't think talking to Bailey's going to get us any further forward. Does he have form?"

"Affray, handling stolen goods, acquitted of GBH last year after a fracas outside the Underground," Val said. "He was on the doors, apparently, but he hasn't worked there since. Or anywhere else, for that matter. He has got a bike, as it happens, but it's a clapped out old 500cc machine, nothing like the bike witnesses have described at the shooting."

"Minor league, then," Mower said, glancing up as DI Cook made his way across the office towards them. "Though worth a look round his house, maybe."

"Kevin, you look rough," Cook said solicitously as he dropped a witness statement onto the desk in front of him. "The DCI wonders if you'd like to sit in on a chat with the security guard who was on duty at the hospital the other morning. His statement's as full of holes as a tart's tights. God knows who interviewed him. Are you up to it?"

Mower got to his feet, tight-lipped with fury, and picked up the statement.

"Are you in on this?" he asked.

"Nope, I'm waiting for a call from the FBI," Cook said. "I reckon there's more to the reverend Burridge than meets the eye, don't you?"

"Worth checking out, I suppose," Mower conceded.

"Mr. Thackeray's in his office waiting for you," Cook said. But when Mower knocked in the DCI's door he found that he had already gone, and he wondered how much time Cook had allowed to elapse before passing on Thackeray's summons. Too much, he concluded, when he joined him in an interview room and was greeted by one of Thackeray's frostiest looks.

"We've asked Mr. Nolan to come in to discuss his first statement," Thackeray said, nodding at the uniformed security guard who was sitting across the interview room table from him. "There are a couple of aspects I'm not entirely happy about. You know each other I think?"

Nolan lit a cigarette from the butt of the one he had just finished and scowled at Mower.

"I took the original statement," Mower said, pulling a chair up to the table and avoiding Thackeray's eye.

"So I gather," the DCI said. "So let's start again, shall we Mr. Nolan, from the time you opened your barrier to let Stella Brady's car through. What time do you reckon that was?"

"Getting on for six," Nolan said. "She's always early, that one. Not due on till half-past."

"And she drove round to the back of the building in the usual way?"

"I can't see the back car-park," Nolan said. "Once they go round the corner they're out of sight."

"Yes, I understand that. So what attracted your attention to the car-park and made you go round to take a look?"

"I heard a noise, didn't I?" Nolan said. "I've told you all this once. Nowt's changed."

"What sort of a noise," Thackeray asked. "You're not very specific in your statement here. Was it the sound of a shot? Or a noise like a shot? Can you describe it exactly?"

"Yeah, it was a sort of a bang, like a back-fire, or summat."

"Not just a car door slamming?" Thackeray persisted.

"Nah, I wouldn't'a bothered about that, would I?"

"So an unusual noise. But you didn't hear a motorbike?"

"Nah, not then," Nolan said. "That were later."

"And you didn't let a motorbike through your barrier?"

"No, I bloody didn't," Nolan said. "So far as I know there's no one at the hospital comes on a bike. So I'd not let anyone in, would I?"

"And no one else arrived for the early shift?"

"No."

"So let's get this straight," Thackeray said. "You raise the barrier and let Stella Brady in. The next thing you hear is an unusual noise and you go and investigate. And while you're round the back of the hospital you hear a powerful bike start up and roar away. Is that right?"

"Yeah, right," Nolan said.

"What exactly were you doing between the time you let Stella into the car-park and hearing the noise which attracted your attention?" Thackeray persisted.

"Doing? I weren't doing owt. I were in my little cabin trying to keep warm. It were bloody freezing that morning."

"You didn't take a nap? Go for a piss? Take your eye off the ball?" Kevin Mower broke in suddenly. "Did someone sneak past you when you weren't looking?"

"I told you. I didn't let anyone in," Nolan said, suddenly agitated.

"No, what you said was you didn't let a *bike* in," Thackeray snapped. "But you never suggested that the bike was in the car-park, did you? You said it started up further away. And no one we've talked to heard it at the back of the hospital. Running a powerful engine there would have wakened the dead never mind wards full of anxious mothers and hungry babies. So what if the killer parked somewhere at the front and then walked into the car-park? Could you have missed him?"

"No. No, I couldn't have," Nolan said.

"But there's no other way in, Mr. Nolan, is there?" Thackeray said. "We've checked. That car-park is pretty secure at the back. So if no one came past you, perhaps there was no one there at all. Just Stella Brady and you."

Nolan licked thin lips and drew heavily on his cigarette, his hands shaking.

"What d'you mean?" he asked.

"Were you on duty the morning that the girl was shot at the front of the hospital?" Thackeray asked.

"No, no, I wasn't," Nolan said.

"So you could have fired that shot too?"

The question hung in the air as Nolan's jaw dropped open and he seemed to find some difficulty in swallowing.

"What d'you mean?" he whispered. "I never fired no shots. What are you saying?"

"Is that the uniform you were wearing that morning?" Thackeray asked, glancing at Nolan's green jacket with the badges of Bradfield Security on the pocket and shoulders.

"Yeah, with my anorak on top," Nolan said glancing at a green topcoat with the same badges behind him on the back of the chair.

"We'll need both coats for some forensic tests," Thackeray said. "Will you organise that, please, Kevin?" Mower nodded bleakly.

"And what about me?" Nolan asked, his voice pitched high with anxiety.

"Oh, you can go, Mr. Nolan," Thackeray said. "But we will almost certainly want to talk to you again. I'm sure you'll be available when we need you. Just leave your tunic here."

Nolan stubbed out his cigarette angrily.

"I'll bloody freeze to death," he said, as he fumbled with his buttons.

When Nolan had scuttled down the corridor in his shirt sleeves, Thackeray handed Mower the two coats he had left behind him.

"If I ever read a statement taken from a potential murder

suspect as sloppy as that again you'll be walking out of here as fast as he did," he said flatly. "Not only that. It had to be a special branch DI who pointed it out."

"You don't really think he's the one, do you?" Mower said, with just a hint of his old combative self in his voice.

"I really don't know, Kevin," Thackeray said. "And I don't very much care. We check him out, just like we check everyone else out. And when I want some other approach I'll let you know. Understood?"

"Sir," Mower said, trying to swallow the panic which threatened to overwhelm him.

Chapter 12

The email message danced up and down on the computer screen in front of Laura as she tried to work out what to do next. She had heard nothing from Nemesis since she had reported her brief exchange of messages with him to Michael Thackeray and she had begun to think whoever it was had thought better of the approach. But now here Nemesis was again, invading her life at a time when the last thing she wanted was to get involved in an on-going police investigation.

This time her emailer wanted a meeting, but he – she felt sure that it was a he, though for no very logical reason – was very cautious. He suggested she drive to an isolated pub on the old road to Manchester, a quiet route since the opening of the motorway with the pub perched high on the crest of a hill where a watcher could spot vehicles approaching for miles in either direction. She was to come alone in her own car, and to bring no one with her. If she was not alone, or was being followed, he would not make contact.

"Oh, sod it," Laura said, pushing unruly strands of hair back from her eyes. The time suggested for the meeting left little opportunity for her to tell anyone at police headquarters, still less for them to organise an elaborate surveillance operation and she guessed that was deliberate. She sent a terse agreement to Nemesis, printed out the exchange and deleted the messages from her mail-box. She left the print-out on her desk. If she failed to come back, she thought, at least someone would know where to start looking although the track-record for finding bodies on the bleak Pennine moors was not encouraging.

When she arrived at the High Pound Inn, a low stone building hunched in a fold almost on the summit of the rolling watershed between Yorkshire and Lancashire, the car-park was empty and for a moment she thought that the pub itself was closed. It could not attract much in the way of passing trade these days, she thought as she tried the main door and was relieved when it opened. Three men were huddled over pints close to the embers of an open fire and as Laura came in one of them rose to his feet, gave the grate a fierce rake with a huge iron poker and hurled on a couple more logs which spat and crackled before flaring into life.

"What can I do for thee, love?" he asked, identifying himself as the landlord as he crossed the room to take his place behind the bar. The room was so low-ceilinged that his bald head almost brushed the exposed rafters as he went. The other two, burly men in dun country clothes and boots, watched with placid interest as Laura took one of the bar stools.

"I'm meeting someone," she said. "I'll have a vodka and tonic while I wait,"

The landlord poured her drink very slowly, scuffling round under the bar for a small bottle of tonic.

"I've no ice," he said, without a hint of apology.

"Lemon?" Laura asked sweetly.

"Nay, we don't get much call for lemon." She could hear a snort of laughter from the table by the fire so she shrugged and accepted her inadequate drink without argument. The high Pennines were a windswept obstruction between the two counties which still defied some of the conventions of what Laura regarded as civilisation: ice, lemon and a measure of pleasantry. She was only ten miles uphill from the outskirts of Bradfield but recognised another world when it clobbered her over the head.

Nemesis was late, and came into the bar so quietly that it was only the waft of cold air from outside which alerted Laura to his arrival behind her. She turned to face a small man in walking clothes – a hooded anorak, woollen hat, hiking boots and with a rucksack on his back - whom she was sure she had never seen in her life before. He hitched himself onto the stool next to her and took off his hat and scarf, revealing receding grey hair and a thin intelligent face, creased around the eyes, with a firm mouth and obstinate looking chin.

"I recognised you," he said.

"We've met?" Laura said, surprised.

"Not really. Dave Randall, Mr. Fenton-Green's technician," he said. He spoke quietly, evidently aware of the group by the fire. When the landlord stirred himself to serve him he ordered a pint and nodded in the direction of a small room off the main bar.

"We'll be more private in there," he said. And when they were settled at an oak table in the tiny snug he continued. "I was in the lab when you were being shown round by Dr. Mahood, but I was in protective clothing. I don't suppose you even noticed I was there."

"I do remember," Laura said. "You had a mask on."

"Are you still writing about the hospital?" Randall asked.

"Well, yes, while this murder investigation is going on there'll be stuff in the paper every day," Laura said cautiously. "I'm working on a profile of your boss. Was it the murders you wanted to talk about? Because I think the police…"

"No, I don't want to talk to the police," Randall said firmly. "I don't know anything about the murders, as such. I was in the lab when the first girl was shot. I've made a statement about that which amounted to the fact that I saw and heard nothing. The second time, like most people, I was asleep in bed with my wife. I'm much more concerned about what Fenton-Green's getting up to in his labs. He thinks I don't know what he does in the evenings when I've gone home, but I've a good idea and I don't like it."

"His research, you mean?" Laura said.

"I came to the hospital from Leeds University. He wanted someone who could help with the day to day stuff for fertility treatment but who understood something about genetics for this joint programme he's working on,"

"This is his collaboration with the university on his fertility research," Laura said.

"Yes, that's it, and most of it is perfectly mainstream and above board. The man's a good scientist as well as a good doctor. But I know he goes into the lab in the evenings, and the work he leaves me to carry on with the next morning doesn't always tie up with the equipment and the materials he's obviously used when he's by himself."

"Materials?" Laura asked, not entirely wanting to know the answer.

"You know what we're experimenting with. Human eggs, sperm, foetal material. But it's all very strictly controlled, what we can legitimately do. And I think the sainted Stephen is pushing the limits of what's permitted. There's frozen material in that lab which I simply can't account for."

"What sort of material?" Laura was even more reluctant to ask this question.

"Well, I'm not sure. It could be from mothers, or babies, taken without permission."

"You mean dead babies, don't you?"

Randall nodded, his face grim.

"I can't prove it one way or the other. But it needs looking at is what I'm saying. It needs reporting and looking at."

"So you're essentially a whistle-blower?" Laura said. "All this secret meeting is a bit dramatic, isn't it? Isn't there some official channel you can use to voice your concerns. After all he could be doing something quite legitimate in his own time, something useful, I mean, for his patients. I agree it should be checked out if you're worried, but you could raise it – with him, or the authorities."

"We're talking a small private hospital here," Randall said. "I don't want to lose my job. If I report him there'll be no doubt where the information has come from – it would have to be me or Dr. Mahood. There's no one else could possibly know. In any case, everyone is paranoid since Stella was shot."

"You don't think that had anything to do with Stephen Fenton-Green, surely?"

"That's not the most bizarre scenario which is doing the

rounds, believe me," Randall said. "But no, that must be something to do with the abortion fanatics. I think what he's up to is something quite different. He's an ambitious man, desperate to make his mark. So far I've not pinned anything specific down. I'll keep trying, though. But it really needs another scientist to take a look. Someone who understands what we're supposed to be doing and can spot anything we shouldn't".

"The only crime I've heard suggested is that he's willing to do late abortions."

"Oh, he certainly does that," Randall said, with a shrug. "Young Dana Smith was one, I'm sure."

"But a pretty deserving case, at her age, surely?"

"Maybe. But there are rules."

"So Stella Brady said when I met her."

"Stella threw a wobbly now and again. She was up in arms about something about six months ago. Came storming in to see the boss. But it all blew over. It was all religion with her."

"But it's not just Catholics, is it? Do you think Dr. Mahood knows what Fenton-Green is up to? Or do you think he's involved?"

"He thinks the sun shines out of Fenton-Green's backside, but I wouldn't think he'd get into anything too way out. He has very little to do with the research anyway. I think he has some religious reservations about that. He does most of the surgery, the obstetrics, routine stuff."

"Would anyone know if tissue had been taken illegally?" Laura asked carefully. "If that's what you're suggesting."

"I don't know *what* I'm suggesting," Randall said angrily. "That's the point. I think it needs looking at, that's all. But if he was experimenting illegally, the patients wouldn't know. The mothers are unconscious or sedated when most procedures are going on. But someone in the operating theatre might have seen something."

"Stella Brady, for instance?" Laura asked quietly.

"She runs the ward. She's not a theatre nurse."

"So how could you find evidence to substantiate your suspicions?"

Randall shrugged.

"It would need a proper scientific investigation to prove one way or the other – DNA testing, all that, to match what should be in the lab to what shouldn't. If I'm right. It's way beyond my capabilities."

"Very Frankenstein," Laura said.

"Yes, well this research is supposed to be helping people, but there are rules," Randall said. "I don't doubt that I'm not the only one who doesn't like to see them broken."

"I'll talk to the medical authorities about what you've said," Laura said. "But I may have to tell the police as well. You may think it's nothing to do with the shootings but I'm sure they'll want to be the judge of that." She could imagine Thackeray's furious reaction if she did not pass this information on.

"I'll deny I've ever seen you," Randall said, getting to his feet angrily. "I'll not be involved in this publicly."

"I'll do my best. Protecting my sources and all that," Laura said. "But if it's relevant to the murder case…That's what the police will be mainly interested in."

"I can't see how it can be," Randall said angrily. "This is minor league stuff, not a reason for shooting anybody."

Laura doubted whether the police would necessarily agree with that analysis as she watched Randall pull his woolly hat back over his thinning grey hair and zip up his anorak.

"I suppose I'll have to trust you then. I must be bloody mad." And he strode out of the bar without a backward glance leaving Laura gazing thoughtfully into the dregs of her iceless V and T and the trio in the main bar gazing thoughtfully at each other.

DCI Thackeray put a head round the interview room door and liked what he saw even less than he had expected. Laura was sitting at the table facing him and glanced up at him with eyes which looked almost bruised with anxiety. She gave him a tentative smile, to which he found it hard to respond. When she had called the station earlier he had deputed an astonished Sergeant Mower to talk to her, which was evidently what he was doing, with DI Cook as ever at his side.

Mower turned in his chair, tension in every inch of him as he met the DCI's questioning gaze.

"D'you want to sit in, guv?" he asked, his voice husky, and Thackeray could see that Laura was watching him with a hurt expression.

"Not unless you find Ms Ackroyd too hard a nut to crack," Thackeray said, though his heavy handed humour raised not a glimmer of a smile around the interview room table.

"We were just finishing," Cook said briskly, getting to his feet, and evidently oblivious to the unease around him. "I'll fill you in, guv, if you like." Thackeray nodded and turned away down the interview room corridor with Cook hard on his heels.

Inside Laura and Mower sat looking at each other for a moment across the table before Mower got to his feet.

"I didn't get the impression your colleague was the slightest bit interested in all that," Laura said. She had not warmed to Paul Cook's supercilious Metropolitan curling lip and wandering eyes.

"He has his own ideas about the case," Mower said shortly. "And if you're not telling us who told you all this stuff about Fenton-Green's lab it's not actually much help, is it?"

"It's the best I can do," Laura said. "If you can convince me the murder case depends on it, I'll think again maybe…"

"Or maybe if the DCI asks you nicely?"

"I don't think that's very likely at the moment," Laura said.

"Like that is it?" Mower asked. "That explains why he's been in such an evil mood for days."

Laura shrugged.

"I don't know how I can apologise for something I did long before I met him," she said bitterly, suddenly angry.

"Hey," Mower said, touching her hand. "It'll work out. I'm sure it will."

"Maybe," Laura said, shrugging herself back into her jacket. "Thanks Kevin. And you take care, d'you hear me." He still looked, she thought, as if he was being pursued by all the torments of hell.

When Mower got back to Thackeray's office, Cook glanced up at him sourly.

"That was a pretty fair waste of time," he said. "Even if he is doing experiments he shouldn't, it's down to the regulators to sort it out. How can we investigate what's going on in a bloody test-tube?"

"Laura has helped us a great deal in the past," Mower said mildly, glancing at Thackeray who seemed to be fascinated by the blank sheet of paper on the desk in front of him.

"You can never trust bloody reporters," Cook said. "That's where the Official Secrets' Act comes in so handy. We don't even have to speak to them if we don't want to. No press officers, no statements, zilch. Marvellous."

Mower opened his mouth to argue but then caught the fury in Thackeray's eyes and thought better of it.

"Tell me about the FBI," Thackeray demanded. "I thought Burridge had been thoroughly checked out before he left the USA."

"There's checking and checking, isn't there?" Cook said. "But there is an FBI file on Burridge. He's never been charged but he's a well-known contributor to one of their more far-out radio stations over there, run by some sect of the Christian Right, a bunch which makes our lot look like pussycats. The Rev. Edgar doesn't actually say go out and shoot abortionists, but the implication's there. And he has some very, very dodgy friends, some of whom have gone out and done just that. He then gets involved in organising their defence funds, that sort of thing."

"Guilt by association, then?" Thackeray asked, his distaste showing. "Is it enough to get him deported?"

"Probably not. But it might be enough to arrest him under the Prevention of Terrorism Act, if I talk to my bosses nicely. How would that do?"

"I'd have to talk to my boss nicely too," Thackeray said. "Which I'm not particularly inclined to do. We've got no evidence against this man. As far as we can see he's behaved impeccably since he arrived in this country. He's due to talk to his rally tomorrow evening and then he'll be away, out of our hair. I've got no reason to even question him again."

"You mean you'll just let him go? In the middle of your murder investigation?"

"I don't see I've got any choice," Thackeray said. "He's staying in the country for another couple of weeks as I understand it. If we need him we can find him. If we have to follow him back to the States eventually, we'll do that too."

"Oh, come on, sir," Cook said. "I'm sure if we took another look round his hotel room, or the offices of his Bradfield friends, we'd soon uncover a reason to hang on to him. They're not hard to find if you know where they are before you start."

Thackeray stood up abruptly.

"Come and tell that to Jack Longley," he said. Cook shrugged.

"Right," he said.

Kevin Mower watched the two officers disappear up the stairs towards Longley's office and drew a deep breath, content that for a time at least Thackeray's attention was distracted from his own shortcomings. He did not envy Paul Cook the roasting he guessed he would suffer upstairs. He would not mind having the Rev. Edgar Burridge at his own disposal for the seven days the terrorist law allowed but Cook had picked the wrong man if he thought that Thackeray would go along with any bending of the rules to achieve that end.

Several heads were raised when he made his way back into the murder incident room where hundreds of statements were still being collated in the hope that the couple of facts that each was likely to contain could be reassembled into a pattern which pointed towards the gunman. It was slow, painstaking work even with the help of the computer systems which had been introduced since those who had hunted the Yorkshire Ripper not far from Bradfield had seen their investigation virtually suffocate in paperwork.

"Anything new?" he asked but was met only with ruefully shaken heads from the computer screens. Unless the murder weapon turned up, Mower thought gloomily, or someone came up with a reasonable description or even an identification of the gunman, the two shootings might remain unsolved. What they needed was a bit of luck, and in his experience strokes of luck were rarer than bluebells in the back streets of Bradfield, notwithstanding the fact that the legendary Ripper had been caught in the end by nothing more sophisticated than a couple of nosy bobbies cruising the red light district on the off-chance.

He threw himself down at his desk and caught Val Ridley's eye across the busy room. She got up and wove her way between the desks towards him, cool and blonde in a blue trouser suit.

"I could cook you a meal tonight if you like," she said, leaning over so that he could see her cleavage down her black top. Suddenly all the frustrations of the job and the depression which had haunted him since Rita Desai's death bubbled up in a frenzy of unfocused rage. He seized Val Ridley's arm and dug his fingers into the flesh until she cried out in pain.

"Leave it alone, you silly bitch," Mower said. "Can't you take no for a bloody answer?"

Val's face flushed scarlet as she pulled away, her eyes full of tears and she rushed out of the room, avoiding the eyes of ranks of startled colleagues.

"You're taking a chance there, aren't you sarge?" said a quiet voice from the back of the room. "She'll have you for sexual harassment if you're not careful. It's what she's been waiting for, that one."

177

Mower put his head in his hands and ground his teeth in furious impotence. If he had bared his chest for the knife with which a woman had once nearly killed him, he could hardly have left himself more vulnerable, he thought. He did not doubt for a moment that Thackeray in his present unforgiving mood would be punctilious in ensuring his departure from the force, if that was what it came to. After years of walking a tightrope he had, he reckoned, finally fallen off.

Chapter 13

Tom Smith hurled himself through the front door of his mother's house in a hail of missiles. Across the street a gang of teenagers howled and hooted in derision. It was becoming impossible for any member of the family to leave the safety of the barricaded doors and windows and neither Maggie Sullivan or Megan Smith would try any longer.

Tom dropped a bag of groceries onto the kitchen table round which his three brothers were sitting.

"We can't go on like this," he said, breathless after running the gauntlet of flying bricks and bottles for the last hundred yards of his walk home from the corner shop. "We're getting nowt done on t'cars. We've had that motor out there three days and not touched it."

"Get t'bobbies up," Mick said. "We'll have to, won't we? There's so many o'them little beggars we can't catch 'em all. And I've got to go down and see to t'horses. I can't leave them, can I?"

"Four big lads like you," Megan said coming into the kitchen un-noticed. "Get out there and bray the little beggars. They'll not come back then."

"It's Bailey putting them up to it," Gavin said. "He's back. I saw him this morning with a bandage round his head and his arm in a sling."

"Police'll do nowt," Megan said. "They'll not lift a finger for gippos, you know that. If you want it stopped you'll have to see to it thisen."

"We can't take on t'whole estate, Mam," Tom objected. "We start laying a finger on them kids and we'll all be on a charge."

"Then we'll have to do what your gran says," Megan said. "Get back on t'road. Though where we'd get a van from God only knows. That old wreck up at Shepley won't move no more. But I'll not shift till we've buried our Dana. I'll not leave her behind."

"I'll not move, neither," Mick said. "I can't leave them ponies. Sal's in foal. She can't go anywhere till t'little un comes. And Charlie's too old to move."

"None of us want to move," Gavin said. "But our mam can't get out o't'bloody house wi'this goin' on outside. It's like a bloody siege, here."

"We'll have to take her out," Terry said. "A bodyguard, like. Where do you want to go, Mam?"

"I'd like to take your gran back to Shepley," Megan said. "It's doing her no good stuck here wi'all this going on. She can't even get her pension stuck in t'house all t'time."

"Right," Tom said. "After we've had us dinner we'll take you and Gran down to t'post office for her pension. OK lads. That'll do for a start." His brothers nodded and Mick got to his feet.

"I'll go down to see to t'ponies now," he said. "I'll go over t'back fences so they won't set eyes on me. I'll be back for me dinner, don't fret."

"Take care," Tom said.

As his brother opened the back door cautiously and slipped out, Maggie Sullivan came into the kitchen with a blanket round her shoulders. She looked frail and ill, a distant look in her eyes and it seemed to take her a few seconds to focus on the group around the table.

"We should be going," the old woman said. "You'll leave it too late if you don't take steps."

"Give your gran a chair and she can help me wi't'dinner," Megan said, beginning to pull groceries out of the bag Tom had brought in. The three remaining brothers got up, filling the room with angry frustration as Maggie sat down and pulled her Tarot cards from beneath the folds of her blanket and began to deal them out on the table with trembling hands. She evidently did not like what she saw because she groaned faintly and shuffled them together again quickly.

"Tha'l't not listen, whatever I say," she muttered. Tom put a hand on her shoulder and could feel the bones close to the skin beneath his fingers like sticks in a sack.

"We can't go anywhere yet, Gran," he said. "Don't worry. You'll be right."

At the front of the house another crash, followed by a ragged cheer, told them that another brick had hit one of the boarded up windows.

"They'll be going home for their dinners in a bit," Gavin said.

"Let's hope it chokes the little beggars," Megan said, picking up a sharp knife to peel potatoes. "If there's not an end to this soon I'll take a big stick to them mesen."

Superintendent Jack Longley drummed his fingers on his desk gently, the only sign of tension as he faced an obviously angry Michael Thackeray who had marched into his office in mid-morning unannounced.

"If you're going to go out on a limb, Michael, you'd best make sure it's not rotten before you put your weight on it. And I can tell you for nothing that this particular limb's good for nowt except the bonfire. You'd fall from a very great height, and I'm not having that."

"He's causing havoc amongst the troops," Thackeray said, his jaw jutting obstinately, although he could see from the look in Longley's eyes that he had hit an immovable object.

"Par for the course," Longley said easily.

"He's a law unto himself."

"Surprise me," Longley said, with a ghost of a smile on his broad face.

"He's driving Mower demented."

"Aye, well, that I'd put a stop to," Longley conceded. "Let someone else mind him. Mower's under enough pressure as it is without adding to it."

"So I can't get rid of Cook?" Thackeray asked, knowing the answer before it came.

"He's special branch. You know better than that," Longley said, wondering whether Thackeray had some ulterior motive for raising the problem with him. "You know they do as they please, that lot, and they've been worse since MI5 was left twiddling its fingers and started poking them into serious crime. I'm not getting on the wrong side of the spooks, Michael. County'd go berserk, any road. They're already getting twitchy about these shootings, asking for progress reports every bloody day. You know the Branch count whatever they like as terrorism if it suits them these days. You'll have to make the best you can of DI Cook."

He watched Thackeray as the DCI gazed out of the office window at the town hall, the ornate sandstone of the Italianate tower golden in the morning sunshine, and he wondered if it was just the importunate inspector from special branch who had washed the colour from the burly detective's face and left dark circles under his eyes. He could not believe a little internal acrimony in CID would hit him so hard. He looked as stressed as he could remember him looking during the years they had worked together but he was sure that there was no easy way of finding out why from a man who guarded his privacy so jealously.

"Mower all right, is he? Apart from not warming to Paul Cook?" Longley inquired blandly.

"He's coping," Thackeray said, wondering how economical with the truth he could be when Mower looked as if he might detonate at any moment with wildly unpredictable consequences. "He's still very strung out." That was one euphemism for usually pissed that no one had come up with when he had been in a similar situation himself, he thought. But while the language changed, the problems didn't, and he knew that very soon he was going to have to issue the regulation ultimatum to Kevin Mower that he very probably would not be able to meet. He sighed and turned away from the busy scene in the square below to meet Longley's pale blue gaze with a shrug. "I'm keeping an eye on him," he said.

"And these shootings? 'Owt new there?"

"Cook's convinced that Burridge is a terrorist over here to foment trouble."

"Well, that would fit the branch's world view, wouldn't it," Longley said. "They'd spot conspiracy to commit something or other at a mother and toddler group. It's an easy crime to spot and a damned difficult one to prove. But do you have any alternative leads?"

"We've still got no description of the gunman who was probably wearing motorcycle leathers and a helmet anyway. The perfect disguise. And we've got no weapon. So no forensics. So no, there's not a lot to go on. It looks like a contract killing but what the hell's the motive? We can find no point of contact between the two victims except the connection with the hospital. We had a go at the security guard who was on the gate when the Brady shooting took place, and could have fired the shot which killed Dana Smith - in theory anyway. I'm waiting for forensic tests on his uniform but I can't say I'm optimistic. If you wanted to hire a gunman I doubt very much if you'd go for Nolan. Burridge probably is the best bet but we've found no serious evidence so far in that quarter. I'll go to his rally tonight and listen to him myself just to see what he's saying in public, but I expect he'll be very cautious and knows the law on incitement and defamation inside out. These sort of people usually do."

"It doesn't look good, Michael. Two innocent women killed and nothing to show for it. Would some sort of TV appeal help? Another appeal for witnesses from Dana's mother or Stella Brady's husband? How do they come across?"

"It might be worth a try, but it would have to be Colin Brady, I think. Dana's mum's not exactly photogenic, or very articulate, come to that. And she's allegedly a Gypsy, which means folk won't instantly warm to her, to be honest."

"And I doubt the whole teenage pregnancy thing goes down too well with the public," Longley said. "But Stella the angel of mercy? That would play well in the *Gazette* and on local TV."

"It's come to something when we have to sell murders on television like packets of cornflakes," Thackeray muttered.

"You have to use these methods these days, Michael, you know that," Longley said. "The results are good."

"Except for the ones when the murderer's made the appeal himself," Thackeray muttered. "That's happened a few times. Then we look right idiots."

"Yes, well it's not likely with these shootings is it?" Longley said irritably. "Any road, the *Gazette*'ll do you proud if you talk nicely to that young woman of yours."

Thackeray held his breath for a long moment to let the red hot anger which welled up inside him subside slightly before he dared to speak again.

"Maybe," he said tightly. He was rescued by an urgent tap on the door.

"Come in," Longley bellowed. Sergeant Mower put his head round the door, looking as if he would rather be anywhere but there.

"We've got problems, guv," he said to Thackeray. "DI Cook's got Edgar Burridge in an interview room and the Reverend is threatening bring in the marines if he's not released by tea-time."

"Who the hell authorised Cook to bring him in again?" Thackeray asked angrily.

"He seemed to think he didn't need authorisation," Mower said. "He took me with him, no argument permitted, and didn't give me a chance to let you know what was going down. He's impounded about a ton of paperwork from the SLL offices as well. It'll take the team a month to work through them, I reckon. I'm sorry, guv. I didn't think you'd be best pleased."

"Sort it," Longley said to Thackeray, after listening to Mower with growing anger. "The man's meeting's at the town hall tonight, isn't it? That's why he's up the wall. I don't want that cancelled unless Cook has come up with hard enough evidence to charge him. We'll have the national newspapers round our necks for a month if we're not careful. So far, by some miracle, they've left us pretty much alone, and that's the way I'd like it to stay. Right?"

"Sir," Thackeray said following Mower to the door.

Downstairs they found DI Cook waiting impatiently in the corridor outside an interview room where, when Thackeray glanced through the window, Edgar Burridge, in dark suit and clerical collar, was pacing, red-faced, around the table under the anxious gaze of a uniformed constable.

"Have you arrested him?" he asked Cook curtly.

"No, no, just asked him in for a friendly chat," Cook said airily. "I've got a whole load of stuff faxed over from Washington, certainly worth giving him a hard time over."

"Has he asked for a brief?"

"Nope," Cook said. "But I left the Knight woman screaming blue murder about harassment. I wouldn't be surprised if she doesn't call a tame solicitor."

"She's more likely to call the *Daily Globe* if we don't watch it," Thackeray said. "Check it out with her, Kevin, will you? Does Mr. Burridge have a legal representative? Mr. Longley wants this played by the book."

"I thought you might want to sit in," Cook said.

"You thought right," Thackeray , his expression grim. "This is *my* murder investigation, remember? Next time you want to bring someone in for questioning you ask me first."

"Sorry," Cook said without any indication that he meant it. "I thought I was making real progress here, as it happens. Sir."

"When we've got a shred of evidence linking Burridge to a gun or a motorbike and we've discredited his alibi for the first shooting, which just happens to be that he was two hundred miles away at the time, I'm willing to be impressed," Thackeray said. "In the meantime, let's get this over with so that he can get to his rally at the town hall without us all having egg all over our faces, shall we?"

As they made to open the interview room door they were joined by a slightly breathless newcomer in a dark overcoat, his broad brow under fashionably short blond hair slightly beaded with sweat.

"Mr. Macdonald," Thackeray said, without enthusiasm as Peter Macdonald of Mendelson, Green and Macdonald, probably Bradfield's most prestigious firm of solicitors, held out a hand which was ignored.

"You're about to interview a client of mine, Edgar Burridge," Macdonald said, slipping out of his coat and mopping his brow with a large white handkerchief. "An American gentleman, I believe. His hosts in Bradfield asked me to join him."

"I'm sure they did," Thackeray said, pushing the door of the interview room open to reveal Burridge slumped, in a chair, his face faintly purple with frustration. When the introductions were over and Burridge's loud battery of complaint at being brought to the police station had been acknowledged though not apologised for, Thackeray picked up Cook's files from the desk in front of him and opened them up, to the inspector's evident annoyance, and briefly scanned the main points.

"Tell me about the Christian Alliance, Mr. Burridge," he said at length. Burridge did not answer immediately and it was evident that the question startled him.

"In Iowa, you mean?" he said eventually.

"Wherever it functions, Mr. Burridge," Thackeray said. "Over there, over here, where else?"

"In Iowa" Burridge said. "And some other states in the west and the mid-west, good Christian communities which have no truck with promiscuity and homosexuality and abortion, all abominations in the face of the Lord."

"A campaigning group?" Thackeray asked.

"We have radio and television programmes. We campaign politically, mainly in the Republican Party, for family values and Christian morality, yes. It's something I'm mighty proud of, Inspector. It's the reason our country hasn't been taken over by the damn' liberals in the way yours has. We are fighting back, sir. And winning."

"Does this line of questioning have anything to do with your current inquiries, Chief Inspector," Macdonald put in aggressively. "I would have thought we're a long way from the American political scene here."

"I wouldn't waste the time of anyone here with anything that didn't have some bearing on my case," Thackeray said glancing down at Cook's notes again. "I merely want to establish Mr. Burridge's connection with this organisation, largely because we have been told by our colleagues in Washington that it has been associated with at least two, and possibly four shootings at abortion clinics in the States. Last time we spoke you told me quite clearly you had no truck with violence. So does that come as news to you, Mr. Burridge?"

"No, it does not," Burridge said, his colour rising again.

"Your group encourages violence?"

"No, it does not. But sadly there have been two individuals who I guess have felt so deeply moved by the sinful nature of these clinics that they have taken the law into their own hands. Deeply regrettable, but nothing to do with the organisation as such, I assure you."

"You've condemned these individuals on your radio and TV programmes then?" Thackeray persisted. "Dissociated yourself personally from this sort of violence?"

"It is not up to me to condemn or condone. The Lord will judge, as he will judge us all."

"Did you know the people who were charged with murder after these shootings?" Thackeray asked.

"No, I did not, sir," Burridge said firmly. "The unfortunate events happened in another State. I had not met the members concerned. I know nothing of them."

"Do you know any organisation in this country which might encourage its members to take the law into their own hands? We've already had one other incident here in

187

Bradfield before these shootings – messy rather than intended to cause injury, I'm relieved to say and we've found the perpetrators - but even something like that raises the temperature. Can you think of anyone in this country, or even in Bradfield, who might be tempted to go too far?"

Burridge glanced meaningfully at his watch and then at his solicitor before replying.

"I can think of no one," he said. "No one at all. I thought after our first meeting I'd made it quite clear, Inspector, that I have no intention of inciting violence at my meeting tonight. In fact I have something to say which may interest you a great deal more than this absurd and fruitless attempt to link me in with the unfortunate events which have taken place here recently. Something you might like to investigate with the same zeal which you seem to be bringing to your murder inquiry, even if in involving me it is a zeal which is sadly misplaced."

"And what is that exactly?" Thackeray asked.

"Something about the May Anderson Hospital which has reached my ears recently," Burridge said.

"From an inside source?" Thackeray snapped.

Burridge shrugged.

"I'm afraid I can't reveal my sources, Inspector."

"Unless the source happens to be Stella Brady, the nurse who was shot," Thackeray said. "Or anyone connected with her. In which case you would be impeding a murder investigation by not telling me. And that, Mr. Burridge, is a crime in this country."

"I assure you your murder victim was not my source," Burridge said blandly. "But I commend my speech to you tonight, Inspector. I'm sure you'll be interested in what I have to say. And now, as I was invited here on the basis that I could leave at any time, I think the time has come to leave. If that is quite convenient to you. I like to pray and meditate for a little time before a major rally. I'm sure you will understand."

To the evident fury of Paul Cook, Thackeray let him go after extracting from him a detailed itinerary for the rest of his stay in Britain.

"We may well want to talk to you again, Mr. Burridge," he said as the clergyman and his solicitor prepared to leave.

Burridge scowled in response.

"I think, if I may say so, you are falling into serious error here, Inspector," he said. "I'll be happy to answer your questions at a convenient time, but I think there is absolutely nothing I can tell you which will lead you to this gunman."

When the two men had been escorted from the building by a uniformed officer, Cook did not conceal his displeasure.

"You let him off bloody lightly, guv. You never touched on most of the stuff the FBI sent over," he said.

"Whatever the FBI think, the man's neither been arrested or charged in America," Thackeray said. "And even if he had been we would still need evidence here before we could move. If you've taken it upon yourself to borrow the SLL files, I suggest you go through them to see what you can glean in that quarter. If the campaigners have anything to do with these shootings, I think it's much more likely that the conspiracy was dreamed up here rather than four thousand miles away in Iowa. You can ask for a couple of volunteers to help you over the weekend. Someone will be glad of the overtime, I expect. And then you hand back everything that isn't material to the investigation – assuming you find something that is. By Monday morning I guess Dorothy Knight's lawyers will be clamouring for the return of their property, which you had no right to take in the first place without a warrant."

"We could use the Prevention of Terrorism Act," Cook said, his face sullen with dislike.

"Is that what you told them?"

"Well, no, not actually," Cook admitted. "There was only a young girl in the office when we got there. She didn't object."

Thackeray said no more though the contempt in his eyes left Cook in no doubt what he thought.

On his way back to his office he glanced into the incident

room where the day's last stragglers amongst the murder team were still sitting at computer screens or leafing through papers. Kevin Mower glanced up, his face haggard.

"I've got the forensic report on the security guard's clothes, guv," he said. "Nothing doing there. There are more dead ends in this case than the Hampton Court Maze."

"Keep going," Thackeray said. "We'll get there." Val Ridley caught his eye as he turned away towards his own office and he wondered why she too looked exhausted. The whole team, he thought, as he tidied away his papers for the night, seemed overwhelmed by the shootings and he knew that if he did not do something to shift the leaden depression which he had carried since he had left Laura's flat his own judgement would be too clouded to be trusted.

It was curious, he thought. For the whole of the time he had known Laura he had never dwelt for more than a moment on the lovers he knew she had had before he met her. Equally, she had never questioned him about his wife or the infrequent liaisons with other women in whose arms he had tried to find peace for a little while. There had been no jealousy there, nor the faintest assumption that he might have the right to be jealous about what had gone before. So why had this single incident, something he knew was a commonplace enough event in many young women's lives, why had this wrenched him apart in a way which he knew was unjustified and dangerous. He thought of the old man in Rome whose iron certainties bore little relation to life as it was actually lived, and cursed the knee-jerk responses he had learned from him so long ago that he had forgotten all about them until they emerged from the past like demons to torment him. His reaction had shocked him as much as it had infuriated Laura. After the American's meeting, he thought, where he would very likely see Laura, they must talk and he must try to find the words to bridge the gulf between them. The possibility that she might not be willing to forgive him was one which he pushed to the very back of his mind

190

Chapter 14

Laura Ackroyd looked at the press release from Saving Lives for the Lord which a heavily perspiring Ted Grant had just dropped onto her desk with distaste.

"What do you want me to do about that?" she asked. "I thought last night that what Burridge was saying was seriously dodgy. We can't print it, can we? Stephen Fenton-Green'll have Sue, Grabbit and Run on the case before lunch-time."

"Don't worry your pretty little head about the legal angles," Grant said, oblivious to Laura's grimace of anguish. "Burridge says he's got evidence that your sainted doc is using bits and pieces he shouldn't be for his research and he's giving it all to the police. Presumably we're talking bits of dead babies here, but I think maybe we'd better not be too specific about that in print. We don't want to upset the grannies. See what you can find out, girl, will you. You've got enough mates down at the cop shop, one way or another."

Laura took a sharp breath. She did not want even to mention her current difficulties with Thackeray to her boss and in any case she deeply resented any attempt to exploit the relationship. Thackeray, she knew, although she could never convince Ted Grant of the fact, would tell her no more – for publication – than he would tell any other journalist, and that was not much.

"They'll tell me to talk to the press office," she said. "I get no favours."

Grant grinned at her evilly.

"Pull the other one," he said. "Any road, you've been into all the angles at the hospital. See if you can find out what's going on up there. Someone must know something if he's been bending the rules. Talk to the regulators. Find out just exactly what he is allowed to do and what's *verboten*. Someone must have blown the whistle for this Yank so I don't see why they shouldn't blow it again for us. You never know, it might have something to do with these shootings. Perhaps Fenton-Green's the mad gunman. You never know. Stranger things have happened."

"That's ridiculous," Laura said. She had so far kept her promise to Dave Randall not to involve him with the police but had not yet worked out a way of writing the story which would keep his name out of the paper. She had been shattered to hear that his version of the allegations had surfaced publicly at Edgar Burridge's packed and rowdy meeting at the town hall the night before, leaving her dangerously exposed if Ted Grant should find out that she's already had contact with the May Anderson's whistle-blower.

She wondered whether Kevin Mower and his colleague, who had barely been able to suppress his lack of interest in Fenton-Green's scientific misdemeanours, had made any further inquiries. If Burridge now knew about Dave Randall's suspicions, she guessed that the police had not bothered to follow up and he had gone to the American in desperation to find a more sympathetic reception. Was it, she wondered, actually a crime to cut corners in your scientific research? If it was, it was not one which Bob Baker, the *Gazette*'s crime reporter, would find easy to handle, though there was a distinct risk that if Bob if began digging around he would uncover the fact that she had already had a long heart-to-heart with the disaffected technician and light Ted's blue touchpaper. She really did not want to go pursuing Fenton-Green herself. It was not that she warmed to the man, she thought. He was as arrogant and self-satisfied as most senior doctors seemed to be. But she approved of the fact that he was brave enough to stand up to the likes of Burridge and Dorothy Knight. All in all she was in favour of anyone who was on the side of women in trouble, and not afraid to do something about it. But it looked as if she would have to take on the story if only to cover her back.

Ted Grant was waiting with increasing impatience, she

realised, and she shook herself slightly to bring herself back to the sweaty reality just behind her chair.

"OK, OK," she said at last, making a show of reluctance which she knew Grant would take pleasure in ignoring. "I'll have another talk with the hospital people. No one ever really explained what Fenton-Green's research was aiming to discover, as it happens. I'll see what I can find out."

Satisfied, the editor continued his perambulation between his reporters' desks, reading computer screens over their shoulders and never failing to put down the most vulnerable or suggest amendments to even the most competent. Ted Grant's management theory had been learned on a London tabloid and he took pride in never being outdone in the fear and loathing stakes. Laura watched him make his way back to his glass-walled office with a veiled expression. She had woken early that morning, feeling tired and irritable, and knew very well the reason why she had slept so badly.

She had not been under any obligation to go to Edgar Burridge's rally the previous evening. The *Gazette* report was being written by a colleague and she had driven into town and parked near the town hall out of sheer curiosity and a disinclination to sit in her flat alone brooding about the desperate state of her love-life. To her astonishment, the queue to get into the meeting was still trailing around the sides of the Victorian building and, once through the great studded oak doors, people were standing three deep up the broad stone staircase which led to the main public arena. By the time she had reached the top of the stairs the body of the hall had been filled to capacity and the rest of the queue was being directed into the gallery one floor up.

From there she had been able to watch the audience relatively unobserved herself, and it had soon become clear that not everyone in the packed hall was a supporter of Rev. Burridge and his views. Down one side and towards the front a small phalanx of women had taken over a block of seats and it was apparent even before the speaker took the platform that they were not planning to give him an easy ride. A few of them she recognised as students from the struggling women's group at the university but most were older, comfortably middle-aged and grey-haired. Laura guessed that they were the sixties pioneers of the new feminism, newly enraged by an attack on freedoms they had fought for and believed were now secure. To her consternation she recognised one white head in the middle of a row. It was her grandmother, Joyce.

At first the proceedings were calm enough. While the major part of the audience, which included a fair sprinkling of priests and other clergy, applauded enthusiastically when the American eventually appeared, the group at the front ostentatiously sat on their hands, watched uneasily by stewards in fluorescent orange jackets ranged with their backs to the speaker beneath the edge of the stage.

Edgar Burridge had been introduced by Dorothy Knight and Father Dermot Burke and began with prayers, for which a large part of the audience dutifully bent their heads, closed their eyes or crossed themselves devoutly. He then launched into his appeal for support and, eventually, for funds to continue the campaign against what he called the"moral debauchery" of extra-marital sex and abortion on both sides of the Atlantic. The interruptions had come slowly and insidiously at first, a groan here, a faint hiss of disapproval there, until, as Burridge got into his oratorical stride and the mellifluous American cadences began to fill the hall, the group of women at the front had stood up as one and begun to chant rhythmically, drowning out the preacher's voice.

To Laura's alarm, the reaction had been immediate and heavy-handed. The stewards who had been watching the proceedings from the front, advanced on the chanting women, cheered on by the majority of the audience, who were by now protesting as vigorously as the protesters themselves. As she saw women being pulled bodily from their seats and hurried towards the exits, Laura struggled from her own seat, pushing past startled neighbours and stepping indiscriminately on toes, as she fought her way downstairs and into the hall. The stewards had not yet got close to her grandmother but Laura was unable to attract her attention over the enormous noise which Edgar Burridge was by now trying to quell from his position on the platform. As far as Laura could see there were no uniformed police in the hall or anyone who seemed to be the slightest bit perturbed that women were being frog-marched out with their arms twisted painfully behind their backs.

Furious at her own impotence she finally fought her way to her grandmother's side and grabbed hold of her arm.

"What on earth are you doing here?" she said. "You're going to get hurt the way these thugs are carrying on."

"I wondered if you'd want to join me, pet," Joyce Ackroyd said cheerfully, her green eyes alive with the brightness of battle. She clutched a walking stick in one hand. "But then I thought the *Gazette* might not like it if their star reporter was seen to be joining in."

"Ted Grant would do his nut," Laura said grimly. "Believe me, I'm his bit player, not his star. Now come on, let's get you out of here before these gorillas do it for you."

She had escorted Joyce from the building, away from the now baying audience inside who seemed to be thoroughly enjoying the discomfiture of their enemies. In the street outside some of the protesters had regrouped and were chanting again, though others were sitting on the town hall steps with their arms around each other, and one or two were weeping quietly.

"You have to write about this," Joyce said firmly. "Those beggars were using far more force than they needed to."

"There's another reporter covering it," Laura said. "I'll talk to him in the morning. Now let's get you home, shall we." She gave her grandmother a hug. "It's way past your bedtime," she said. Only as she led Joyce slowly away towards her car did she notice Michael Thackeray standing in the shadows at the top of the town hall steps. She turned towards him, suddenly overcome with anger at what had happened inside.

"Why is it you can never find a bloody policeman when you want one?" she called bitterly. Thackeray had looked for a moment as if he was about to make his way down the steps to join them but as the crowd of angry women surged suddenly between him and Laura he had shrugged and turned away.

Joyce glanced at the granddaughter who was so like her in so many ways that she felt her to be part of herself and sighed.

"I see you're taking the hard road again, pet," she said. "There's no point telling you, I suppose."

"None at all," Laura had snapped.

Gazing at her reflection in the blank computer screen she sighed. To make the situation between herself and Thackeray worse should have been enough for one evening, she thought wryly. To upset her grandmother as well was unforgivable. When would she ever learn?

At police headquarters the morning briefing of the murder squad detectives had gone badly. Paul Cook, looking smug, and a small group of colleagues looking seriously disenchanted, sat in one corner surrounded by the piles of files Cook had appropriated from Saving Lives for the Lord. Their task was prescribed for the duration. Sergeant Kevin Mower sat at his desk in almost total silence, looking ill and avoiding the eye of his boss as far as he could. DC Val Ridley contributed to the discussion with suggestions of such forced enthusiasm and total irrelevance that Thackeray eventually decided to ignore her to save her the embarrassment of speaking. By the end of the meeting the only new development of any significance which had emerged was that the bullets that killed Dana Smith and Stella Brady bore a close similarity to two which had been recovered from a body of a man, still unidentified, who had been found in the Thames in London ten months earlier.

"If it was used in Bradfield this month and in August, Manchester in May, and London a couple of months before that you're into serious crime," DI Paul Cook offered lazily from his file-stacked corner of the room. "D'you want me to check out the London end, guv? I reckon you could have something drug-related here after all. Do we know if the pharmacy at that toy-town hospital is secure? Perhaps our lily-white nurse isn't the angel everyone makes out she is."

"A long shot, but worth checking out," Thackeray conceded, sufficiently baffled by the case to clutch at any straw. He assigned another member of the team to venture down what he was convinced was another dead end at the pharmacy, and agreed that Cook should talk to his colleagues in London about the possible migration of the murder weapon from one end of the country to the other.

Kevin Mower raised his head from his intense study of the surface of his desk and focused first on Cook and then on Thackeray with a truculent gaze.

"I looked at the pharmacy records," he said. "They looked OK to me. They don't keep much morphine for the obvious reason that they don't deal with terminal cases. It's not that sort of hospital. The pharmacist's one of those meticulous beggars who records every last aspirin dished out to a nurse for her period pains. I'd be surprised if you found a gram of bicarbonate of soda's gone astray."

"Check it again anyway," Thackeray said and Cook made no effort to hide his satisfaction at that. "Kevin, you can get down to the security firm and make sure that Nolan hasn't done a runner. Just because there's no forensic evidence to link him to the killings, and he's got no criminal record, doesn't let him off the hook. I'd be much happier if he hadn't had the opportunity to fire the shots on both occasions."

Mower nodded his assent to that, though it crossed Thackeray's mind that perhaps he should have entrusted the interview to someone who didn't look as if he had spent the night in the gutter.

"Come and see me as soon as you get back, Kevin," he said sharply. "Right," Thackeray went on. "I know this one is as frustrating a case as we've had, but we'll get there in the end through attention to detail. Nothing is too small, nothing should be regarded as irrelevant until we've proved it is. Someone somewhere in this town knows where that gun came from and who fired it – twice. Someone knows the bike which was used, where it came from, where it is now. If there's any connection between the two victims, apart from being in the wrong place at the wrong time, someone knows about that too. So we keep going, we keep checking every detail, if there's anything you're not happy about, the slightest hint of something not right, you go back and take another look at it."

As the meeting broke up and Mower hurried out of the door without a backward glance, watched by Paul Cook and Val Ridley with close interest and a distinct lack of friendliness, a uniformed officer hurried into the room and approached Thackeray.

"That American preacher's downstairs again, sir," he said. "Asking for you. Says it's urgent and he doesn't look as if he's going to take no for an answer."

Thackeray groaned faintly. He had seen and heard enough of Burridge's methods the previous evening to sicken him of the SLL campaign in spite of the applause and cheers which had greeted the uninterrupted climax of the American's speech. He might have some sympathy with Burridge's views, he thought, but he had none with the idea of browbeating or terrifying anyone facing the sort of life and death decisions Burridge saw in such clear cut terms. The man was a bully and the last person he wanted to talk to again until he had clear evidence, which he still seriously doubted anyone would find, that he was involved in the shootings in some way.

"Did he say what he wanted?" Thackeray asked.

"No, sir," the constable said. "But he's very insistent."

"I'm sure he is. He seems to make a profession of it," Thackeray muttered sourly to no one in particular and followed the uniformed officer down the stairs to an interview room where he found Edgar Burridge pacing up and down impatiently.

"Good morning to you, Chief Inspector," the American said amiably enough when Thackeray walked in. "I thought I saw you at the town hall last night. I hope you were impressed by that overwhelming support I got there."

"I was less impressed by your stewards," Thackeray said.

"Minimum force, Chief Inspector, minimum force. That's what I always tell them. We can't have misguided bra-burners and hippies going away with broken bones, can we, however ungodly their views?"

"You were treading a very fine line," Thackeray said.

"Well, I have to confess I like my meetings orderly," Burridge said, his smile expansive. "We try to make sure that tickets are only distributed to supporters but obviously that hadn't worked out too well last evening. I guess I'll have to talk to Dorothy Knight about it if I come again."

"Is that likely?" Thackeray asked, not disguising his fervent hope that it was not.

"Well, now, I just don't know about that," Burridge said. "I get the feeling that this little old country is just waiting for a movement like ours which has been so successful Stateside. I guess there's a time for moral regeneration in every country's history and I get the impression this might just be your moment to take on the forces of darkness which have been allowed to dance around God's acre here for so long. To take on the abortionists and the faggots and the satanists and the rest and rebuild a God-fearing society here."

"Don't you think that might be down to us?" Thackeray said.

"Well, I guess I never feel any compunction in offering help where it's needed, sir. No compunction at all. Which is why I was so anxious to see you this morning to make sure you had the evidence of wrong-doing at the May Anderson Hospital, one copy of which is amongst those files which your colleagues so inconveniently helped themselves to yesterday."

"And what's in this file?" Thackeray did not bother to hide his scepticism. He had heard Burridge's allegations at the meeting the previous evening. "Unless you can substantiate what you're saying there's not a lot we can do on the basis of anonymous allegations which were pretty vague, to be honest."

"I have a tape-recording from an witness who is in a position to know exactly what could be taking place under the cloak of Dr. Fenton-Green's alleged research project," Burridge said angrily. "There is a transcript in the files which you are welcome to read. What I'm hoping is that he will make contact again and firm up on what he knows."

"And are you now going to tell me who this witness is if it wasn't Stella Brady?" Thackeray asked.

"I'm still not prepared to tell you at this juncture. The person concerned needs to make arrangements to secure his position before he allows his name to be made public. But I can assure you there is enough in his statement to justify an investigation at the hospital. Enough for me to go to the media immediately. I have informed the local paper here in Bradfield what's going on. I could hardly not after what I said at the rally last night. And later today I shall be faxing press releases to the London papers. I'm sure there will be plenty of reporters and medical writers who will be anxious to find out just what the local police are doing about these allegations, Chief Inspector. Plenty, praise the Lord."

"I'll look at your file, Mr. Burridge," Thackeray said. "And if I can see anything which leads me to believe that a crime has been committed, rather than just a breach of the medical regulations, then I'll consult my superintendent about what we should do next. Thank you for your help."

Burridge looked at Thackeray for a long moment, his colour rising again.

"Well, I sure hope you will, Chief Inspector," he said. "I sure hope you will."

* * *

Laura Ackroyd stood at the top of the steps leading to the front door of the May Anderson Hospital, at the spot where Dana Smith had died, and glanced up and down the deserted road outside. The only person in sight was the security guard on the gate, huddled in his little hut against the chilly wind which was blowing down from the high moors. She must make a perfect target, she thought, and shuddered slightly before pushing open the door.

But she was more puzzled than afraid. She had driven up to the hospital in the hope of talking to Stephen Fenton-Green again, only to be told that he was away at a conference. As she stood at the reception desk wondering what to do next, she heard the front doors swing open again behind her and an enthusiastic voice bid her good morning.

"Dr. Mahood," she said, meeting the doctor's broad smile with a more guarded one of her own. "I was hoping to see your boss to talk some more about his research," she said.

Mahood shrugged.

"I can't help you there," he said. "Not my baby, you know." He laughed at his own choice of words. "Or babies either," he said.

"What about Mr. Randall, is he around?" Laura asked, throwing her question evenly between the doctor and the receptionist. But the girl shook her head.

"Dave's taken a couple of days off," she said. "Some family problem, apparently. No one seems to know where he's gone. Mr. Fenton-Green was hopping mad about it yesterday. Apparently he couldn't get him by phone. Very odd. He'll get the push if he's not careful."

Mahood had just shrugged again.

"I expect there's some good reason," he said. "Dave

201

Randall's not the irresponsible kind who'd take time off for no good reason."

But as Laura turned away to leave she felt a sick fear settle somewhere deep in her stomach. This was the man who had told her emphatically that he did not want to put his job at risk. She would, she thought, find out where he lived and try to contact him there. But she did not think she would have any success. Either Dave Randall had got frightened and gone to ground, she thought, or maybe Dave Randall was also dead.

Chapter 15

The Kawasaki hit a hundred miles an hour where the motorway began to snake down from the summit of the trans-Pennine route and it moved smoothly to the right to overtake a cluster of traffic in the other two lanes. The weather was cold but fine and visibility perfect and the black-clad rider had no intimation of danger as the road took him east, snaking across miles of open moorland and bog beneath an opalescent sky. He never knew that it was a blown tyre on one of the lorries on his nearside that caused several other speeding vehicles on the steep gradient to swerve wildly out of the way of the suddenly slewing artic and across the trajectory of his bullet-like machine. The bike cut clean through the first car it hit, took the roof off the next and set in chain a pile-up which blocked the entire three-lane motorway within seconds. The now airborn biker somersaulted several times ahead of the vortex of colliding, screeching metal behind him and came to rest, his neck snapped like the stem of a flower, in a black leather bundle like a crumpled rubbish-bag against the crash barrier where a smoke-blackened fire officer found him an hour later as he took a breather from cutting casualties from the wreckage. It did not take an expert to tell him that the biker was dead and it was another hour before an ambulance crew found the time to collect the broken body, the sixth for which they could do no more than provide a stretcher and a blanket for transport to the mortuary at Bradfield Infirmary.

It was well into the evening before the police and mortuary staff came to search his leathers for evidence of his identity and uncovered much more than they bargained for. Inside the now torn and bloodied jacket they found first a black automatic pistol and then a small roughly square package wrapped in brown paper and, inside that, thick plastic. When a corner was unwrapped it was not hard for the police-officer who was supervising the search to identify a consignment of illegal drugs.

The young police constable who had been at the crash scene on the motorway and seen more than his fill of death and destruction that afternoon made his decision quickly.

"Leave him here, and make sure that no one touches him," he said, with unaccustomed assurance to the baffled mortuary attendant. "This is one for CID."

Barry Foreman leaned back in his leather executive chair behind his extensive desk at the headquarters of Foreman Security Services and smiled encouragingly at his visitors.

"He hails from Hull, I believe," he offered helpfully. "Has it crossed your mind that's probably where he was going, Chief Inspector, if he was heading east on the M62?"

"Hull?" Paul Cook said incredulously. "I thought you said he worked for you. I've heard of commuting but that's ridiculous."

"You've not been listening," Foreman said, the faintest hint of irritation clouding a face which had remained untroubled since Thackeray and Cook had arrived fifteen minutes earlier. "I said he *used* to work for me. I sacked him. Six months ago. You can look at my employment records if you don't believe me. If Carlo Fantoni has been getting up to things he shouldn't since then I know nowt about it and there's no reason why I should. I've not seen him since."

"Why did you sack him exactly?" Thackeray asked, not for the first time.

"He was unreliable," Foreman said. "Took days off, turned up late, couldn't be bothered to wear his uniform, things you can't put up with if you want to build a reputation in the security business. You know that, gentlemen. It's exactly the same in t'police force, isn't it? You've a reputation to keep up, a certain standard to maintain. Fantoni was sloppy and unreliable – just like some coppers I know - so I let him go."

"Had you any reason to suspect that he was involved in

anything illegal while he worked for you?" Thackeray persisted, refusing to rise to Foreman's sneer. "You run the doors at local clubs. Was he in cahoots with the dealers trying to get inside?"

"Not to my knowledge," Foreman said.

"And would you have come to us if he had been?"

Foreman shrugged.

"You know we have to be whiter than white in this game. I'm not stupid. I know your colleagues are watching every move I make. I employ honest staff and if I suspect they're not honest, they're out. I'd no evidence that Fantoni was into drugs but I had my suspicions. That were enough. I got rid – two weeks' money and out t' door. We didn't bother with the niceties. He's not the type to take me to a bloody industrial tribunal is he?"

Thackeray gazed at the six foot something of impeccably tailored and immaculately groomed impassivity on the other side of the desk and sighed. Foreman was known as a hard man, but he was not the tough, muscle-bound sort of thug who he had met often enough in his early days in the force. This was a new breed of criminal – and the DCI had no doubt Foreman was a criminal – computer literate and intelligent enough to keep his Italian loafers well out of the muck and his hands well clear of the blood which he was sure supported his more than comfortable lifestyle. "You have to admit it's odd, though, don't you," he mused aloud. "An ex-employee of yours is found with drugs and the gun which probably killed two women in Bradfield. Another employee of yours is there when one of the murders occurs, and could well have been for the other? Just coincidence, you think?"

"You'll have to ask Steve Nolan about that," Foreman said. "I don't even know if they ever worked together, them two, though I suppose I could get someone to find out if you think it's really important."

"I'll let you know," Thackeray said shortly. "But if you recall anything else that might link Nolan or Fantoni with the May

Anderson Hospital let me know straight away. I don't believe in coincidences."

Back in the car, Paul Cook glanced at the DCI with a chilly expression.

"Load of bollocks, all that, don't you think, guv?"

"I'm sure," Thackeray said coldly. "But it may not be so easy to prove it."

"The drug squad'll want in on the case now and my lot'll be pricking up their ears if they hear about heroin doing a ton down the motorway from Manchester to Hull."

"I want no one else sniffing about until I'm sure that we've really got our murderer," Thackeray said. "If it was Fantoni fired the shots I want to know why. In particular I want to know who, if anyone, hired him."

"Foreman wouldn't think twice," Cook said.

"I'm sure you're right. But we need evidence."

"Let me turn his place over," Cook offered eagerly.

"You'll take it easy," Thackeray said. "You've done enough unauthorised turning over. Foreman offered to show us his employment records. Check those out and talk to anyone else there who knew Fantoni. Especially Nolan. If Fantoni was the gunman there must be a chance Nolan recognised him or at least knew him as a man who rode a powerful bike. He was far too unobservant to be credible, was Nolan. Ask him to come down to the station again and we'll see if his memory has improved."

"I thought Kevin Mower talked to him already," Cook said. "I haven't seen a report, come to think of it."

Thackeray glanced at the special branch officer with an inscrutable eye.

"We'll check that out when we get back, too," he said ominously.

Laura drove down the M1 with a sense of liberation, the Golf touching eighty as she skipped around the late rush-hour traffic and the queues for the Meadowhall shopping centre outside Sheffield and on south into open, hilly country where little clusters of orange lights gave a blurred glimpse of an isolated village huddled against the Pennine foothills. Somewhere between Derby and Nottingham she slowed down and pulled into a service station as she had been instructed by Dave Randall's email earlier in the afternoon. If there was any sign that she had been followed, he had said, he would not make contact. Filled with relief that he was safe and well, even if consistently mysterious in his comings and goings, she had followed his instructions to the letter. She glanced into her mirror as she pulled into the slip-road which led to the car-park, but the only vehicle she could see behind her was a heavy truck which veered off towards the lorry park. Ahead the car-park was only half full. Anyone watching, she thought, would have little trouble in seeing her arrive unaccompanied. She slid the car into a space facing the brightly lit restaurant and shops, switched off her lights and undid her seat belt so that she could stretch her legs. Wait, Randall had said, so she waited.

She had told no one about the latest message from the lab technician. The police, she was sure, would be interested in her meeting with the absent member of the May Anderson hospital's staff, but she had felt no obligation to call them ahead of it and a distinct disinclination to speak to Michael Thackeray at all. She still found it hard to believe he was no longer with her and she did not suppose that her angry reaction when he had seen her on the town hall steps the previous evening, clearly on the side of the evicted protesters, would have made him any more conciliatory than he had been before he left. Well, she thought, with a shrug, this was something he would have to come to terms with or not, as the case might be. Her own past could not be undone and she felt no particular guilt about the decisions she had made so long ago. They had seemed right at the time, and still seemed right to her. But as Vicky had said the last time Laura had spoken to her friend, Thackeray had no talent for bending and nor, perhaps, did

Laura herself. It might be that they were temperamentally incapable, Vicky had suggested sadly, of the sort of accommodations marriage demanded. That's not true, Laura had cried, devastated by her friend's prognosis but deep down she wondered now if Vicky had not been right.

Her reverie was interrupted by a sharp tap on her window and she recognised Dave Randall standing at the passenger door. She lowered the window.

"Sorry," she said. "I was miles away."

"We'll go in my car," Randall said. "I don't think anyone followed you but we'll take no chances."

"Go?" Laura asked, getting out of the Golf and locking the doors. "Where are we going?"

"Not far," Randall said. "I thought you might like to meet Fenton-Green's first wife."

He left the motorway at the next junction and drove fast along unlit country lanes for what seemed like miles. Laura noticed that he glanced constantly in his rear-view mirror but he seemed satisfied that they were not being followed and after half an hour of what she suspected was a deliberately devious route, he pulled up in a village street outside a substantial cottage. She had asked him at one point who he was afraid of but he had not answered.

"She's still a nurse," he said. "But married again with a couple of kids. She agreed to see me this evening because her husband would be out. She said she didn't want to talk about Stephen Fenton-Green when her husband was there. Not a subject they ever discuss, apparently. Her name's Deborah, by the way, and I haven't told her you're a reporter. She'd probably have a fit. Just let her think you're from the hospital as well."

The door was answered quickly when they raised the brass knocker and a plump woman in her early forties gazed at them cautiously.

"Dave Randall," he said. "We spoke on the phone. This is Laura, who's also very interested in what Stephen Fenton-Green is getting up to with his research."

Deborah opened the door with some apparent reluctance and when she had settled her visitors in the comfortable sitting room she stood in front of the wood-burning stove and twisted her wedding ring around her finger awkwardly.

"It's all a long time ago," she said. "I'm very happily married now with a son and a daughter. Teenagers. I've almost stopped thinking about Stephen, you know? Almost – but not quite."

"You know he's big in fertility research now?" Randall asked.

"Yes, I see his name mentioned from time to time," Deborah said. "I suppose it makes sense for him, after what happened to us."

"What did happen to you and Stephen?" Randall asked quietly. "This is what we don't understand. Mr. Fenton-Green seems to have had dreadful trouble having a child himself ever since you and he split up and at one point I got the distinct impression he was infertile. I thought that must be what motivated him. But it's not, is it?"

"We had a child," Deborah said. "We got married because I was pregnant. He seemed to think it was the right thing to do, although he was older than me and I wasn't so sure. Anyway, he persuaded me he really wanted the baby, and we had Toby. He was born two months early and barely survived. It probably would have been better if he hadn't as it turned out."

"Something was wrong?" Laura asked.

"He seemed to be fine at first. Rather slow to develop but everyone just put that down to his premature birth. But by the time he was about eighteen, months, old it was obvious he wasn't normal. They did every test in the book. Stephen dragooned every paediatric specialist in London to look at him. But he never walked and he never talked and from about two and a half he began to deteriorate rapidly. As did our relationship. Stephen couldn't come to terms with a son who was less than perfect. He had such plans for him…" Deborah shrugged, her eyes shining with tears.

"He left in the end," she said. "By this time Toby screamed almost permanently and Stephen shouted. I was on the verge of a breakdown. It was all horrendous. Finally I just told Stephen to go. I couldn't cope with both of them. It was impossible. We divorced and he got a job in the Midlands soon afterwards and I never saw him again. His solicitor kept in touch over the arrangements for Toby, until he died. He was three years and seven months old. Stephen didn't even come to the funeral."

Deborah gazed at the carpet for a moment and Laura saw a single tear fall onto her hand, which she brushed away impatiently.

"It's all a long time ago," she said eventually. "And I have a new life now and two beautiful completely normal kids. But you never forget your first baby, do you?"

Laura shook her head sharply.

"I'm sure you don't," she said.

"Did they discover what was wrong with Toby?" Dave Randall asked.

"No," Deborah said. "Not definitely. Though in one of his hysterical rants, cursing me, and God and anyone else he could think of to blame, Stephen admitted it must be genetic – and from his family. Apparently he had an older brother who had died in similar circumstances as a young child. His parents would never talk about him but he had found photographs of him as a baby, unknown to his mother, and wheedled the rest out of the family nanny. He comes from quite a wealthy background. They never thought I was good enough for him." She smiled ruefully and shrugged.

Randall drew a sharp breath.

"So he directed his energies into fertility research," he said softly. "I wonder why?"

"You think he's trying to find the cause?" Deborah asked. "Is he that good?"

"Oh yes, he's that good," Randall said. "But I think he's trying to find the cure as well as the cause. This is a red hot area, genetic research. There could be a fortune in it if he really came up with something new."

"Stephen always had his eye on the main chance," Deborah said. "He once told me that he hated pregnant women but if he wanted to make money in private practice it had to be that or heart surgery and he wasn't a skilful enough surgeon to make it as a cardiac specialist."

"Nice," Laura said. "What's surprising is how popular he is. His patients seem to adore him, the nursing staff worship him and he has no difficulty picking up wives and girlfriends along the way."

"That's the charm I fell for," Deborah said ruefully. "There was never any shortage of that, in public anyway. But my mother always used to say you need to see a man at seven o'clock on Monday morning in mid-January before you can really claim to know him. He wasn't so pleasant then, especially if the baby had been crying all night."

"There've been no more babies, though," Randall said harshly. "In fact his second wife needed fertility treatment – which failed. And now his girlfriend is on the hospital's books as well."

"I can't imagine he would want another baby," Deborah said quietly. "It would be monstrously unfair to his partner, if what he suspected is true. But then Stephen was never a very fair man."

Laura glanced at Randall, another question on the tip of her tongue, but he shook his head imperceptibly.

"It was good of you to see us," he said.

Randall drove slowly back to the motorway service station and by a more direct route, saying nothing until he had pulled up beside Laura's Golf again.

"You think he's working on some sort of gene manipulation?" Laura asked.

"If you'd been through something like that and you had the skills, isn't that where you'd put your efforts?" Randall came back quickly.

"But if he's trying to create a baby for himself without the faulty gene he's not had much luck so far, has he? The treatment his second wife had was a total failure."

"None of this is easy," Randall said. "I told the Rev. Burridge that."

"You spoke to Burridge?"

"Only in general terms. I thought they were the people who would be most likely to push for some sort of investigation. That's all I'm looking for, really."

"So you *were* the person he was talking about at the town hall?" Laura said, as the cogs slotted into place. "I thought it must have been you."

"I suppose so. I wasn't there."

"He played it for all he was worth," Laura said. "Fenton-Green must be furious. Can you really not get any idea what he's been working on from the lab?"

"Not personally, I'm not enough of an expert, but I think I know someone who can," Randall said. "Leave it with me. I'll be in touch by email."

"Perhaps we should contact the police…"

"Not yet. There's nothing to tell them yet," Randall insisted. "It's no more than suspicion, is it? And what he's doing is probably not criminal anyway, just unauthorised and possibly unethical. It's the General Medical Council we should be reporting him to."

"But you've decided to keep out of the way? I was worried about you. You don't think there's any connection between this and the shootings, do you?"

"Oh, I shouldn't think even Fenton-Green would be that crazy, even if Stella Brady had her suspicions, which I don't think is very likely. She was in his office again carrying on like crazy last week but I think it was the Dana Smith abortion she was agonising over. She had an over-sensitive conscience, that one. I just decided to keep out of his way for a bit. He can make life pretty uncomfortable for me if he finds out I've been whistle-blowing about the direction I think his research is headed. Which is why, if there's any public whistle-blowing to be done I'd rather it was done by you than me. I don't want to be quoted, thank you very much. I'd quite like to go on working somewhere, though not for Fenton-Green for much longer, I don't think."

"You won't go back?"

"I'll probably go back to hand in my resignation and pick up my P45. I don't suppose he'll want me to work my notice in the circumstances."

Chapter 16

Maggie Sullivan eased open the back door of her daughter's house just as dawn was streaking the night sky with silver as she had done every morning since she had arrived there from Bradfield infirmary. The hours the family were spending cooped up in the tiny kitchen or the cluttered front room were torture to her. For most of the time the predatory young of the neighbourhood, hurling abuse or worse at anyone who ventured to open a door or a window at the Smith's house, deterred even Maggie from venturing out. But she had guessed, rightly as it turned out, that the grey small hours before seven would see most of the estate's population still sound asleep.

The voices in Maggie's head were quite clear. She acknowledged their presence now and again with a murmur of assent or disapproval, but she had given up passing on the messages to her daughter or her sons: they did not want to know about the warnings which she heard quite clearly. Sometimes they came from the clump of trees she could see from the window of the bedroom she was sharing with Megan, where she glimpsed the hanged man swinging in the breeze. Sometimes they came from the dark pit which opened up in front of her as she shuffled from room to room, an abyss which sent her stumbling backwards to escape the chilly, airless depths from which her persecutors, death and the devil in dreadful tandem, whispered their instructions. Go on your way, Maggie, they told her relentlessly, as she picked listlessly at the food Megan put in front of her, or when she woke in the night to the sound of her daughter's wheezing breath in the bed next to hers. Go on your way, you're not safe here, get out, they said, as Mick slipped out across the back gardens to tend to his ponies. On your way, they repeated, as the other three lads joshed and tussled over games of cards round the kitchen table, increasingly incensed by their enforced idleness. But she could not go anywhere while bricks and rotting rubbish constantly thudded against the boarded windows, and Tom's car languished in front of the house with its tyres slashed and windscreen smashed into a thousand fragments which glittered in the mud. There was no where to go.

Glancing this way and that with quick, bird-like movements of her head, she edged round the corner of the house, past the demolished car and out into the street in the faint morning light. She walked slowly, her knees protesting at the now unaccustomed exercise. "Go home now," the familiar voice whispered, but she shook her head irritably, knowing that she could not face the long bus journeys back to Shepley or the scramble down the muddy lane to her caravan, which was where she longed to be.

At the end of Benwell Lane, where the houses ended and the rough grassland leading to the moors began, she strode out more confidently, knowing that she had outstripped her persecutors and happy to fill her lungs with the frosty morning air. As the sky lightened she could see the huddle of houses around the Green and the Cricketers' Arms, and beyond that the shed at the end of the field where Mick's ponies spent the night during the cold weather. Hurrying she followed the muddy path across the green and came to the dry-stone wall, topped with a couple of strands of barbed wire, and clucked and whistled until six familiar shapes loomed out of the gloom breathing mistily over her as she reached into her coat pocket for the mints they loved.

Maggie had grown up with horses. She could still remember her father swinging her up into the saddle for the first time as a small child and parading her proudly up and down a street filled with bustling crowds of buyers and sellers of horse-flesh, big broad men in cloth caps and mufflers, smelling of hay and tobacco, feeling legs and peering at teeth and sealing a bargain with a smacked palm against palm. That had been long ago, in the old days when home was on wheels and a sturdy cob hauled the caravan from farm to farm and campsite to campsite and the police were interested only in what the lads might have stolen not in where you spent the night.

"Not long now, pet," Maggie said fondly to the little piebald mare who was heavily pregnant. "Not long, and then maybe Mikey'll tek thee up to Shepley and, let thee run wi'thi foal up theer. We've got to get away from these little beggars round here, haven't we? There's nowt to keep us down here now, wi' Dana gone."

She handed out her mints to the ponies and let them nuzzle her shoulder as the light strengthened and the first pink streaks of winter sunlight crept over the dark shoulder of the hills to the east before she reluctantly turned away and began her slow plod back to the house and let herself in to the gloomy interior as silently as she had crept away. She filled the kettle and put it on before hanging her coat on the peg behind the kitchen door.

"Tha'rt up early, Gran," Mick said as he came down the stairs stretching and yawning.

"Always an early riser, I am," Maggie said. "Best thing would be for us all to get off early and away to Shepley before those little beggars do summat desperate," she said, lifting the kettle with difficulty to brew the tea. "Safer theer."

"We'll be reet, Gran," Mick said cheerfully. "You're not to fret. Only another week or so and I'll tek thee down to't field to see the new foal."

"You're a fool, Michael, and so are your brothers," his grandmother said. "I've told you, there'll be no more peace here for you, or for your ponies, I dare say. We have to go."

"Aye, well, you talk to me mam about that," Mick said as he shrugged on his jacket and unlatched the kitchen door. "I'll be back in half an hour, tell her, over't back gardens. She's not to worry."

Maggie sat down at the table with her mug of tea, staring into its tannic depths and listening to the faint sounds of the sleeping household. Megan no longer got up early, she had noticed. Her daughter tossed in her narrow bed all night and eventually stumbled down the stairs in a torn dressing gown looking pale and puffy around the eyes. She glanced across the kitchen to where the devil had slipped into a seat close to the door, a flickering cloak wrapped tight around him, his horns nodding slightly as if in time to some internal tune of his own.

"Chilly down there today, is it?" Maggie inquired.

"Take your toes off, will frost-bite," the old boy said cheerily. "And your fingers. Rots 'em black and takes 'em right off. You'll be wanting the fire then to warm you up. Won't be long now. You won't listen, will you? Think you know best. I'll not warn you again."

Even as Maggie stared at the now empty chair, she heard the scuffle at the front door behind her and turned to see flames licking under the sill and into the narrow hallway.

"Megan!" she shrieked, fear tearing at her heart. "Megan, get down here. Tom, Gavin, we're on fire. Will you come away now, all of you. We've got to go."

* * *

"There must be someone else involved apart from Carlo Fantoni," DCI Michael Thackeray said, his jaw set in an obstinate line which superintendent Jack Longley recognised only too well. "Why would a drug courier who's been living openly in Hull for the last six months, just as Foreman said he'd been, suddenly come back to Bradfield and shoot two women dead. It makes no sense at all unless someone hired him to do it."

"I'm sure you're right, Michael," Longley said. "Forensics are OK on the gun, are they?"

"It's the gun which killed both women. A powerful bike was heard on both occasions. If he'd just been injured in the smash instead of killed I've no doubt I'd have a confession by now."

217

"But you're still not happy?" Longley almost sighed.

Thackeray shook his head and gazed at his boss bleakly.

"Means, opportunity, fine. But what the hell's the motive?" he said.

"Drugs, you think?"

"We've checked the hospital pharmacy twice and as far as we can see security there's watertight. The chief pharmacist is a stickler. The order book and the prescription records match up down to the last Panadol. The drug squad have got Barry Foreman in their sights because of the Fantoni connection but I'd be amazed if they can find any link to the May Anderson."

"So what else could it be if not drugs?" Longley asked slightly wearily. "Do you reckon this Yank hired him to take pot-shots at anyone and anything up there?"

"I want to look at Fantoni's mobile phone records for starters. When we know who he's been talking to we may be a bit further forward. And we'll do the same for Burridge's out-fit. And Stella Brady's husband. I suppose it's just possible she had a fling with this Fantoni, broke it off, God knows…"

"When does Burridge go back to the States?" Longley asked cautiously. "Considering you've almost certainly got your killer this could push the overtime bill through the roof if you're planning to follow the Rev. Burridge back to Iowa."

Thackeray allowed himself a faint smile, and Longley was surprised to realise how seldom he had seen the Chief Inspector's face lighten over the last few days.

"I'll try to avoid that, but there is the question of what we're to do about the allegations he's making against Fenton-Green."

"Wait till he comes up with something concrete and crimi-nal," Longley said. "That's a can of worms we can do without unless there's hard evidence to work on."

"Right," Thackeray said, evidently relieved.

"Laura all right, is she?" Longley ventured.

"As far as I know," Thackeray snapped, his face closing again like a slammed door and Longley's mind did a somersault

218

as he took in the implications of that and decided that he had ventured down an avenue he had no desire – or even right – to pursue.

"Aye well, don't waste too much time on the motive for the shootings now we've got the gunman," he said, his voice hardening. "There's plenty of other crime to keep your lads busy. I reckon you can scale the murder investigation down unless you get some really definite lead on who might have hired Fantoni, if anyone did. Perhaps Brady did have an affair with Fantoni and he had reasons of his own to want her dead. In which case, we'll never know. Talk to the press office about some form of words for the papers – we've found the murder weapon, person carrying it's no longer with us, the case isn't closed but there may never be a prosecution – you know the score."

"I'd like Paul Cook off our backs now, too," Thackeray said. "He and Mower are at daggers drawn."

"Aye, I'll see what I can do about that. Perhaps we can get him seconded to the drugs squad," Longley conceded. "What about Mower? Is he up to par now?"

Thackeray shrugged wearily.

"Not so's you'd notice," he said. "Leave him to me. I'll read him the riot act. I should have done it before now but I've put it off."

"The trouble with giving someone enough rope to hang himself is that it often gets tangled round someone else's neck an'all," Longley said. "Sort him out, Michael. You know it makes sense."

Thackeray walked slowly back to his office, his anger growing with every step. He felt no satisfaction that they had found their gunman. Fantoni's death, he thought, had cheated not only the police but the victims' families of any chance that the unanswered questions surrounding the shootings would ever be answered. That could be frustrating enough at the conclusion of even the simplest domestic murder investigation. The man, and it was generally a man, who slaughtered his wife and children and then killed himself, always left a cancerous, guilt-inducing question-mark over his motives, enough for any grieving relative to torture themselves with for the rest of their lives. But the shooting down of two apparently blameless women by a man whose criminal activities he had no doubt would soon be the subject of speculation in the *Bradfield Gazette* - if not the national newspapers - left so many agonising questions unresolved that he had no doubt the case would linger like a bad smell around the hospital, the families and the police for years to come. If this was really as far as it went, he thought, it would satisfy nobody, least of all him.

He strode into the incident room like a thunderstorm only to find that neither Mower nor Cook were there.

"Did they say where they were going?" he asked Val Ridley who was hunched over her computer like a blonde wraith.

"They wouldn't tell me anything, would they? D'you want me to try Kevin on his mobile?"

Thackeray's lips tightened.

"No, leave them be. Just tell them to see me as soon as they come in," he said.

"Is it all over then?" Val asked. The question froze Thackeray's mind for a moment until he realised that she meant the case. He was aware that everyone in the room was waiting for his answer.

"We'll review the options at the briefing in the morning," he said and no one had the courage to press him any further. But as he walked miserably back to his office he knew there were other options that he needed to review even more urgently before they closed down on him completely. He flung his jacket on the back of his chair and lit a cigarette, watching the smoke rise to the ceiling through half-closed eyes. Laura, he thought, might be better off without him and the feeling which had been haunting him ever since she had turned away from him angrily in front of the town hall was that she might have come to that conclusion herself. He could curse God and his representatives on earth, he thought, but in the end he suspected that the only person to blame was himself.

Five miles away at Benwell Lane, DI Cook and Sergeant Mower were sitting in an unmarked car outside Megan Smith's increasingly dilapidated house. That morning's fire had scorched the front door and one of the boarded up windows and the rendering above but had not apparently gained any significant hold inside the building.

"If they'd tried that on when they were all asleep they'd never have got out alive, the way it's been turned into a fortress," Mower said sombrely. "Their good luck the old girl's an early riser."

"Don't talk too loud or you'll put ideas into the little bastards' heads," Cook said, nodding at the cluster of youths who were hanging around the bus shelter a hundred yards further down the street.

"You don't want to start interviewing them again, do you?" Mower asked wearily. "Uniform got nothing out of any of them and according to his mother, Nick Bailey's still safely tucked up in bed at home while his cracked ribs mend."

"Oh, Bailey's probably too smart to chuck a petrol bomb himself, anyway," Cook said easily. "He'll have found some little toe-rag who owes him to fling it on his behalf. Anyway, it wasn't petty feuds between thieves up here I wanted to talk to you about. Uniform can look after the Smiths and the Baileys – or let them fight themselves to a standstill for all I care. There's another way I thought you and I could earn ourselves a few brownie points, if you're interested."

"Oh yeah?" Mower said without enthusiasm. "What would that be then, guv?"

"Barry Foreman," Cook said.

"I thought the drug squad was going to follow up his links with Fantoni." Mower did nothing to disguise his lack of enthusiasm.

"Well, I guess they will, when the spirit moves them. But

from what I'm told they're going to start at the Hull end. It might be weeks before they get around to any Bradfield connections. In the meantime I thought we might keep an eye on him ourselves. Just see who's coming and going around his office, nothing heavy, though I might be able to get into his phones if I pull a few strings with mates of mine in the Smoke."

"You think Mr. Thackeray'll sanction that do you?" Mower said. "You've gotta be joking."

"Who said anything about Mr. Thackeray," Cook said. "I'm talking about you and me, Kevin. A little unpaid overtime and a lot of kudos if we pull something off. And don't tell me you're not in need of something useful to put on your record just now because I know that's not true. You're on a knife-edge and you know it. Anyway, I don't think Fantoni came all the way to Bradfield to shoot two women without something pretty substantial to show for it, do you? And who does he know over here who can come up with the sort of money a contract like that would fetch? It has to be Foreman. There's no one else within miles."

"There's no evidence," Mower said. "Not a shred. Nolan swears he's not seen Fantoni since he was sacked. Noone else at the company admits to seeing him in Bradfield since he got the push."

"So you're going to call it a day, are you, like your wimp of a boss? Case closed? Do me a favour."

"He's not closed the case. There are lines of inquiry still being followed up," Mower protested.

"But not this one, and my hunch is this is the best one we've got," Cook said. "Still if you can't get your head round it, perhaps I'll just talk to Val Ridley about the complaint I think she should make about your sexual assault on her the other day. And then there's the fact you're hungover most of the time, when you're not actually drunk on duty. You had your moments at Paddington Green, I seem to remember, and I don't see any good reason why I should be

222

part of the cover-up you've got going here with your mates in CID..."

Mower looked at Paul Cook with loathing in his dark eyes.

"OK, OK," he said. "We'll follow up your hunch. I know how important it is for you to get one over the Yorkshire hicks."

"Oh, come on, Kevin," Cook said, starting up the car. "You know as well as I do that most of them are as thick as the proverbial short planks. It takes someone with a bit of nous to handle bastards like Foreman. I wouldn't ask anyone else."

"Fuck you," Mower said wearily as Cook slid away from the kerb and the besieged Smith house under the anticipatory gaze of the cluster of youths further down the Lane who sped them on their way with jeers and obscene gestures.

"If I were a gippo up here I'd have been on the road long before this," Cook said as he accelerated away. "Some people never learn."

Dave Randall met his visitors in the corridor outside the maternity ward and beckoned them to follow him up the stairs to the second floor of the May Anderson Hospital.

"It's good to see you again, sir," he said to the tall, grey-haired man who stood aside to allow Laura Ackroyd to pre-cede him through the swing doors leading to the staircase.

"You realise this is completely unprofessional," Professor Edwin Cave said. He had met Laura in the centre of Bradfield and allowed her to pose as his wife as the two of them talked their way past security on the pretext of visiting a patient who had just had a baby. The patient was as genuine as the flowers the professor carried rather self-consciously – Dave Randall had made sure of that – although the excuse for their presence in the hospital was certainly not.

"I didn't know who else to turn to," Randall said as he led the way along the empty corridor to the laboratories. "I just need to know whether what's going on here is above board or not."

"And Ms. Ackroyd?" the professor asked, his thin face screwed up with distaste. "I assume her knowledge of genetics and fertility treatment is pretty rudimentary."

"Dave came to me first with his worries," Laura said, thrown on the defensive. "If what he suspects is true I think there's a public interest, don't you?"

"Maybe," Cave said, not disguising his distaste at the idea of helping to throw a colleague to the media lions. "But you do realise, don't you, that we may find nothing at all amiss? Even if Fenton-Green is stepping over a few boundaries, it may be impossible to spot. He may not keep any records here. He may even take tissue samples and so forth away with him. We're talking experiments with single cells under a microscope, not some Frankenstein monster springing lifesize from the operating table."

"I'd really feel happier if you took a look, professor," Randall said as he unlocked the laboratory doors. "Mr. Fenton-Green is at a seminar in Manchester today, so it seemed like a good opportunity."

Once inside with the doors closed and locked behind them Randall put on protective clothing and handed white coats to his two guests.

"There's nothing wrong with the fertility treatment which goes on here," he said. "I don't want the place contaminated. A whole lot of desperate women depend on it."

"I'm sure they do," Cave said drily. "I understand Stephen Fenton-Green has had problems in that department himself. Perhaps you're confusing the urgency that tragedy might provoke in a good doctor with something suspicious, David. Is that a possibility?"

"I suppose so," Randall admitted unhappily. "I know I'm asking a lot but.." He shrugged. "You were the only person I could turn to."

"Could he be trying to create an embryo free from a genetic defect?" Laura asked.

Cave looked at her sombrely.

"A lot of people are trying to do that, Ms Ackroyd," he said. "It's one of the major objectives of genetic research, to get rid of some of the genetic diseases like haemophilia and cystic fibrosis. But…" He shrugged as he glanced around the benches and stacked shelves of the lab. "I don't think Stephen is in that league, scientifically speaking. We're not exactly at the cutting edge here. Still, as I've allowed myself to be persuaded into this dubious errand, I'll take a look."

Methodically the professor began to inspect the lab, taking samples out of liquid nitrogen, examining slides under microscopes, flicking through notebooks and records, peering into cupboards, even, at Dave Randall's insistence, peering fastidiously into waste bins and unscrewing discarded slips of paper.

"Look," he said to Laura at one point, a hint of enthusiasm in his chilly grey eyes, waving her to a microscope under which he had placed a sample. "This is what it's all about. That is a fertilised human egg, what those mothers downstairs are waiting to have implanted." Laura peered into the eyepiece as much to hide the tears which had sprung unbidden into her eyes as because the misty blob at the other end could tell her anything comprehensible.

"I hope I don't have to do it this way," she muttered, turning away.

"Better this way than no way at all," Cave said briskly. Laura perched herself at a bench on one of the tall stools and contented herself with watching the two men as they spent the best part of an hour examining the lab from top to bottom but she guessed from Cave's increasingly distant expression that he had found nothing which caused him any serious concern. At length he took off his glasses and put them away carefully in a leather case.

"I'm sorry," he said. "I can see nothing untoward here. Of course, it could be that some of the stored eggs or tissue samples were illicitly obtained, but there is no way of proving that short of DNA analysis and you would need very strong evidence to authorise that. Perhaps there are more samples than I would have expected to find for the number of patients being treated, but that could merely be caution on Stephen's part. The only other slight oddity I've seen is one set of fertilised eggs which are entirely female. That could be pure chance or it could be related to a patient carrying a male chromosome-linked defect – muscular dystrophy, for instance, in which case there would be strong reasons for not implanting a male foetus. Do you know any cases of that sort, David?"

Randall shook his head.

"No, and I don't have access to the codes Mr. Fenton-Green uses for his samples. He's always been very insistent on storing everything anonymously."

A small bell rang at the back of Laura's mind, but she could not place the connection Cave's words had suggested.

"I'm sorry," the professor said. "But I really think you're letting your imagination run away with you, David. I can see nothing amiss, and the more I think about it the more I'm convinced I shouldn't have agreed to come here today." Looking unhappy, Randall helped Laura and the professor off with their white coats and unlocked the door of the laboratory. But as he opened the door they became aware of a commotion echoing from somewhere down the long tiled hospital corridors. As they hesitated, the door was pushed open in their faces and they found themselves face-to-face with a furious Stephen Fenton-Green, hair dishevelled, expensive overcoat half-hanging from his shoulders, his eyes blazing.

"What…?" he said, obviously as astonished to meet the trio on the way out of his laboratories as they were to see him. "Edwin?"

"I'm sorry, Stephen," Professor Cave said quickly. "I was passing and came in on the off-chance of catching you. David here kindly let me in…"

"You knew about the demonstration?" Fenton-Green said, glancing anxiously over his shoulder to where the sounds of shouting were getting nearer. "They've broken in somehow, half a dozen of them, looking for the labs."

"Yes, yes," Cave said quickly. "But you weren't here…"

The two men stood face-to-face for a second and Laura knew that the misunderstanding Cave had encouraged had thrown the panic-stricken Fenton-Green off his stride, perhaps just sufficiently for them to get away with it.

"My office was warned what was going to happen," she lied happily. "Have you sent for the police?"

"Yes, yes, of course. I came up to make sure none of them had got this far," Fenton-Green said, his eyes darting beyond David Randall to the neat and tidy laboratory that his illicit visitors had left behind them.

"Everything's fine, sir," Randall said. "I'd no idea anything was wrong until Professor Cave turned up…"

"They could create mayhem in here." Fenton-Green was beginning to look desperate as the noise behind them grew to a crescendo. Then as suddenly, it faded and they could hear a single voice taking some sort of control of the situation.

"That sounds like the police," Cave said. "Thank God for that. I'm very glad we didn't have to man the barricades for you."

"They'll get everything under control," Laura said soothingly. "And then perhaps you could give me a brief interview for tomorrow's paper..?"

"I don't think so," Fenton-Green snapped, his colour slowly returning to something like normal as he slipped off his coat and stepped into his lab.

"Perhaps a drink later, Stephen?" Cave asked, but his colleague shook his head angrily.

"There's work I need to get on with," he said ungraciously. "Some other time perhaps?"

Dave Randall gave an imperceptible shrug behind Fenton-Green's back as his boss ushered him back into the lab, leaving Laura and the professor outside in the corridor as the door was closed and locked in their faces.

"Do you think he believed us?" Laura asked as they made their way back to the main reception area of the hospital where half a dozen uniformed police-men were escorting four burly young men from the premises. Outside the usual placard-wavers were safely corralled on the other side of the street.

"For the moment," Cave said grimly. "Though when he thinks about it later he may well realise what a fairy story we told him."

Chapter 17

The morning was the coldest yet as Maggie Sullivan made her way unsteadily down the path to her grandson's paddock, her feet sliding on frosted patches of mud and dead leaves, leaving her feeling perilously adrift as she reached out to steady herself against a dry stone wall she could barely see in the dawn light. After skinning her knuckles, she stood for a moment, trying to make out the shed where Mick kept his hay and tackle, her breath wafting in misty clouds in front of her face.

"Eeeh, but it's time we were away," she said to helplessly to the shadowy figure who followed her now wherever she went.

"Freeze your tits off," the devil said companionably.

"Bugger off," Maggie said sharply. She hurried on, conscious of her companion muttering and mumbling behind her, evidently finding it as hard as she did to keep his balance on the icy surface beneath their feet. This morning she had wrapped a blanket from her bed around her shoulders before leaving the house and as the light imperceptibly strengthened she looked like an ancient Arab huddled within a shapeless bundle of clothes as she struggled, shivering, up the slight incline to the wall where the horses usually trotted across the grass to greet her.

But this morning there was no welcoming whinny or thud of hooves as she approached. Beyond the wall, as she leaned against it to recover her breath and still her thumping heart, all was grey, frosty silence.

She reached out a hand and cursed as she caught it on a strand of barbed wire.

"Sal, Bonnie, come on my lasses," she said softly. "Come on, Prince. Where are you, my precious?"

"Stupid animals, horses," the devil whispered in her ear.

"Best if they've got out o't'field and run off. Then we can all get back to Shepley. Back where we belong."

"Sal," Maggie called. "I've got thi mints, my lass. Come on now."

As she spoke she edged her way along the wall to the field's five-barred gate as the thin light from the east began to catch the tussocky grass of the paddock, the humps silvered by the frost like a choppy sea. At first she thought that the field was empty, that the ponies had gone, but then as she peered through the gloom she became aware of humped and scattered shapes on the ground close to the shed. Her heart thudding like a steam engine now, she used every ounce of her strength to open the rusted iron latch on the gate and push it open. She stumbled across the field terrified of what she would find on the other side, and when her eyes confirmed her worst fears, she let out a low moan and sank to her knees beside the first of the lifeless forms sprawled across the grass.

She reached out feebly and felt the stickiness of blood, the stiffness of limbs which would never move again, the edges of the gaping wounds with which the ponies had been struck down, their soft lips drawn back over teeth in terror, and she felt as if her heart would burst.

"Time to go now, Maggie Sullivan," the seductive voice murmured in her ear but the old woman merely shuddered convulsively, pulled her blanket around her shoulders as she lay her head along the rough flank of the nearest pony and let the darkness overtake her.

"He's moving early this morning," Sergeant Kevin Mower murmured into his mobile phone as he watched Barry Foreman run down the front steps of his house and wave an electronic controller at the garage doors which slid open at his command. "He's off like a bat out of hell."

"Shit," said DI Paul Cook at the other end of the line, his voice indistinct as he tried to swallow the mouthful of bacon sandwich with which he had answered Mower's call. "I'll follow you in my car," he said. "Keep me in touch."

"Right, guv," Mower said, his own voice husky. He had taken up his station outside Foreman's house just after six, far too early for mind and body to adjust to a new day after the quantity of lager and whisky he had sunk the night before. It was only the sure knowledge that his career was now on a knife-edge which had persuaded him not to burrow back under the bedclothes when his alarm went off at five. Since then he had sat hunched over the steering wheel listening to breakfast chatter on the radio and swigging coffee from a polystyrene cup to prevent himself falling back to sleep. Foreman had not previously emerged from home much before nine thirty. What, Mower wondered, was so different this morning to persuade him into his garage and behind the wheel of his Range Rover so early.

He ducked down in his seat as the bigger vehicle passed him and then slipped into gear and took up a position a car or two behind Foreman as he followed the morning stream of cars and lorries down the hill and into Bradfield town centre. There was little chance that Foreman would realise he was being followed in the heavy traffic, Mower thought, but when the Range Rover failed to turn towards Foreman's company offices and began the equally steep climb out of the town on the north side, against the rush hour flow, Mower became more anxious and dropped back.

"He's heading north, guv, but there's a risk he'll spot me now," he muttered into the car-phone. "I need you to take over."

"I'm stuck behind some bloody truckload of sheep," Cook snarled in reply. "Don't bloody lose him. I'm trying to raise the drug squad. They must have a tap on his phone by now and may know where he's headed."

Mower gritted his teeth and put his foot down on the accelerator, falling into close convoy behind the Range Rover which had now negotiated the narrow townward end of

Aysgarth Lane and was making good speed out of the built up area towards Broadley. "If he gets into open country he'll suss me," Mower said under his breath. But just as the sergeant was sure that he must have been spotted, the Range Rover took a sharp left without a flicker of an indicator. Mower slammed on his brakes and then let his car run on beyond the intersection before pulling into the side of the road.

"He's gone up to Benwell Lane, guv," he told Cook, feeling his heart protesting. "If I'd followed him he'd have spotted me for sure. I'll give it a couple of minutes and then mosey on up. There's not that many places you can hide a Range Rover there. It'll stick out like a sore thumb and someone'll have it away if he leaves it for ten seconds."

"I'm right behind you," Cook said.

"The gore's all the horses'," Amos Atherton said as he finished his first examination of Maggie Sullivan's body, on his knees in the blood-soaked grass and mud. "I can't see any sign of an injury on the old girl, but I'll not be able to give you a definitive answer till the PM." He glanced up at DCI Thackeray who was standing above him as aloof and unbending as a mute at a funeral.

"She could have had a heart attack when she found all this," Atherton said with distaste as he glanced at the six mutilated horses, roughly covered now with sacking. The heavy pathologist scrambled back to his feet with a sigh, then reached down again and picked up something round and white from the mud and passed it to Thackeray.

"A mint," Thackeray said. "She probably brought it up for the ponies. They like mints. Didn't you know?"

Atherton shook his head angrily.

"The mentality of people," he muttered vaguely in Thackeray's direction. "I doubt you've got a murder here, though what you'd call the rest of it I'm not sure."

"Right," Thackeray said. "We can move her then."

"Oh aye, she can go to the mortuary," Atherton said. "And you'll need the knacker's yard for the rest, if they still have knackers, do they?"

"It's been arranged," Thackeray said bleakly.

"Nowt gets any better, does it," Atherton said. Thackeray had seldom seen him so depressed, he thought. Animals and children, it was always the same, and this incident had an elemental viciousness to it, the ponies hacked and slashed almost to pieces, the pregnant mare's foal pulled from the womb, which had shocked not only Atherton but most of those who had been called to the scene. He gritted his teeth, knowing that the next interview with the Smith family might be more than DC Val Ridley, who had accompanied him and was now leaning against Mick Smith's shed looking green, could bear.

"What sort of sick bastard could do that?" Val asked helplessly.

"Where's the lad who found them?" Thackeray asked. "What's his name? Mick?"

"He waited till the ambulance arrived, told them it was his grandmother and then made off, apparently," Val said. "Uniform were slow getting here so noone stopped him. Presumably he's told the rest of the family what's happened by now."

"That saves us the shock element, at least," Thackeray said. "Come on, we'd best get it over. It's not going to get any easier."

They walked in silence the short distance from the paddock to the Smiths' house where a small group of curious onlookers had already assembled on the opposite side of the road.

"The old girl, is it?" one woman asked as the two detectives, accompanied by a uniformed PC, picked their way past the wrecked car in what had once been a garden. "Mad as a barrel of frogs, that one."

Megan Smith was waiting for them at the open back door and in the kitchen the police found themselves facing the three older Smith sons sitting stony faced at the kitchen table.

"Is she dead, then?" Megan asked.

"Mick told the paramedics that the old lady was your mother, and yes, I'm afraid she's dead," Thackeray said quietly.

"Murdered, was she?" Megan asked, glancing at the glowing dark eyes of her sons.

"We don't know," Thackeray said. "It seems unlikely as far as the doctor can tell at this stage. We think she may have had a heart attack."

"That's what you call it, is it, if you frighten an old woman to death," Tom said bitterly. "They wanted us out and it looks as though they've gone the right way about it now, an'all."

"You'd better tell me who *they* are," Thackeray said.

"That's for you to find out," Tom said, his face as shuttered as those of his brothers.

"I want to take her back to Shepley for t'funeral," Megan said. "Her and Dana together."

"There'll have to be a post-mortem, Mrs. Smith," Val Ridley said. "They're not sure of the cause of death yet."

"Where's Mick?" Thackeray asked suddenly but four pairs of dark eyes glanced away from his and there was no answer.

"I need to speak to him about what he found when he went up to the field this morning," Thackeray persisted. Tom Smith shrugged.

"Mick's got business to teck care of," he said.

Thackeray glanced at Val Ridley who nodded imperceptibly and left the house. Outside she used her mobile to call the station and put out a call for Mick Smith who, she guessed from his family's reticence, might well be seeking revenge. She was as sure as Thackeray was that the family knew very well who their tormenters were. The crowd across the road had grown larger now and she was acutely conscious of their unforgiving surveillance. But it was an elderly woman with a kindly face who eventually plucked up the courage to cross the road and approach her.

"I heard what they did to young Mick's horses," she

whispered, taking Val Ridley's arm in a firm grip. "Little beggars. There's no call for that, is there? Dumb animals."

"Do you know who might have done it?" Val asked, without much hope of a constructive answer. The woman looked across the road at the watching crowd and tightened her grip.

"They'll not say a word, most of 'em," she said. "But everyone knows. It'll be them lads from down t'other end o't'street. They've been on at the Smith lads for weeks now, chucking bricks, swearing and chanting, setting that fire the other day. It's not right you know. A lot of 'em…" She glanced back at the bunch of women she had left behind. "They're right scared of Nick Bailey, you know. But if you don't stand up to them when they're little, they just grow into bigger thugs, and then where are we?"

"I thought Nick Bailey was still in bed with his cracked ribs and a broken arm," Val said.

"Well he's not so housebound he wasn't racing up and down t'street last night on that noisy little bike he rides," her informant said waspishly.

"Right," Val said, but as she turned back towards the Smith's house to relay this new information to the DCI she saw Thackeray hurry out of the back door, his face grim. Unexpectedly he took hold of her arm and hurried her down the street away from the crowd.

"The control room just called," he said. "They've had word that a lad armed with a shotgun is hiding outside the Bailey's house shouting for Nick Bailey to come out. They've sent for the armed response unit, but we'd better take a look, see if there's anything we can do."

"Mick Smith," Val said, with complete certainty.

"Who else?"

As Thackeray and Val Ridley arrived at the Baileys' house, which stood silent and apparently undisturbed in the faint rays of morning sunlight, a Range Rover pulled up with a screech of brakes behind their car and a tall burly man leapt out of it and made towards the gap in the fence where the garden gate had once hung.

"Mr. Foreman," Thackeray shouted, recognising the visitor. "I don't think that's a good idea."

Foreman spun round to face Thackeray, his eyes alight with fury and his hands clenching and unclenching at his side but any idea he had of dismissing Thackeray's warning became redundant as a shotgun was fired alarmingly close by, although none of the pellets seemed to come in the direction of the little group on the pavement.

Foreman turned on Thackeray.

"Where's the heavy mob then?" he asked. "Where's the SWAT team or whatever it is you call it these days? My girl-friend and kids are in there so what the hell are you doing about it?"

"The armed response unit is on its way," Thackeray said calmly, propelling a now rather more willing Foreman away from the danger area. "It's no more than five minutes since we were told there was trouble here. How did you know there was a problem so quickly."

"Karen rang me, didn't she," Foreman muttered angrily. "Half an hour ago."

Thackeray glanced at Val Ridley.

"Check out the ETA of the troops," he said. "And the time of the first call we received." Val pulled out her mobile phone and nodded, wondering, as Thackeray did, just why Foreman should have been told about Mick Smith's threatening pres-ence long before the police were.

"Right, Mr. Foreman," Thackeray said. "Now tell me just what you think is going on here, could you."

"It's that mad little toe-rag Nick, isn't it? Karen's little brother. She told me he'd been pestering the gippos for weeks. Got a good hiding for it, as you well know. Anyway, sum-mat's gone pear-shaped this morning and this lad turned up with a shotgun, threatening to blow the door in if Nick didn't come out."

Thackeray forbore to tell Foreman just what Nick had done to enrage the Smith family this time and why he too would like to speak to him at length about his morning's work.

"Did Karen tell you where Smith is now?" he asked, intent on keeping an explosive situation under control.

"He's hiding in the back in an outhouse where Nick keeps his bike, isn't he? She's got the babies upstairs in the bedroom. She didn't say where Nick and her mum are."

"And has he said what he wants?"

"He wants Nick to come out, doesn't he. He's been ranting and raving at him. But Nick won't budge."

"Very wise, I should think," Thackeray said drily.

Thackeray glanced down the narrow side access to the semi-detached house's main door and beyond that the garden. The passageway had been built long before council properties were assumed to need garages and was not wide enough to take a car but adequate for a motorbike to get through to the back of the house. Beyond that he could see little and as he considered the options he was surprised to see Sergeant Kevin Mower's car speed round the corner and halt with another squeal of brakes close behind them. Mower joined them, his bloodshot eyes and unshaven face failing to inspire much confidence in either of his colleagues.

"I heard we had big trouble," he said.

"You moved fast to get here before the heavy mob," Thackeray said.

"I wasn't far away," Mower said, evasively. "Is there anything I can do?"

"Get my family out of there," Foreman snarled. "Or I'll get my own lads up here and do it myself. And there'll not be much left of either of those stupid little beggars when I've finished with them."

"Smith's taken cover in an outhouse at the back," Thackeray said to Mower. "It's going to be difficult to get him out of there without someone getting hurt. He'll need talking down."

"Let me suss out the back of the house from next door," Mower suggested, but Thackeray shook his head sharply.

"You look like death warmed up, Kevin," he said unsympathetically. "Go and wait in your car. I'll want to talk to you later."

Val Ridley made as if to say something but the anger which suddenly blazed between the two men silenced her. Mower shrugged and turned away.

"Talking the little bastard out could take days," Foreman said. "My Karen's doing her nut in there. I told them to get out of the windows at the front..."

"Too dangerous," Thackeray snapped. "He could be round there in seconds if he got a hint what was happening. When the armed police arrive we'll consider that again but not now. It's far too risky."

"I told her that. There's two babies to think of," Foreman said. "I told her that so long as they all stayed in the house they'd be safe enough."

"So long as we keep him calm and don't provoke him into forcing his way inside," Thackeray said. "We have experts to deal with these situations, Mr. Foreman. The only thing we can do is wait for them to turn up. Trust us." A single glance at Foreman's face told Thackeray that trusting the police was the last thing the big man was likely to indulge in.

"Can you call up your girlfriend again?" he asked, trying to distract him. "It would be a good idea if I spoke to her and found out exactly what's going on in there, and what they can see from the back of the house. It'll save time later."

Foreman pulled his mobile phone from his pocket and punched in a number.

"Karen, is that you?" he asked. "Are you all OK? There was a shot.."

He listened intently and then grunted.

"She says Smith screamed at them to keep people away," he said. "He took a pot shot at the upstairs windows at the back when he saw my car pull up. There's glass everywhere."

Thackeray took the phone out of Foreman's hand.

"This is DCI Thackeray," he said. "There are more police on the way and we'll deal with this without anyone getting hurt if you do as you're told and stay well away from the doors and windows. Call me on this number if anything changes. Anything at all." He gave her his mobile number.

"Is there a fixed phone in the house," he asked Foreman when he had rung off.

"No. Karen's using her mobile, isn't she?"

"Pity," Thackeray said, knowing that if they were in for a long siege a mobile was dangerously prone to battery failure when communication from inside the house to outside might be vital.

In the distance they could hear the sound of police sirens approaching up the long hill from Bradfield and within minutes they found themselves on the edge of a military style operation as armed and uniformed officers spilled from vans and fanned out around the house, blocking off the roadway in both directions, taking up positions behind parked cars and other vantage points, weapons at the ready. A uniformed Chief Inspector approached Thackeray.

"Martin Meacher," he said. "You must be Thackeray. I don't know how we've never met before. Will you fill me in?"

Thackeray explained everything that had happened at Benwell Lane that morning to push Mick Smith into his present murderous rage.

"So it's the son he's after, not the family generally?" Meacher asked.

"I wouldn't bank on it, the state he must be in after seeing his horses and his grandmother dead," Thackeray said. "He probably reckons they were all murdered."

"Volatile, then?" Meacher said sombrely. "They're always the worst to deal with. A professional crook trying to blag his way out with a hostage is far more rational."

"Rather you than me," Thackeray muttered.

"Has anyone been round the back?" Meacher asked.

"No, Kevin Mower was all for a recce but I stopped him."

"We'll evacuate the neighbouring houses and then have a look," Meacher said. "But from the look of it he'll have a clearer line of fire that way than this."

As he turned away towards his officers who were waiting for further instructions, the tension racked skywards as two more shots were fired. For long moments there was complete silence and then a shout of surprise as two figures appeared round the side of the house into the line of fire of half a dozen edgy police marksmen.

Almost, but not quite frozen with surprise Thackeray put a hand on Meacher's arm as he opened his mouth to shout orders to his men.

"Hold your fire", Thackeray said firmly as Mick Smith, red-eyed and shaking, emerged from the garden of the Bailey's house, his arm held tightly by a far more villainous-looking Kevin Mower who had the boy's shotgun broken harmlessly over his arm. "That's my sergeant with the boy."

Firm hands took hold of Mick Smith as Mower handed the gun to Meacher and then glanced at Thackeray and shrugged.

"I've not cautioned him," he said. "I hadn't the heart. I found him crying his eyes out at the back of the shed."

"And the shots?" Thackeray snapped.

"My fault," Mower said. "I reckoned on one but I thought he wouldn't have reloaded the second barrel. Anyway, he missed."

He held Thackeray's eyes for a moment and then glanced away and Thackeray knew that the sergeant had hoped the boy wouldn't miss. He drew him out of earshot of Meacher's men who had Mick Smith handcuffed already and were bundling him into a van.

"Go home, Kevin. Sleep off whatever it is you need to sleep off . I'll see you in my office at nine in the morning."

Mower nodded and walked slowly back to his car. In the slumped shoulders and almost aged gait Thackeray suddenly saw himself twelve years previously and the knot of anger in his stomach tightened. He glanced at Val Ridley, who had been listening to the exchange, and could see the pain in her eyes. His instinct was to offer comforting words but he could not find them and the moment passed as DI Paul Cook, looking bright-eyed and keen, made his way towards them through the now relaxed uniformed squad. "Good job I got Mower out of bed early, I hear," Cook said cheerfully.

"I'll want a word later about the deployment of my officers without my knowledge," Thackeray said coldly.

"Foreman's a legitimate target," Cook snapped back.

"But Kevin Mower isn't," Thackeray said. "But we'll talk about that later with Superintendent Longley, shall we? Val, go and tell Mrs. Smith what's happened and where her son's been taken. I've a post-mortem to attend."

Even as they spoke Foreman emerged from his Land Rover and hurried towards the Bailey's house.

"Mr. Foreman, just a minute," Thackeray shouted, but his quarry took no notice and disappeared inside as the door was flung open and a blonde woman in a dressing gown threw her arms around his neck.

"We'll need statements from everyone in the house," Thackeray said curtly to Cook. "See to it will you."

Chapter 18

The boy who dropped the first edition of that day's *Gazette* onto Laura Ackroyd's desk glanced over his shoulder for no more than a second as she absorbed the front-page headline and pictures of the crime reporter's lead story and gasped. She recognised in the blurred image of a woman carrying two babies and being helped into a car the features of Karen Bailey, whom she had last seen in the maternity ward of the May Anderson hospital. In spite of Ted Grant's interest, she had never succeeded in making contact with Karen again. The hospital had refused to reveal her home address and her own research had drawn a blank, with no phone number listed. Now, to her astonishment, which only grew the further she read, she found her quarry on the front page. She glanced towards Ted Grant's glass-walled cubicle and wondered whether he had linked the woman who had just escaped from an armed siege to the May Anderson coverage, and whether his reaction would be as volcanic as it often was when his plans were knocked off course.

Well, the whole of Bradfield knew now where Karen Bailey lived with Barry Foreman, and why an enraged teenager had laid siege to the house in Benwell Lane where her mother and brother lived and which she had been visiting the previous night. Bill Baker, the crime man, had dwelt lovingly on every detail of the feud on the estate which had left six ponies massacred in a scrubby field, an already bereaved family terrorised and an old woman dead. Comments from police sources were minimal in the report but reading between the lines Laura guessed that Maggie Sullivan's death was probably from natural causes, and that the second young man who was helping police with their inquiries was likely to be Nick Bailey, Karen's brother. She did not think that Ted would be very interested any longer in her proposed description of the

Bailey twins' miraculous conception and birth given the even more dramatic events which had now engulfed them.

She glanced across the office to a desk on the other side where Bill Baker sat with a telephone receiver hunched to his ear as he scribbled furiously in a notebook. She strolled across and leaned over his desk in as friendly a fashion as she could muster as he put the phone down. She and Baker did not always see eye-to-eye on the details of crime reporting and she had more than once borne the brunt of Thackeray's anger when her colleague had embroidered too inventively in print.

"What's the latest on the old woman who died at Benwell Lane?" she enquired as casually as she could. Another murder, she thought, would be as much as Thackeray could cope with and might put her own plans for a reconciliation out of bounds even longer.

"Oh, they reckon she collapsed with a heart attack when she found the dead horses," Baker said casually. "No sign of foul play, according to my sources at the mortuary. They've arrested Bailey for butchering the horses and Micky Smith for trying to blow Bailey away. Why are you so interested, anyway? Worried about lover boy's overtime? He's got his work cut out with the shootings at the hospital, hasn't he? They seem to have run into the sand on that one. Unless you know different of course?"

Baker looked up at her slyly and she shook her head.

"You know Michael and I don't talk about his cases," she lied. "I've told you often enough."

"Yeah, yeah, and the boss is about to launch a column for gays and lesbians. Tell me about it. Anyway, Sergeant Mower seems to have made himself a bit of a hero, disarming this Gypsy lad."

"What?" Laura said.

"You're not paying attention," he said, opening the *Gazette* on his desk to the second page where he had described the siege in the sort of detail which relied more on his imagination than reality but all Laura saw was the half-page photograph of an almost unrecognisable Kevin Mower, semi-bearded and looking exhausted, staring out at her.

"Shit," she said under her breath and hurried back to her desk and grabbed her phone. She failed to locate Mower at police HQ and without much hope of success dialled his home number. She was on the point of giving up when the receiver at the other end was eventually picked up.

"Kevin?" she said, unsure that the voice at the other end was really his.

"Who's that?" Mower asked, his voice slurred, though whether from drink or exhaustion she could not tell.

"It's Laura. I read about what happened. Are you all right?"

"As well as can be expected in the circumstances, I guess," Mower said.

"I couldn't believe what you just did," Laura said. "You could have been killed."

"No such luck," Mower said in a tone which made Laura shiver. "It was close, but not close enough."

"You don't mean that," she said, her mouth dry.

"Don't I? I've got an interview with the boss tomorrow and I reckon he's going to give me the chop, heroics or no heroics. That was my last throw, Laura, and it's not going to work, is it? It can't. It was a bloody crazy thing to do and won't cut any ice with the brass. They know how many risks I took and how many standard procedures I ignored. I'm history."

"What a mess," Laura breathed. She guessed that Mower's assessment of his future prospects might well be accurate. In different circumstances she might have leapt to his defence with Thackeray but at present she knew that would certainly do more harm than good.

"The weird thing is that I was looking for Karen Bailey myself," she said. "I wanted to interview her about the fertility treatment she got at the May Anderson."

"You what?" Mower asked, surprise sharpening his voice to something closer to normality. "Karen was one of Fenton-Green's patients, you mean?"

"Yes," Laura said. "Is that important?"

"I'm not sure," Mower said. "But it just might be."

"You'd better tell Michael, then. He and I are not really on speaking terms just now."

There was a long silence at the other end of the phone.

"I'm sorry to hear that," Mower said. "I thought you two had something really good going there."

"So did I," Laura said. "But it seems not."

"Life's a bitch," Mower said before he hung up.

Thackeray wasted no time in ringing Laura. She was still making a dispirited attempt to finish the feature she was writing when the familiar voice turned her heart over.

"We need to talk," Thackeray said. But before she could frame a suitable response which did not give him the chance to conclude that she had been sitting by her phone waiting to hear from him, he plunged her into despair again. "Officially, I mean. I hear you've been making your own inquiries into Stephen Fenton-Green's activities," he said.

"I was supposed to be writing about fertility treatment. Before things got out of hand at the May Anderson," Laura said cautiously. "You know that. It's got nothing to do with the murders."

"I think I'd better be the judge of that," Thackeray said ominously. "Meet me at the Woolpack at five, will you? Unless you'd rather come over to the station..."

Laura could not work out how much of a threat lay behind the invitation.

"The Woolpack," she said and put the phone down hard.

She made sure that she got to the pub first and had ensconced herself comfortably at a corner table with a double vodka and tonic before Thackeray arrived. He got himself a soft drink and pulled out a stool so that he could sit opposite her across the small table. His expression was grim and he made no attempt to greet her as slipped off his coat, flung it on the bench beside her and sat down.

"Is Stephen Fenton-Green a suspect in the murder case now?" Laura asked. "I thought you had it pinned to the anti-abortion lobby?"

"I've a good idea now who fired the shots," Thackeray said. "What I don't know is who else was involved and why. Kevin tells me that you know of a connection between Fenton-Green and a man called Barry Foreman? Is that right?"

"I tried to interview his girlfriend after she had twins," Laura said, keeping her voice level with a great effort. "Fenton-Green was her consultant for the fertility treatment. I'd no reason to think she was important to your investigation."

"She used her own name, so no one made the connection," Thackeray said shortly, obviously unwilling to reveal whether the connection was important or not. "You actually met Stella Brady, didn't you? What was your impression of her?"

Laura thought back to the brief meeting she had had with an intense nurse who had seemed to wear her conscience on her sleeve.

"You'd have got on well with her," she said waspishly. "She wanted nothing to do with the terminations. Implied Fenton-Green was doing some of them too late. But she was keen enough on the fertility work. Enthusiastic even. She said Karen Bailey's babies were a miracle. She seemed a very professional woman."

"She didn't want to blow any whistles, then? She didn't take the opportunity to grab a nosy reporter and bend your ear about anything dodgy going on at the May Anderson?"

"No, she didn't. She said no more than Edgar Burridge has been saying about the late terminations. I'd have investigated what she said if there'd been anything else. And I'd have passed it on to you when she got shot. I'm not completely without moral scruples, Michael, whatever you think of what happened years ago."

Laura took a gulp of her drink to hide her distress, annoyed with herself for saying so much. Thackeray watched her, his face a mask which successfully concealed the turmoil he was feeling. Laura tried again.

"What you might be interested in, if you've got Fenton-Green in your sights, is his wives," she said. " I managed to track them down. But as far as his scientific work is concerned, I've drawn a blank. If he's up to something he shouldn't be in those labs, I've no idea what it is."

"I think you'd better make a formal statement, covering everything you know about Fenton-Green and the hospital, his wives, his research, the lot," Thackeray said. "Can you do that this evening? I'll tell Val Ridley to expect you. And you'd better tell Ted Grant that your inquiries are material to my investigation."

"He'll be over the moon about that," Laura muttered. But Thackeray got to his feet and picked up his coat while Laura watched him, mutely seething with hurt and frustration.

"I'll see you soon," Thackeray conceded. "But this case is coming to a head, so I don't know when." After he had gone Laura drained her drink and sat for a moment, oblivious to the noise of the rapidly filling bar. She would do as Thackeray had asked, she thought, because she had little choice, but then she would continue her own inquiries. The time had come, she thought, to interview Stephen Fenton-Green again in person.

Michael Thackeray did not believe in miracles. When he had sought one from a God he now believed was both deaf and blind, as well as uncaring, it had not been forthcoming. His son had remained as dead and his wife as deranged as he had discovered them on the day which shattered his life into pieces that even now had barely been put back together. And if he did not deserve a miracle, which he accepted might be true, then he could see no reason at all why Barry Foreman, a man whose gains were certainly ill-gotten and sins far more wide-ranging and destructive than he was ever likely to be able to prove, should have been vouchsafed one either. A torrid telephone call to the administrator at the May Anderson Hospital confirmed his suspicions. If his medical records were accurate, Barry Foreman's achievement of fatherhood after ten years of trying was less miraculous than possibly fraudulent. And that gave Thackeray the key he was looking for.

Sitting in Foreman's office, accompanied by a seething DI Paul Cook, who had been very reluctant to see Foreman come under the cosh in case it compromised inquiries into his drug connections, Thackeray leaned back in his chair and savoured the moment.

"You haven't wasted much time getting back to work," Thackeray said.

"Things to do," Foreman said. "A business to run."

"Your girlfriend's OK, is she? And the babies?"

"They're fine now you've got that little toe-rag under lock and key. All kids' stuff, him and Nicky, wasn't it? Six of one and half a dozen of the other… Is that what you wanted to talk about?" Thackeray shook his head.

"Fantoni," he said quietly.

"Fantoni's history," Foreman said. "I've told you all I can about him. Bad business, that pile up."

"He was one of the victims, yes," Thackeray conceded. "But we didn't tell the *Gazette* everything about the crash. It didn't suit us at the time."

"Tell them what?" Foreman asked, not noticeably perturbed.

"What Fantoni was carrying," Thackeray said. "Which might interest you."

Foreman raised no more than an eye-brow. He believes he's fire proof, Thackeray thought. And in normal circumstances he might be. But no one knew better than he did himself that there were cracks in even the most apparently impregnable fortress if children were involved.

"Did you ever introduce Fantoni to anyone with an interest in the May Anderson Hospital?" Thackeray asked, changing tack and, judging by the faint flicker in Foreman's eyes, successfully.

"What do you mean, an interest?" Foreman asked.

"For or against, I suppose," Thackeray said. "Did you put any of the anti-abortion protesters in touch with him? Or Stephen Fenton-Green?"

"Why the hell would I do that?" Foreman asked.

"They might have been looking for a man with a gun. And Fantoni certainly had a gun. He had it on him when he was killed. Also a large quantity of heroin. Does that surprise you at all?"

"I told you. I've no idea what Fantoni's been getting up to since he left here. I sacked him for being soft on dealers on the doors, so no, I suppose it doesn't surprise me if he got into that game himself. But it's nothing to do with me."

"The gun Fantoni was carrying is the one which killed Dana Smith and Stella Brady. Does that surprise you?" Thackeray asked.

"Or that he was well-known in Hull as a man who would break a leg, or a head on demand? Or worse?" DI Cook put in suddenly. There was that faint flicker in the eyes again.

"What's your view of abortion, Mr. Foreman?" Thackeray asked. "Are you in favour of a woman's right to choose? Or do you think it's a sin, if not a crime, like Edgar Burridge?"

"If you'd taken as long as I have to have kids you'd know it's not something I've ever given much thought to," Foreman said, irritated now.

"Ten years, was it?" Thackeray said thoughtfully. "A long wait to be a father. I suppose when Fenton-Green offered you some hope on that front there wasn't much you wouldn't have done for him, was there? It's a pity he's a man who can't be trusted."

Foreman stared at Thackeray, his eyes cold, his face rigid and Thackeray felt that sense of exultation that a marksman achieves when a shot hits the bulls-eye.

"A lot of what he's doing is experimental," he went on. "Of

course, you can always set your mind at rest with DNA tests. I'm sure the hospital will arrange that for you in the circumstances."

Foreman said nothing but Thackeray and Cook could see the nerve on his temple throb with the effort of keeping of keeping the volcanic emotions which had seized him under control. His eyes bulged and his fists clenched and unclenched for half a minute before he could trust himself to speak again.

"Are you saying there's summat wrong with my twins?" he said at last.

"We don't know, Mr. Foreman, but we think Stella Brady thought there was. With your medical history she thought there was no way you and Karen could produce a child, in a test-tube or anywhere else. Maybe he did produce a genuine miracle. Or maybe what he wanted from you was so important to him that he manufactured one. After all, if *you're* not fertile there's plenty of people who are."

"I'll fucking kill him," Foreman said, smashing a fist down onto his desk and filling Thackeray with an enormous sense of relief as he saw his gamble pay off. "If those babies aren't mine, I'll fucking kill him."

"There's been enough killing," Thackeray said. "But you can put him away for a very long time."

"Right," Foreman said. He drummed his fingers on the desk irritably. "But it makes no sense, you know. Karen had dropped the litter before he came to me asking about getting hold of a gun. For self-protection he said. He was worried about all these demonstrations. Said he'd read about doctors getting shot in America. I wanted nowt to do with it, so I gave him Fantoni's phone number, left it at that. What happened after that was nowt to do with me. I was grateful to the man, for God's sake. I had two baby daughters courtesy of Mr Fenton-Green and he asked me a favour. I'd no idea they'd go around shooting women and kids, had I?"

"This was so recent?" Thackeray was thrown slightly

by Foreman's revelations. "Not before Karen had the treatment?"

"Last week, when I went in to visit them," Foreman snarled. "So all this about my twins is bollocks, isn't it? Fenton-Green had no reason to be doing me special favours nine months ago, had he? I was just another patient. He treated us and the treatment worked. There's nothing wrong with those babies, is there, you lying bastard? You're just trying to wind me up."

"I don't know, Mr. Foreman," Thackeray said. "I only know that a very experienced nurse thought there might be. And she was shot by a gunman you introduced to your consultant. Make what you can of that. If the twins are fit and healthy maybe you should just accept the miracle and leave it at that." But he knew Foreman wouldn't. No father could.

The voice on the intercom was female and faint when Laura tried to gain admittance to Stephen Fenton-Green's country house later that evening.

"Stephen's not home yet," Fiona Madeley said. "I'm expecting him any minute."

"Could I come in and wait?" Laura asked, not really expecting a positive answer, but to her surprise the wrought iron gates in front of her car began to swing open and as she got out in the glare of the security lights the front door opened as well.

The woman who opened the door was about her own age, pale and blonde and stunningly beautiful. But there were dark circles under her anxious eyes and when Laura was over the threshold she closed the door and locked it firmly behind her.

"Stephen will kill me for letting you in, he's going mad about security, but I've been here by myself all day. The cleaning woman called in sick and I've not been feeling too brilliant myself." The words poured out in a torrent as she led Laura into a sitting room where the embers of a fire glowed in the grate and waved her into one of the deep armchairs.

"I'm pregnant, you know, and I'm so excited and so scared. Stephen has waited so long for this. Do you have children?"

Laura swallowed hard and shook her head.

"Not yet," she said.

"It's a huge thing, isn't it?" Fiona said. "I'm quite terrified, especially as it's been so hard for Stephen. He's had to wait so long. We couldn't conceive naturally, you know. I had to have treatment at his hospital. It's a fantastic thing, isn't it, what he does? Like a miracle."

That word again, Laura thought and she shivered, wondering just what sort of miracles Stephen Fenton-Green was achieving.

"That's why I'm so keen to finish this series of articles about the May Anderson that I'm working on," she said quickly. "Mr. Fenton-Green said I could contact him any time for additional help and I was in the area, so I thought I'd drop in on the off-chance of catching him." Fiona seemed to accept this flimsy excuse for her presence and waved towards the drinks cabinet.

"Would you like something while you wait?" she asked. "I'm giving alcohol a miss at the moment. I have to look out for the baby now. No booze, no cigarettes, lots of vitamins…" Laura accepted a vodka and tonic gratefully.

"Perhaps it was a mistake for me to bother Mr. Fenton-Green at home," Laura said suddenly, realising that the sort of questions she wanted to ask the consultant would throw this nervous woman into a panic. "Perhaps I should see him at the hospital tomorrow…"

"Too late," Fiona said, raising a hand, which shook slightly. "Here he is now. I can hear his car."

Trapped by her own impulsiveness, Laura was not surprised by the evident anger with which Stephen Fenton-Green greeted her when he discovered her sitting in his living room with a drink in her hand. She stood up awkwardly as his expression darkened and he flashed Fiona a glance of furious inquiry.

252

"Why do I keep finding you intruding into my life, Ms. Ackroyd?" he asked

"I was keen to continue our discussions about your research," Laura said. "I was in the neighbourhood and thought you wouldn't mind if I dropped in…"

"I do mind," Fenton-Green said. "I mind having my privacy invaded like this and I will be telling your editor so when I speak to him tomorrow. Now would you do me the courtesy of leaving."

"If we could perhaps make an appointment for tomorrow? There are one or two things I'm not clear about…"

"Please leave," Fenton-Green said. Laura put her drink down carefully on a coffee table and picked up her bag with a shrug. But before she could make her way to the front door past a glowering consultant and an evidently embarrassed Fiona Madeley, the intercom buzzed loudly.

"See who that is, Fiona," Fenton-Green said. "I'm not at home to anyone."

Fiona went out into the hall.

"I understand congratulations are in order," Laura said quietly. "You're going to be a father again."

Fenton-Green could not disguise the shock in his eyes.

"What do you mean, again?"

"I spoke to your first wife," Laura said as Fiona came back into the room looking even more anxious.

"It's the police at the gate," she said. "I've let them through. They insisted."

"Have you been able to solve your little genetic problem with this new baby?" Laura asked quickly. "That must be quite a breakthrough."

By this time Fiona had tuned into the conversation.

"What genetic problem?" she asked.

"I don't know what you're talking about, Ms Ackroyd," Fenton-Green blustered. "Now, please, if you don't mind, it seems I have yet more unwelcome visitors."

And ones you can't turn away, Laura thought to herself as

the doorbell shrilled and Fiona left the room again to answer it.

Michael Thackeray looked even more surprised than Fenton-Green had been to find Laura in the living room, but he was closely followed into the room by Paul Cook and made no overt comment.

"Mr. Fenton-Green, I have officers outside and a warrant to search these premises," he said.

"What the hell for?" Fenton-Green asked, his face flushed now. Fiona subsided into a chair with a faint moan.

"I'd also like to invite you to accompany me to police head-quarters to answer some questions," Thackeray said.

"About what, for God's sake?" Fenton-Green snapped.

"There are two matters," Thackeray said, avoiding Laura's eyes. "There are the deaths of Dana Smith and Stella Brady, and also the matter of a possibly illegal operation on Karen Bailey."

"Good God, man, you're out of your mind," Fenton-Green said. "I was the one being shot at when that girl died. How could I possibly have murdered her? And what's all this about an illegal operation? There's nothing illegal about fertility treatment."

"Well, we'll know for sure about that when we have DNA tests done on Ms Bailey's twins, and their supposed parents, won't we?" Thackeray said. "Unless you want to save time by telling us exactly what those tests will show?"

For a second Laura thought that Fenton-Green would attack Thackeray physically but gradually the tension in him relaxed and his shoulders slumped and from where she was standing close to Fiona, Laura thought that she could see the man age ten years in as many seconds.

"I'll tell you nothing," Fenton-Green said, his voice faint now as he glanced at Fiona who was visibly shaking. "Are you arresting me? I'll want to call my solicitor now, if you don't mind. I'll tell you nothing without him present."

"Take him to the car," Thackeray said wearily to Cook. "And send the search team in."

When the two men had gone he turned to Laura, who had sat down beside Fiona and was holding her hand.

"Can you stay with her until I find a woman PC to take over?" he asked.

"Of course," she said quietly. " You won't know yet but Fiona is expecting a baby."

"That's a great pity in the circumstances, Ms Madeley," Thackeray said. "I don't think Mr. Fenton-Green will be around to give you much support with the child."

"What has he done to that woman?" Fiona asked urgently. "What's all this about his first wife? Stephen told me he couldn't have children and now you're saying he did have one." Laura told her about the short life of Toby and the suspicions about Fenton-Green's research.

"So he could have fiddled about with our baby too?" Fiona asked, her voice breaking. "What has he *done* to me? You don't even know, do you? You don't know what experiments he'd been doing."

"I suggest you see another doctor if you're worried," Thackeray said. And as Fiona collapsed into hysterical tears he glanced at Laura with a look of total defeat. "I'm sure they'd consider a termination in the circumstances," he said.

He left the house, swarming now with uniformed officers conducting a thorough search, but as he was about to get into the car where Cook and Fenton-Green were waiting for him, he became aware of another vehicle pulling up sharply just outside the open gates, the driver's staring face just visible where the beam of lights from the house penetrated the darkness of the lane outside.

Thackeray walked slowly ahead of the car and through the gateway and leaned into the open window of the newcomer's Range Rover. Barry Foreman gazed back at him impassively.

"I did think I might put a bullet between his eyes," he said conversationally. "But as you got here first I decided he'll suffer one hell of a lot more doing it your way. In fact I'll make bloody sure he does just as soon as I know which nick he's in."

"And you have the gall to complain about Nick Bailey's vicious tendencies?" Thackeray said. "Perhaps it's just as well your twins are girls. There may be a little more hope for them."

"You're a vicious bastard an' all, Inspector Thackeray," Foreman said, gunning his engine.

"It takes one to know one," Thackeray said, turning away as Foreman let the car into gear. "We'll be in touch."

It was two days before Thackeray could find the time to go round to Laura's flat and even then he could not find the courage to go in. He sat in his car smoking, emotionally drained by the events of the previous forty-eight hours. They had needed to keep Stephen Fenton-Green in custody for the whole of the time the law allowed before he felt able to charge him with the murder of Dana Smith and Stella Brady. Item by item the evidence Thackeray needed had filtered in: the phone records of his calls to Fantoni, who actually shot both women, the statement from Barry Foreman that he had put the consultant in touch with his former employee, the grudging admission from the security guard Nolan that the motorcyclist he had seen, in full leathers, could well have been Fantoni, the analysis of the notes and samples which had been found in Fenton-Green's small laboratory at his home, and finally the production by the May Anderson Hospital itself of its record of Stella Brady's suspicions about Fenton-Green's procedures, filed away and conveniently forgotten ten months previously at the point when Karen Brady must have become pregnant. With each turn of the screw Fanton-Green had blustered more unconvincingly, in spite of his solicitor's advice to say nothing, until finally, with time running out he had deflated like a pricked balloon and admitted the conspiracy to murder Stella and pin the blame on the anti-abortion protesters.

"And the girl? Dana? How did she fit in?" Thackeray had spat at him through dry lips, his eyes half closed with fatigue, thinking of the wrecked family at Benwell Lane.

"He wasn't supposed to hit anyone that day," Fenton-Green had muttered. "It was just supposed to be a warning shot that looked as if it was aimed at me. The stupid bugger could have killed me just as easily."

Thackeray had charged him then, promised him more questioning about the medical malpractice, joined briefly in the CID celebrations in the Woolpack, gone home, fallen into his bed fully dressed and slept for twelve hours.

He stubbed out his cigarette at last and picked up the bunch of roses that were lying on the back seat. When Laura opened the front door to him she could not help laughing, so unexpected was the sight of Thackeray half-hidden by what looked like the entire contents of a florist's shop.

"A peace offering?" she asked.

"A first instalment, anyway," he said, shamefaced.

She let him in, and allowed him to take her in his arms and kiss her with as much tenderness as the first time.

"You can't get out of it as easily as all that," she said at last, pushing him away gently.

"I know. I'm sorry," he said. "I had no right, no right at all. It was a knee-jerk reaction, something I thought I'd left behind me long ago. It was unforgivable."

"But you want me to forgive you anyway?"

"I've had a week without you," he said. "That's just about seven days too long."

"Some week," she said, her face clouded. "I see from Bob Baker's front page story today that you've charged Fenton-Green with murder. Even though he didn't pull the trigger?"

"He commissioned the pulling," Thackeray said shortly.

"And the rest of it? His so-called research?"

"We're not entirely sure yet. He had a lot of material and notes stashed away at the house. The final test results will take some time. But the murders were undoubtedly linked to whatever it is Fenton-Green's been up to in his lab. We think he began to panic when the demonstrations thrust the hospital into the news. We think Stella must have seen the couple's medical records much earlier and realised that there was no way Barry Foreman could produce a child. She knew there was something wrong as soon as the IVF pregnancy was confirmed but the hospital, or Fenton-Green, or both of them, fobbed her off. When the twins were actually born we guess she must have threatened to blow the whistle seriously. Whatever Fenton-Green's motive was for giving Foreman a baby – and it may simply have been to prove that his experimental techniques worked – he had realised by then that he could call in a very big favour from a very serious criminal."

"So is there something wrong with those beautiful babies?" Laura asked. "And Fiona's baby? What exactly has that monster done?"

"We don't know yet but the experts think there are two possibilities: that Fenton-Green fathered Karen's children himself, as a dry run for Fiona, after trying to eliminate the faulty gene. Or the babies have no father at all."

"Clones?" Laura breathed. "If they can do it with calves and lambs…why not? They kept telling me there were too many girls being born. They'd have to be girls, wouldn't they?"

"Even the women he treated for free had a part to play, apparently," Thackeray said. "He built up his reputation as a latter-day saint while he plundered their bodies for experimental material. We're going to have to check out every abortion and fertility patient Fenton-Green's treated for years back. We don't know how long he's been experimenting. Of course, if Stella Brady had breathed a word – to the General Medical Council, or to the Press – Fenton-Green's career would have been ruined."

"Oh yes," Laura said, horrified. "Wouldn't it just."

Thackeray went over to the window and looked out into the garden silvered by an almost full moon and pressed his head against the cool glass. He could feel the room behind him vibrating with what he and, he guessed, she wanted to say and he did not know how to break the log-jam of hurt which stood in the way.

"How's our hero Kevin?" Laura asked at last.

Thackeray groaned.

"Kevin has got three months leave to get some treatment and sort himself out," he said. "It was what someone gave me once. I couldn't believe I was hearing myself go through that ritual with him but Longley gave me no choice. Our man from special branch had made a formal complaint about him."

"Do you think he'll come back?"

"I don't know. I did, but I'm not sure what that proves."

"Michael," Laura said, moving to join him at the window and slipping an arm around his waist. "This has been an awful case for you. If you want to try and salvage what we had together I'll give it another go."

"You need a man to give you lots of babies," he said. "I've seen you with Vicky's kids. I'm not brave enough to do that again."

"I'll have to take you as you are," she said. "You may turn out to be braver than you think."